BLOODY ROYAL PRINTS

REBA WHITE WILLIAMS

TYRUS
BOOKS

Published by
TYRUS BOOKS
an imprint of F+W Media, Inc.
10151 Carver Road, Suite 200
Blue Ash, OH 45242. U.S.A.
www.tyrusbooks.com

Hardcover ISBN 10: 1-4405-8548-2
Hardcover ISBN 13: 978-1-4405-8548-7
Paperback ISBN 10: 1-4405-8545-8
Paperback ISBN 13: 978-1-4405-8545-6
eISBN 10: 1-4405-8546-6
eISBN 13: 978-1-4405-8546-3

Printed in the United States of America.

10   9   8   7   6   5   4   3   2   1

Library of Congress Cataloging-in-Publication Data
Williams, Reba.
Bloody royal prints / Reba White Williams.
    pages cm
    ISBN 978-1-4405-8548-7 (hc) -- ISBN 1-4405-8548-2 (hc) -- ISBN 978-1-4405-8545-6
(pb) -- ISBN 1-4405-8545-8 (pb) -- ISBN 978-1-4405-8546-3 (ebook) -- ISBN 1-4405-8546-6
(ebook)
    I. Title.
    PS3623.I5594B58 2015
    813'.6--dc23
                            2014048190

This is a work of fiction. Names, characters, corporations, institutions, organizations, events, or
locales in this novel are either the product of the author's imagination or, if real, used fictitiously.
The resemblance of any character to actual persons (living or dead) is entirely coincidental.

Many of the designations used by manufacturers and sellers to distinguish their products are
claimed as trademarks. Where those designations appear in this book and F+W Media, Inc. was
aware of a trademark claim, the designations have been printed with initial capital letters.

Cover design by Stephanie Hannus.
Images © kritchanut/123RF, iStockphoto.com/Michal Boubin.

This book is available at quantity discounts for bulk purchases.
For information, please call 1-800-289-0963.

Dedication

Bloody Royal Prints is dedicated to Dave: Without his patient assistance, it never would have been completed.

Bloody:

1. *Adjective* Resembling or pertaining to blood
2. *Adjective* Covered, smeared, or stained with blood
3. *Adverb* Unpleasant, deplorable, perverse
4. *Adverb* Damnable, cursed (considered profane or obscene)
5. *Verb* Make bloody: stain with blood

PROLOGUE

Dinah

April, New York

Dinah was certain Jonathan would forbid her to accept the Samuel Palmer Fellowship in London. She was determined to stand up to him. She must. It was a great honor, and it would be a great adventure. She couldn't let it go.

She chose her moment carefully, on a Saturday afternoon. They had enjoyed a delicious lunch at Orso, where they broke all their diet rules and stuffed themselves with pizza bread and roast pork. Jonathan had followed lunch with a nap, and after his wake-up shower, settled down in the living room with *The Economist*. She approached her husband before he began to read.

"Jonathan, the most wonderful thing has happened," she said.

He looked up from his magazine and smiled. "Tell me about it."

She forgot her prepared speech and handed him the letter from the Art Museum of Great Britain. She couldn't wait for him to finish reading it. She began to babble, explaining how prestigious the award was, and what a wonderful time they would have, if he would take the time to go with her to England. He didn't comment, but put the letter aside and seemed to be listening.

She talked about getting to know London and taking trips to the country to visit Bath and Oxford and gardens and castles all over England. When she had said everything she could think of that might persuade him, she braced herself for a tantrum.

"That is wonderful news. Congratulations!" Jonathan said. "It fits in perfectly with something I want to do. I'd like to open an office in London. I haven't mentioned it to you because I didn't think you'd want to leave the gallery, and your friends here, especially Coleman. I need a few months over there for leasing and setting up an office, recruiting staff, and, most of all, signing up a few new clients by convincing them I can raise capital not just in the United States, but worldwide. Your letter says your appointment is for four months, and that amount of time is right for me, too. How soon can you be ready to go?"

Dinah was astonished by his reaction. "Bethany can take care of the gallery," she said. "Coleman and I can e-mail, text, and phone. We'll be fine. I can go as soon as you're ready."

For the next two hours, Dinah and Jonathan made plans for the move to London. Jonathan would contact realtors to find office space and a place to live. They argued about what their London home would be like. Dinah wanted an apartment with a weekly cleaning service; Jonathan wanted a large house fully staffed— butler, cook, housekeeper, the works.

"We'll need a big house and servants for entertaining," he said. "It's important for my business. And you can't run a house that size on your own; you'll be far too busy at the museum."

"You may be right," Dinah said. "I'll be at the museum all week. I don't much like the idea of a house full of servants, but they might make it easier to adjust to living in a new city, a new country." She began to think about closing the house on Cornelia Street, turning over the gallery to Bethany, telling Coleman . . .

"Clothes!" she said. "I don't know what I have that will be suitable for London. I'll have to go through my closet."

He laughed. "Buy a whole new wardrobe," he said.

"Maybe I will," she said. "But first I'll call Coleman and Bethany."

By the time she talked to them, Dinah was more than resigned to having servants to wait on her. She envisioned coffee and a croissant in bed every morning before going downstairs for a healthy breakfast someone else had prepared. Every day she'd spend a little time in the kitchen with the cook, planning the meals, and making out a grocery list, but someone else could do the shopping.

She'd come home in the evening after work to find an exquisitely prepared meal—sometimes just for her and Jonathan, other nights for guests. She'd go up to her room, shower, and change into something glamorous, and enjoy being served. She could hardly wait.

CHAPTER ONE

Dinah

Monday, late April, London

Dinah was dreaming that she was snug in her New York bed in the Cornelia Street house. Her alarm, set to wake her while not disturbing Jonathan, buzzed. She reached over to shut it off and was startled by the frigid air on her bare arm. Instantly awake, she remembered she was in London, in the house from hell. She had been in London for nearly a month. She missed her home in Greenwich Village every day.

She slipped out of bed, put on her blue cashmere robe and furry slippers—both bought at huge expense from Harrods because the house was so cold—and set about her morning tasks.

Fortunately, the master bedroom suite had large bath- and dressing rooms on either side of the bedroom. She had converted her dressing room to a mini-kitchen. She could still use the bathroom for showers and baths and the like, but a coffeemaker and an electric juicer had replaced toiletries on the countertops, and a small refrigerator occupied a third of the floor space.

The coffeemaker was on a timer, and the coffee was nearly ready when she entered her make-do kitchen. She washed her face, and brushed her teeth and hair: Jonathan did not like seeing her untidy. When she was presentable, she unlocked the door to the refrigerator. Like the coffeemaker and the juicer, the refrigerator—and the padlock she had bought to go with it—had been among her first London purchases.

She set the breakfast tray on the counter, put Jonathan's mug on the tray, ready for his coffee, and took the glass of orange juice she'd prepared the night before out of the refrigerator.

She glanced at her watch. Not quite time. Jonathan's loud alarm, the signal that she should take him his tray, would go off any minute.

Jonathan had, since he was old enough to make his preferences known, demanded that his parents' servants bring him black coffee and fresh orange juice every morning as soon as he was awake. She had wondered what he had done in his early teens at Deerfield Academy. Prep school room service must have been hard to come by, let alone a tray brought to one's bed. She knew from his friends' jokes that Jonathan had always found someone he could pay to make that tray appear—not only at Deerfield, but at Yale and Harvard Business School. In his New York bachelor apartment, he'd employed a cook and a maid. The maid had brought him his tray, and served the second course of his breakfast in the dining room.

Dinah had been amused by his fixed habits and demands. It had been easy to deliver his wake-up tray in New York. Every evening before she went to bed, she set the coffee timer to begin perking at the same time her alarm sounded, and had used the electric juicer to squeeze the orange juice and put it in a pitcher in the refrigerator. In the morning she poured juice into a glass, put it on the tray with a cup of freshly brewed coffee, and delivered it to Jonathan's bedside. The kitchen and the bedroom in the Cornelia Street house were on the same floor, and were only about fifty feet apart. Everything had been convenient in her New York home.

But the kitchen in the London house was three floors below the bedroom floor, and lacked an elevator—or "lift," as they said here. The London house came with a butler, a cook, a housekeeper, and an assistant to the cook, all of whom lived on the fifth floor, and a cleaning woman who, like the chauffeur, came in daily.

Dinah had assumed that one of the servants would appear at the designated time with Jonathan's tray. She'd explained Jonathan's tastes to Mrs. O'Hara, the cook, and prepared a notebook describing his preferences, dislikes, etc., and when meals were to be served. But the morning after their first night in the house, Mrs. O'Hara had appeared with a tray of tepid tea, milk, sugar, and a yellowish chemical-tasting drink that had never been near an orange.

Jonathan, furious, blamed the unacceptable tray on poor directions from Dinah, and after frowning at Dinah, turned to Mrs. O'Hara.

"I'm sure you didn't understand that I drink coffee, not tea, first thing in the morning, and that the juice must be freshly squeezed. I assumed Mrs. Hathaway told you about the oranges? And the coffee?"

Mrs. O'Hara glared at him. "I have always served morning tea to those living at 23 Culross—that is the way it's done in England. Coffee is not served until ten or eleven o'clock in the morning, or after dinner at night. The juice is quite fresh—in England it is produced at the store. I do not lower myself to squeeze oranges. The juice has been acceptable to all of the previous tenants."

Dinah was amazed. O'Hara seemed to imply that Jonathan—and Dinah—were ignorant about the better things—English things—like tea and "fresh" orange juice. Dinah expected Jonathan to blow up, but he ignored Mrs. O'Hara's impertinence and held his temper.

"Mrs. Hathaway will explain more carefully what I want, and I expect you to bring me a proper tray tomorrow."

Mrs. O'Hara glared at him and stalked off. Jonathan showered and dressed and went down to the dining room, where he encountered Mrs. O'Hara's second rebellion. Dinah had explained Jonathan's breakfast likes and dislikes: Above all, he didn't eat fried food or anything fatty. For breakfast he ate one of several special cereals—unobtainable in London, but his cereals had been imported and stored in cases in one of the kitchen pantries. He liked skim milk and blueberries with his cereal, and a special sweetener, also unobtainable in London, also stored in the pantry with the cereal.

He was horrified when, instead of his usual breakfast, he faced an array of greasy eggs, doughy sausages oozing pork fat, barely cooked fatty bacon, gummy oatmeal, smelly kippers, canned baked beans, fried bread, and black pudding. Mrs. O'Hara stood proudly by the buffet, as if waiting for his thanks.

"Mrs. O'Hara, I cannot eat this food," Jonathan said.

Mrs. O'Hara announced that she had always served a full English breakfast to the tenants, and had never had complaints. Jonathan again ignored her impertinence.

"Mrs. Hathaway will explain what I want for breakfast, and I expect to see what I want on this table tomorrow morning," he said. He left for the office breakfast-less, and angry with Dinah.

When on their second morning in the house Mrs. O'Hara appeared at the bedroom door with a tray loaded with a gray beverage she described as coffee, a pitcher of heavy cream, a bowl of sugar cubes, and the same ghastly juice, Dinah knew Mrs. O'Hara had no intention of serving the food and drink ordered by the Hathaways. The woman looked like the agreeable Mrs. Bridges from *Upstairs, Downstairs*, but had the personality of Kreacher, Harry Potter's ill-tempered house elf. Every time she ignored Dinah's instructions about food, Dinah had to listen to another tirade from Jonathan about her inability to manage the servants.

When he went into his dressing room, she ran downstairs to set out his cereal, but the only milk in the refrigerator was creamy, not skim, and there were no blueberries. She loaded the same indigestible English breakfast as yesterday's, laid out on the buffet exactly as it had been the day before, on trays, and took all of it into the kitchen. She had done the best she could.

Mrs. O'Hara, Mrs. Malone (the housekeeper, who reminded her of Mrs. Danvers, the sinister housekeeper in *Rebecca*), and an enormous woman she'd never seen before (could she be the cook's assistant?) grabbed the dishes out of her hands, and settled down at the table like pigs at the trough. They began to cram the food into their mouths, slurping and smacking. Dinah, sickened, could hardly wait to leave the room.

Jonathan was somewhat appeased when he saw his cereal, but annoyed by the lack of blueberries and skim milk. Again he blamed Dinah. He gagged on the gray drink Mrs. O'Hara described as coffee.

"Is there no good coffee to be had in England?" he asked. "Order it from New York, if you have to."

"London has dozens of Starbucks," Dinah said. "They must sell the same coffee here as in New York. I'll buy some today."

Once Dinah knew what she had to do, she set about doing it. After she bought the coffeemaker, she took it into the kitchen and explained to Mrs. O'Hara how it worked. The cook ignored it, and sneered at the juicer and the oranges Dinah bought. When Dinah left freshly squeezed orange juice in the refrigerator overnight, however, it disappeared. That was when she bought the refrigerator, where she also kept oranges and orange juice, skim milk and blueberries. She learned to keep her bathroom-kitchen locked, but that meant the cleaning woman couldn't get in her bathroom, and Dinah had to clean it.

After his early breakfast, Jonathan showered and dressed, which gave Dinah time to run downstairs, remove the greasy buffet—the same spread appeared every morning—and set out Jonathan's cereal, with blueberries and skim milk. Since everything was exactly as he wanted it, he congratulated Dinah on having finally given Mrs. O'Hara the appropriate instructions. She didn't tell him what she had to do to make sure his morning began exactly as he wanted.

Dinah knew that what she was doing was ridiculous, but having a major scene every morning would be far worse. If only she could dismiss the cook, and hire someone else, or if Jonathan would let her do the cooking herself. But once Jonathan made up his mind, he was immovable, and he insisted that she manage the servants who came with the house. She was doing her best to make him happy and prevent scenes. Her inconvenience was the price of peace.

Jonathan didn't come home for lunch, and Dinah made sure she was out of the house at lunchtime. But dinner, like breakfast, had been a nightmare, featuring inedible food and a tantrum by Jonathan, until Dinah had started bringing in takeout of one kind or another, and substituting it for the dinner Mrs. O'Hara prepared. She became an expert on takeout. Indian, Chinese, Thai, French, Italian, Spanish, Japanese, Moroccan, Korean, Turkish, Vietnamese, and many more varieties were available, but unfortunately Jonathan did not care for exotic food. Harrods, Fortnum & Mason, Whole Foods, Marks & Spencer, and the wonderful markets—Borough Market was a favorite—enabled her to keep him happy with the familiar foods he preferred.

CHAPTER TWO

Dinah

Monday, May, London

The only sunny spot in Dinah's dreary London existence was her friendship with Rachel Ransome. Dinah had liked Rachel when they'd met during Dinah's brief visit to London in January, and with frequent overseas phone conversations and e-mails, their friendship had grown. Dinah hadn't realized how much the art dealer's hospitality would mean to her in London. She knew no one else in England, except, of course, Jonathan, and her cousin Coleman's half-brother, Heyward Bain. But Heyward was always on a plane headed to Dubai or Beijing or some other exotic far-away place for his mysterious business activities.

Jonathan worked even longer hours than he had in New York. He was in his new office all day and sometimes well into the night. He joined her for dinner every night, but often went back to the office after dinner. Dinah wished they could go to some of the great restaurants in London, but he said he was too busy.

Nothing was going well. She hadn't started the work at the museum that had brought her to London, but she had met the people with whom she'd be working. They had been polite, but distant. No one had suggested a get-acquainted lunch, or seemed interested in her. She'd heard that the English were standoffish, but by American standards, the museum crowd was cold and unfriendly. Her fellowship required her to catalogue a large collection of American prints the museum had received as a gift.

Did the museum staff resent her being invited to do this? She had no idea, and knew no one with whom she could discuss the problem.

Rachel's invitations to visit an art gallery, or to join her for lunch or tea, helped stave off Dinah's loneliness and her frustration with her domestic situation. She didn't discuss her house and servants problems with Rachel; it was good to forget them for an hour or so.

At lunch with Rachel, she had almost forgotten how miserable she was. They had finished their crab salad and lemon tart, and were sipping coffee by the gas fire in Rachel's library when the maid, looking flustered, announced that Princess Stephanie was in the gallery, and wished to speak with Rachel.

"She says it's a 'matter of life and death,' madam. Shall I show her in here?"

"Yes, please," Rachel said, and turned to Dinah. "You do not mind, do you? I doubt that whatever she wants is quite that important—she tends to be overly dramatic—but she would not trouble me with a trivial matter."

"Of course I don't mind. Do you know her well?" Dinah asked.

Rachel shook her head. "Not at all. She comes into the gallery to look at paintings or jewelry occasionally—" She broke off, and stood while the maid ushered in a slender blonde, exquisitely dressed, and well-sprayed with Joy.

Dinah, following Rachel's example, also rose. She didn't know the protocol for greeting a princess, especially a very young one. She'd heard Princess Stephanie interviewed on television, and knew that she was in her twenties, ten years younger than Dinah, and probably twenty years younger than Rachel.

"Oh dear, you have a visitor—I'm so sorry—I should have rung, but I was so upset, I didn't think." The young woman appeared to be on the verge of tears.

Dinah, feeling de trop, said, "I should be going, Rachel—"

Rachel held up her hand. "Stephanie, may I present Dinah Greene? Dinah is an old friend. She owns a print gallery in New York, and is in London on a Samuel Palmer Fellowship, cataloguing a major gift of American prints to the Art Museum of Great Britain. You may speak freely in front of her."

The young woman turned to Dinah. "Please call me Stephanie. May I call you Dinah? It's actually about a problem involving prints that I've come here today. Perhaps you'll remain with us a little longer? I'd be most grateful. It's confidential, but I'm sure I can trust a friend of Mrs. Ransome's. I need help desperately."

The young woman's cotton-candy pink lipstick was smeared, and a lock of ash-blonde hair had straggled loose from its chignon. On television, she looked meticulously groomed. Whatever her problem, it was serious enough for her to make an appearance looking less than perfect.

Her blue eyes, like those of the late Princess Diana, were her best feature, but they were an even brighter shade of blue, so vivid that Dinah suspected tinted contacts. Her high-pitched voice was grating, as was her tendency to end her remarks on an upward note. Every statement sounded like a shrill question.

Still, Dinah was fascinated by an up-close view of a princess, even a minor one with an annoying voice. She was also intrigued by the young woman's story. What could she have to do with prints?

"Yes, please call me Dinah. I'll be happy to stay if you think I can help," Dinah said.

"Please sit down," Rachel said.

Stephanie smiled weakly. "Thank you," she said. She perched on the edge of a chair until Rachel returned to her seat by the fire.

Dinah sat opposite Rachel, feeling as if she were in church. Up, down, up. At least she didn't have to kneel or curtsey.

"I expect you know that Queen Victoria and Prince Albert made etchings?" Stephanie said, looking at Rachel.

"Certainly," Rachel said.

Dinah nodded. Dinah owned Prince Albert's etching of the Queen's Cairn terrier, *Islay*, and Queen Victoria's etching of the Prince's greyhound, *Eos*. The miniature prints were a gift from Jonathan. Framed in antique brass, they stood on the mantle in their New York living room.

Thinking about that living room, Dinah felt a wave of homesickness. She wished she'd brought the Victorian prints to London. They'd be a pleasant reminder of home in the depressing sitting room of their rented house. She must stop thinking about that hateful house. She forced herself to concentrate on what Stephanie was saying.

"Over the years, many of our family have engaged in some form of art as a hobby—painting, mostly—but I knew about Queen Victoria's printmaking and thought it would be fun to etch. So I learned how—it's not very difficult—well, actually, it's awfully difficult to make a really good etching—but anyway, I've made a lot. And the thing is, they've been stolen," she said, tears rolling down her cheeks.

Rachel frowned. "I do not understand why you are telling me this. The Ransome Gallery does not deal in prints. No one is likely to try to sell them to me, if that is what you wished to discuss."

"No, no. I wasn't actually thinking anyone would try to *sell* them to you. But I understand you have assisted with investigations involving prints—identified the criminals?"

"I have been able to assist friends in the United States with a few art-related problems, but my role has been minor. Dinah has done a great deal more detecting than I," Rachel said.

"I see," Stephanie said. She turned to Dinah again. "Will *you* help me?"

Dinah was curious to learn more, especially why this theft was "a matter of life and death."

"I'll try," she said.

"Would you like coffee?" Rachel asked Stephanie, ringing for the maid.

"Oh yes, please, black. Thank you."

The maid served Stephanie, and refilled Dinah's and Rachel's cups. When the door closed behind her, the young woman continued.

"The images in the Queen's and Prince Albert's prints were *very* proper—their dogs, the children, copies of pictures from their collections—that sort of thing? They were private, kept under lock and key at Windsor."

Rachel nodded. "But despite all that security, about sixty of them were stolen from the man who printed for Their Highnesses. The thieves prepared and circulated a sales catalogue of the prints. Prince Albert was furious and, in 1848, took the matter to court. Prince Albert won, of course, and the catalogues were destroyed and the sale prevented," she said.

Stephanie nodded. "Since then, if we—that is, those with a connection to the throne—make etchings, we are not allowed to have them printed outside the palace. Actually, that means outside wherever we live, since hardly any of us live in a 'live' palace. But most of us are housed in approved and secure quarters. As I think you know, Mrs. Ransome, I live in a flat in what is nicknamed the Little Palace." Stephanie looked at Dinah. "It's not a palace at all; it's a modern building. Calling it a palace is a bit of a joke: It is a very un-palacey palace. I print my etchings on an old-fashioned hand press in my spare bedroom. I make only a few impressions, and when they're done, I lock them in the safe in my flat. But someone stole them—every one." She broke into tears again, took a handkerchief from a pale blue bag the exact shade of her suit and shoes, and blotted her wet cheeks.

Dinah was fascinated by Princess Stephanie's clothes and puzzled by her distraught manner. Why all the fuss? Even if the plates as well as the prints were stolen, why would it matter? This woman wasn't a professional artist whose livelihood depended on selling prints. She was an amateur—a hobbyist—and from the look of her, rich.

Dinah was not warming to Princess Stephanie. The young woman was so artificial, so Barbie-dollish. Her every gesture seemed rehearsed. She cried without disturbing her mascara, and she didn't smear her foundation when she dried her tears. That required practice. Her clothes were too perfect, matchy-matchy. Even her white handkerchief was embroidered with her initials in pale blue. Could one buy lingerie that color-matched designer outfits? If so, Dinah was sure Her Highness was wearing a pale blue thong.

Dinah looked at her watch. At this rate, Stephanie's story was going to take all afternoon, and so far, it was boring.

Rachel must have thought so, too. She intervened, her tone stern. "Stephanie, please control yourself, and come to the point. Why has this theft upset you so much?"

"Well, you see, sometimes I draw from life. There are a number of people in the Little Palace connected in one way or another with the Royal Family. And they—we—occasionally have royal visitors. I sketched them when they were relaxed, not posing. Perhaps they didn't know I was drawing them. Sometimes I photographed them and worked from the photos. Actually, in my prints, people are often engaged in private activities, casually dressed, or in—uh—dishabille."

Rachel looked horrified. "Are any of these etchings of nudes? Behaving inappropriately? Surely not engaged in sexual activities?" she asked.

The girl nodded, tears pouring down her face. "I'm afraid so. Actually, some people may describe a few as pornographic. I don't think they are—they're works of art. But others may see them differently."

Dinah now understood why the theft of the prints was catastrophic. The young Royals' inappropriate dress or lack of dress, and the paparazzi's constant spying on the Royal Family, had led to scandal, and had left the press hungry for more. They would feast on Stephanie's etchings.

Rachel frowned. "I agree that you have a serious problem. Stop that whining and tell us exactly what happened. When did you discover that the etchings were missing?"

Her words acted like a splash of cold water in the girl's face. Stephanie stopped crying, and replied, if not calmly, at least comprehensibly.

"This morning. Actually, I didn't know they were gone until a man rang me. He says he has the prints, and won't return them unless I give him money. If I don't pay, they'll appear in the newspapers. As proof that he has them, tomorrow one of them will appear in *Secrets*, that dreadful scandal sheet."

"How much money did he ask for?" Rachel asked.

"One million pounds, which is absurd. I have no money—only a tiny allowance from a family trust. It takes every penny I have to live," Stephanie said.

"Tell me exactly where and how the prints were kept," Rachel ordered.

Dinah was surprised at Rachel's dictatorial manner, and angry expression. She had never seen this side of her friend, even during Rachel's struggles with her vicious assistant, Simon, who'd stolen from her, cheated her, perhaps planned to kill her.

"They were in the safe in my closet—the kind of safe they have in hotels? After I spoke to the man, I opened it, and it was empty."

"When had you last looked in it?" Rachel asked.

"Friday night before I went to bed, when I put some new works away."

"So they must have been stolen Saturday, Sunday, or this morning?" Rachel said.

"I suppose so. I was in and out all day Saturday and Sunday—a few friends came for drinks on Saturday, and I gave a little dinner

Sunday night. Most people in London go away for Saturday and Sunday, of course, but I was able to round up some friends who, like poor me, are forced to stay in town, unless we are fortunate enough to be invited somewhere."

"Did you keep other valuables in the safe? Or just the prints?" Rachel asked.

Stephanie shook her head. "Nothing else, just the prints."

Rachel raised her eyebrows. "What about your jewelry? Wasn't it in the safe?"

"Actually, all I own is costume jewelry. If I need jewelry for an important occasion, I borrow it from a jeweler. I keep my inexpensive bits and pieces in a box in a dresser drawer. Nothing else in my flat was touched, just the safe," Stephanie said.

"Does the safe work with a combination?" Rachel said.

"Yes, it's my birthday—twenty-one eleven—November twenty-first."

Dinah and Rachel exchanged glances. Stephanie's birthday celebrations had probably been covered by the press every year since she could toddle. Most of England would know that November 21 was her birthday. Only an airhead would choose such an obvious code.

Dinah wondered what advice Rachel would give the princess. And when. The "when" was increasingly important. She needed to get back to the house of horrors at least an hour before Jonathan arrived for dinner, and before she went home, she had to pick up food for dinner. She had a list she rotated—mostly cold food. Smoked salmon. Sliced ham or roast beef. Roast chicken. Cheese and fruit. Anything to substitute for the ghastly meal Mrs. O'Hara would serve. The cook's dinners were even worse than her breakfasts. O'Hara insisted on serving dishes Jonathan detested—mostly offal, which he couldn't abide, as the cook had been told repeatedly. Every day Dinah had to purchase food that would prevent Jonathan's nightly tirade about Dinah's inability to manage the servants.

When Rachel asked who had a key to Stephanie's flat, the young woman claimed that only the building manager had a key to use in case of emergency. She seemed rattled and hesitant when Rachel wanted to know the names of those who'd visited her flat on the critical days. Dinah thought her reaction suggested that the list would be long, or that she didn't want to disclose the information. When Rachel insisted that she couldn't help Stephanie without the names, the girl reluctantly agreed to compile a list when she could consult her diary.

"Is there anyone in the palace in whom you can confide? Someone who would help you?" Rachel asked.

Stephanie shook her head. "Actually, anyone I told would be forced to take this to the highest level. That would be disastrous for me. Isn't there anything else I can do?" She looked as if she might cry again.

"I suggest you wait until tomorrow, and see if one of the prints appears in that paper you mentioned—*Secrets*, I think you said? If it does, you *must* speak with someone at the palace. Come for coffee tomorrow morning at eight thirty. Bring the newspaper if the photo of the print is in it, and most important, your list of weekend visitors. We then shall see where we stand," Rachel said.

At last Stephanie left.

Dinah took a long breath. She felt as if she'd listened to that piercing voice and constant use of the word "actually" for weeks. She should get on with her errands, but she was too full of questions.

"Is Stephanie really a princess? I never heard of her before I came to England, but since we've been in London, I've seen her on television several times," Dinah said.

"Yes, she is very popular with both the public and the media. And, no, she is not a princess, although she is said to be distantly connected to the Windsors—or rather, to the House of Saxe-Coburg and Gotha, as the Windsors were known until 1917. The title 'princess' began with newspaper stories when she was a child. Stephanie was a pretty little girl—very photogenic. Many pictures of her appeared frequently, and the press christened her the Little Princess, or maybe her family gave her that name. But as she grew older, there were objections in high places to her using the title. Stephanie was annoyed by what she considered interference in her affairs. She had her name changed legally. Her first name is Princess," Rachel said.

"Good grief, I never heard of such a thing. I wouldn't have thought she had it in her. She seems so—I don't know—feckless?" Dinah said.

"Do not underestimate her. She seems to have inherited some of the famous Victorian grit and stubbornness. Whatever else she is, she is definitely a descendant of Queen Victoria," Rachel said.

"I'm impressed," Dinah said.

"Do not be. Queen Victoria's descendants are myriad. Victoria had nine children and thirty-eight grandchildren, including twenty-two granddaughters, five of whom married reigning monarchs. In any case, Stephanie's connection to Queen Victoria does not make her a princess. There are only a handful of designated royals in England. Of course, Europe and Africa are full of princes and princesses and tribes of other royals. There are said to be six or seven hundred surviving Habsburgs, a host of people who call themselves Romanovs, and many more, with various names and titles, from dozens of countries."

"I had no idea. I've never met a prince or princess in the United States," Dinah said.

"There must be some who live in New York, or at least visit there. Most of those living in exile, or hoping to someday claim a throne, drift back and forth between London, Paris, and New York. Some are legitimate; some are frauds. There are a few reigning royals who identify themselves by first names only, which may be awkward for the uninformed," Rachel said. "I understand that when a lady introduced herself to Prime Minister Blair as 'Beatrix,' he asked her what she did. She was forced to explain that she was the Queen of the Netherlands."

"Good grief!" said Dinah. "Mr. Blair must have been terribly embarrassed!"

"Perhaps," Rachel said.

"There's so much I don't know. What is the 'Little Palace'? And what's a 'live' palace? Is it one that's empty—just for show?"

Rachel smiled. "I forget that you are an American, and would not necessarily know these things. The Little Palace is the nickname for the building where Stephanie and a number of people like her live—inexpensive for those who can get a flat—almost a grace-and-favor building. The building has exceptional security. I am certain Stephanie's thief is someone she knows. One cannot enter the Little Palace without an invitation and proper identification."

"What does 'grace-and-favor' mean?" Dinah asked.

"'Grace-and-favor' once meant free accommodation by permission of a sovereign or government. Grace-and-favor residents were typically retired members of royal households, or members of the armed forces who had served the country or the Palace. The practice dates back to the eighteenth century, but officially it no longer exists. Still, some people who would once have been given grace-and-favor accommodations pay very little rent—what is called a 'peppercorn' rent," Rachel said. "That, I believe, is how the flats at the Little Palace are awarded—almost free. I don't know who manages the building or awards the flats—some charity, I think. I'm sure the building has no connection with the Royal Family."

Dinah frowned. "But why does Stephanie have a 'peppercorn' flat? Did someone in her family do something important?"

"I have wondered about that, too," Rachel said. "I only know what I have read in the papers, which may not be accurate. Her parents, about whom I know nothing, died in an automobile accident when she was an infant. She was brought up by distant relatives. Perhaps one of them is powerful. Someone influential has made it possible for her to live in the Little Palace, and that is surprising, since she was criticized by many important people for changing her name as she did. She was scolded by a Royalist group who are said to handle matters like this by dealing with people they think might embarrass the Palace. Some people call them the 'Pal Pols'—short for Palace Police. I think they are volunteers, not real police, but they can be difficult. I have never encountered them, but they are said to be unpleasant to those who behave inappropriately."

Dinah's head was reeling. None of this had been covered in her English history class. "What's a 'live' palace?" she asked.

"One where the queen or king and their families live. The 'live' palaces are Buckingham Palace, where the Queen lives during the working week, and Windsor, where she spends weekends, and which she officially occupies for certain functions at Easter and in June. At Christmas and for the month of January, Her Majesty is at Sandringham, her private estate in Norfolk. In August and September, she moves to Balmoral, a property in Scotland Queen Victoria bought in 1852," said Rachel. "Sandringham and Balmoral are not palaces, of course."

"Wow! That's a lot of real estate. Taxpayers in the United States complain because they have to support both the White House and Camp David. Some presidents have their own places as well, and the people have to pay for security when the president goes to his ranch, or his beach house or whatever. People say it isn't right for the president to have so many houses when Americans live in poverty, or are homeless," Dinah said.

Rachel nodded. "I am not surprised. There are those in England who feel that way about the wealth of the Royal Family. Some people do not even think there should be a Monarchy. I, of course, disagree. I am a Royalist and proud of it."

Dinah stood up. "I must go, but before I do, two more questions. If Stephanie's so poor, how can she afford those clothes? And why doesn't she want to tell you who was in her flat over the weekend?"

"Designers beg her to wear their clothes. She does not pay for them—they are given to her, and she shows them off. As for who was in her flat: she would not want her friends to think she threw them to the wolves—that is, to the police—if she has to turn to the police about the theft of the prints. I suspect she does not want me to know she spends her time with low-life Eurotrash. I think she is lying about the key, and gives it out indiscriminately. She probably has no idea who was in her flat during the critical period. I shall know better when I see her list."

"She's annoying, but why are you so angry with her?" Dinah asked. "You seem furious."

"I do not trust Stephanie. I am not certain we have the full story, or that she is telling the truth about anything. But if those prints are as she describes, and appear in print or on television, they will damage the Monarchy. I admire the Queen, and regret the pain she has suffered because of the behavior of some of her family, and the loathsome press. I will do all I can to make this scandal disappear, even if it means having to spend time with that little fool," Rachel said.

"She *is* a dope, isn't she?" Dinah said. "Thanks so much for lunch. The crab salad was marvelous, and eating in this lovely room is a treat. Stephanie's story was interesting. I'm curious about her and her problems. Will you call me tomorrow and tell me the next chapter in the case of the stolen etchings?"

"Since you have not yet started work, why not join Stephanie and me for coffee, and hear it directly from her?" Rachel said.

Dinah, with a blank engagement book, was happy to accept. She couldn't bear hanging around that horrible house, being bullied by those wretched women. Although London was full of fascinating places to visit, she was tired of sightseeing, and didn't enjoy going around by herself. She longed for a warm, comfortable house where she could read, or write letters, or nap, or cook a delicious meal, without anyone disturbing or harassing her. She longed for friends around her. She missed being in the Greene Gallery, surrounded by people she liked, and who liked her.

More than anything, she wished Coleman would come to London. Coleman would deal with the impossible people in the awful house. If anyone could persuade Jonathan to fire them, it was Coleman.

CHAPTER THREE

Rachel

Monday, May, London

Every morning Rachel set aside time to be thankful for her life in London: thankful for the inheritance that made that life possible, that gave her the house and gallery, that gave her the time to write scholarly books on Renaissance jewelry; and thankful for, above all, the recent changes that had restored so much that she had lost.

Her partner, Simon, had cheated her, stolen from her, and left her impoverished until Heyward Bain, an American billionaire whom she hardly knew, came to her rescue.

Bain, who believed that he was partly responsible for creating the monster Simon had become, had restored all she had lost. He had managed to banish Simon to Australia, where he could no longer hurt Rachel.

She could do little to thank Heyward Bain for all he'd done for her, but she was befriending his young relative Dinah Greene, who was in London for several months on a fellowship at the Art Museum of Great Britain. Dinah hadn't said so, but Rachel thought she was unhappy. Dinah rarely mentioned her husband. Apparently he was submerged in his work, opening a London branch of his financial firm. Dinah's job at the museum had not yet begun, and she seemed to be lonely and at loose ends.

Rachel had invited Dinah to tea and lunch, and taken her to several exhibitions. She had enjoyed it. She liked Dinah. The young woman—she was in her early thirties, about ten years younger than Rachel—had lovely manners and a soft Southern voice, and she was very nice to look at, well-dressed in a quiet way. She was also knowledgeable about art, especially American art. Rachel was proud to introduce Dinah to the acquaintances they'd encountered at the museums and galleries.

Rachel was glad that Dinah had been with her when Princess Stephanie had turned up with her strange story. Rachel neither liked nor trusted Stephanie, and would rather not be involved in her sordid activities. Since she was, it was good that she had a witness, and one who knew prints. Dinah's expertise might be helpful, if this problem of Stephanie's turned out to be more than a tall tale to get attention.

She settled down to some serious thinking.

She flipped the switch to turn on the electric fireplace, and pulled her chair closer to the glowing faux logs. She missed wood fires—so much more attractive than electric—but the restrictions on their use had cleared the city's notorious smog, and for that she was grateful. The electric fire, with its softly whirring fan, kept the room warm. London could be chilly and damp any time of the year. The cold troubled Rachel. Her body could not forget, even after more than ten years in England, that as a girl she had lived in hot places in the United States. Oh, well. Her house was well heated, and her closets were filled with warm garments.

She should work on the book she was writing, about some newly discovered Medici jewelry—she tried to write five pages every day—but Stephanie's story was disturbing. Why had the little fool produced art potentially embarrassing to the Queen? She must have known it could cause trouble, not only for the Royal Family, but also for herself.

Something was odd about the theft, and the money the thief—or thieves—demanded. The "or else" was the publication in a rag called *Secrets* of a print that would embarrass the Queen. Those who'd stolen the prints must know that Stephanie had no money.

It would be easy to ascertain her income, or lack of it. Stephanie and her kind had no secrets. The press pursued them like foxes after chickens, and delved into every aspect of their lives. Could the thief possibly think the *Palace* would buy the prints back?

Ridiculous. No matter what the tabloids threatened to print, the Palace would not pay blackmail or tolerate extortion. Could this be yet another piece of the unpleasant campaign to damage—even abolish—the British Monarchy? Was it not bad enough that reporters had attacked the Royals for years, egged on by Republicans? Rachel detested the hack who'd written that the Monarchy was "the rotten core of Britain's decrepit democracy." The Queen was the rock on which Rachel's adopted country stood. She would never forget the Queen's 1992 speech, when she referred to her *annus horribilis*.

How could she prevent Stephanie's foolishness turning into yet another disaster for the Queen? She wished Professor Ransome was here to advise her. He had been dead for twelve years, but she still missed his counsel.

Rachel had been in her early thirties when she moved to London, armed with the fortune inherited from Ransome, the great Renaissance scholar. She had served him well as housekeeper and factotum. He had been her teacher, her inspiration, her model. After his death, she changed her name to Ransome, and gave his name to the gallery she opened. But she had never implied that he and she were married: Mrs. was a courtesy title, given her by Ransome's friends, in acknowledgment that the frail old man had lived longer than had been expected because of her care. He had left her everything, even made her his literary executor.

People speculated about their relationship, but they had not been lovers. Still, she had loved him. Her love was respectful, admiring, grateful. He had depended on her, trusted her, advised her. He would know what she should do about Stephanie and the theft. He would not care about the fate of the girl—she was obviously shallow and stupid—but he would agree that helping Stephanie would help the Queen. He would tell Rachel that solving this problem was her duty.

Duty aside, having been a part of the investigation of two mysteries involving Dinah and Coleman Greene, she might have found it difficult to resist this one, which had landed in her lap. The satisfaction of solving a mystery, like solving any complicated problem, was addictive.

Before she did anything else, she needed to know more about Stephanie. Her old friend Julia Fitzgerald lived in the Little Palace, where Stephanie also lived. Julia undoubtedly knew Stephanie, and perhaps some of her circle. She would be interested in Stephanie's story. Rachel picked up the phone and dialed Julia's number.

Sure enough, Julia knew Stephanie well. She was intrigued but not surprised by Rachel's story.

"She's an idiotic little creature and she travels with a crowd of brainless Eurotrash," Julia said. "Come to lunch tomorrow and I'll tell you all about her and her suitors. She's very popular—even has a girl-in-waiting—not officially, of course. More of a hanger-on. But I'm not surprised she's in trouble. Stephanie has flirted with disaster for years."

Rachel wanted to see Julia, but she couldn't accept her invitation. Julia would have to cook the meal after shopping for the ingredients, and paying for them out of her meager income. Rachel could not let that happen.

"You must let me take you to lunch, since I intend to ask your advice. I shall book a table at The Goring, and collect you in the car tomorrow at 12:45," Rachel said. The Goring dining room was Julia's favorite.

"That's an offer I can't refuse," Julia said.

"Good. I will see you tomorrow," Rachel said.

CHAPTER FOUR

Coleman

Monday, May, New York

Coleman, sitting at her desk in the immense office her half-brother, Heyward, had designed for her, wondered if she would ever get used to so much space around her. She was only five feet tall, and felt dwarfed by the high ceilings and the great glass window, with its magnificent view of New York skyscrapers. She missed the snug little office she'd used when she edited *ArtSmart*. She'd occupied it for years, and it fit her like a much-worn glove.

She'd done her best to make her giant office feel smaller and more comfortable, by enlarging magazine covers of *First Home* and *ArtSmart* to poster size and hanging them every twelve inches on the walls. She bought several tree-like plants to fill in the corners, and discarded the enormous basket the decorators had purchased for Dolly, her tiny dog. Any Maltese would be lost in that basket, and five-pound Dolly ignored it. Dolly spent most of her time in the office in her favorite Kitty Kup underneath Coleman's desk. These days Coleman was almost always at that desk. She didn't like being inside all of the time, but the job required it.

Coleman had completed the reorganization of her new magazine, assisted by the consultants she had hired at the time of the acquisition of *First Home*. After terminating nearly half of *First Home*'s underworked and overpaid staff, and combining the magazine's back office with *ArtSmart*'s, Coleman had moved the trimmer and more productive *First Home* staff out of their expensive space and into the CH Holdings building, which she and her half-brother owned, and where *ArtSmart* had its offices.

With all the fat stripped away, Coleman was able to assess *First Home*'s strengths and weaknesses. The gardening department was popular and much admired: It won prizes, attracted lively correspondence from readers, and was a favorite in its field. The young woman who managed it was talented, knowledgeable, and flexible.

The food department was also a winner. *First Home*'s chef had grown up in Mississippi and been famous as the head cook in a Jackson restaurant before joining the magazine. Miraculously, he was able to keep the Deep South flavors in his delicious dishes, but reduce the sugar and fat content. Coleman was amused to see that the staff lined up to taste the meals he prepared in the sparkling new test kitchen. The odors floating out of that kitchen were so enticing, Coleman had to struggle not to join the queue.

That was the good news. On the other hand, the two remaining departments clamored for immediate attention, restructuring, and dismissals.

She'd had an unpleasant conversation with the young man in charge of architecture, pointing out that the house plans he brought to the magazine were too extreme for the magazine's audience, and far too expensive. Irate at her criticism, he'd screamed at her, called her names, and, as she'd hoped, threatened to resign. She'd accepted his resignation and seen him ushered out. Today she was on her way to implement her plan for his replacement.

She took a taxi to the Architects' Library Club on East Eighty-Seventh Street, where she met with Janet, an old friend, also the librarian and general manager of the club. Coleman had given her friend a brief description of what she had in mind on the telephone. Janet was eager to pin down the details and launch the program Coleman had proposed.

"I am so excited about your idea," Janet said. "We have lots of young architects who would be thrilled to have their plans featured in *First Home*."

Coleman smiled. "I'm excited about it, too. As you know, *First Home* is a monthly. I'd like to have a new plan in every issue, each a design for a first home. Price is important, but the houses should also be attractive, appealing, charming. I suggest that you head a panel of senior architects to choose each winner. The architect you select will receive a financial prize—you should suggest an appropriate amount—in addition to our publishing his or her plan, a story about the design of the house, and an interview with the architect in the magazine. Do you think your judges will expect an honorarium?"

Janet laughed. "No, they'll love doing it, especially if you list their names in the magazine every month."

"Done!" Coleman said. "Let's get started today. Can you give me some material on the history of the Architects' Library Club? We'll publish an article in *First Home* about the club, and announce the new program."

Coleman returned to her office, confident that the new architecture department would be exactly what *First Home* needed.

But the important interior design department was in worse shape than the architecture department, and its problems were more difficult to solve. Its editors were two dowdy women who shared an apartment as well as the job, and who had similar tastes. They were not old, but they *acted* old, and *selected* old. Neither was imaginative or creative. They stocked samples of the few materials they used, and used them over and over—for years. Most of what they recommended was too expensive for *First Home* readers, as well as being unappealing and dated.

Coleman knew the Drab Drones would have to go, but she didn't know how to replace them. In the short term, she cut back their territory, turning the decoration of kitchens and dining rooms over to the food team. Patios, porches, and glass sunrooms were now gardening team responsibilities. The department heads had accepted their new assignments—and the accompanying raises—with enthusiasm, while the foolish Drabs didn't seem troubled by losing a big hunk of their territory. They shrugged off the loss and continued down their unsuccessful paths. Bad as they were, they were all she had. She was stuck with them until she found replacements.

Coleman knew nothing about interior design. How many times had her cousin Dinah or her friend Debbi suggested she get another apartment, or at least redecorate the one she had? She'd refused, didn't want the mess, the distraction, the bother. She didn't tell them she had no idea how to decorate her apartment, and she wasn't interested in learning. But drastic times called for drastic measures: She had to learn about interior design in order to understand what the department should do, and how it should be managed.

She had no choice but to plunge in and try to learn all she could as fast as she could. She asked several schools of interior design for catalogues and reading lists, and whether they allowed auditing. They assured her she'd be welcome to audit courses, and sent her videos to watch, piles of paper, and lists of books she should read. She soon found herself walled in by great stacks of magazines and books.

One of her half-brother's most welcome additions to the new office building was a magnificent library on the fifty-fifth floor, the floor he shared with Coleman. Like Coleman, Heyward loved books. He'd stocked the library with a huge number of volumes on topics that interested him: paper production, forestry, air pollution, and dozens of other arcane subjects. All the books that *First Home* and *ArtSmart* owned were shelved in the library, and generous donations from Heyward had expanded their collections. The library even had a card catalogue: Heyward had commissioned it from a man who still made them.

The books she was studying would eventually go in the library, but for the moment, she wanted them where she could reach them. She arranged them by subject—Furniture, English; Furniture,

French; Frames, picture; Mirrors; Color (paint and wallpaper); and so on.

She was enjoying her studies and learning, but what she was doing was catch-up. She had to be out in front of the crowd. She needed new ideas, fresh approaches, fashionable materials for the decorating department. How was she to find them? Or identify them?

She had asked her old friend Zeke for ideas; he was managing *ArtSmart*, her other magazine, and in touch with much of the art world. He'd referred her to Bethany, his brand-new bride, who was in charge of Dinah's gallery while Dinah was in England. But while Bethany had marvelous taste in clothes, like Coleman, she'd never paid much attention to interior design.

"I sympathize with you, and I'll be happy to go shopping with you anytime, but I don't know a single decorator," Bethany said. "I was mighty glad to move into Zeke's apartment. It's perfect. I didn't have to do a thing."

Coleman would ask Dinah for advice if she weren't in London, adjusting to a new country, a new house, and new and important work at the Art Museum of Great Britain. That left Debbi Diamondstein.

Debbi, whom Heyward had chosen to decorate the offices of *First Home* and *ArtSmart* as well as his own office, was Coleman's publicist, a friend, and aware of everything fashionable, avant-garde. Debbi wasn't an interior designer except as a favor to her favorite clients, who were also her best friends. The rooms she designed were much admired, and she was sure to come up with some good ideas.

Debbi laughed when she heard why Coleman was calling. "All these years Dinah and I have been trying to get you to move or at least fix up your apartment—but no! You didn't care. If you'd listened to us, you wouldn't be at such a loss," she said.

"Okay, okay. Say 'I told you so' a few more times, and be done with it. You're right, of course. I'm reading, studying, and learning from books, but I need to get out in the world, check out the new. But which stores should I visit? And do you know people I should be talking to? People with original ideas? And where can I find not-too-expensive, attractive houses to look at? Do you know anyone I might hire to work with me? The women running the decorating department are hopeless. I need to hire someone to take over the department as soon as possible." She paused to take a breath, and Debbi leaped in.

"About stores: Start with ABC, Nineteenth and Broadway, a fabulous store. Full of ideas. Their goods can be expensive, but they have great sales, and you'll be inspired by what you see. You can sometimes chase down less expensive versions of what they're showing," Debbi said.

"Got it," Coleman said.

"As for people you should talk to, start in your own backyard. The harpies running your decorating department are doing their best to destroy a talented young woman who works for *First Home*. She's smart and attractive and competent, and naturally they hate her. Rescue her, listen to her. You won't regret it. Her name is Evelyn Cartright—Lyn, for short. She's the daughter of one of my clients."

"Why don't I know about her?" Coleman asked. "Why haven't I met her?"

"You weren't interested in the kind of thing she does, remember? Lyn got the job through your gardening lady, who was embarrassed by how bad the decorating department is, and knew Lyn could spark it up. The old crones reluctantly took her on as an assistant. They were supposed to give her a chance, but she's spending most of her time going out for coffee or food for them. They have no interest in her ideas."

"How old is she? What's her background?"

"You've heard of her mother, Sylvia Cartright. She's in the top echelon at Nelson-Taylor, the LA clothing store. Sylvia has a great eye for fashion, and her daughter has her taste, but Lyn is interested in interior design. She's twenty-five, been out of college a few years, and was a very successful decorator in Texas. She wanted to get out of her mother's shadow, so she came to the Big Apple. She could take over your interior design department today. She's more than qualified.

"Lyn will have lots of ideas, but here's a lead she might not know about: A friend recently told me about a cluster of villages in Connecticut where the houses sound perfect for *First Home*—charming cottages with pretty little gardens and original decoration. The biggest and most attractive village in the area is called Merriweather. There's an art colony on nearby Eelgrass Island, so a lot of artists and writers have settled in the area. That's why the houses are so colorful and original."

"Whom do I contact?" Coleman asked.

"A woman named Frances Forester owns what's said to be a charming inn in Merriweather. She also owns several rental cottages. You should call her, go see her, look at the cottages. But be careful not to annoy her—they call her the Cranky Yankee, easily offended. Before you do anything else, promote Lyn! She can take over inside while you're out scouting for ideas."

As soon as she hung up, Coleman headed for the decorating department, Dolly at her heels. She could hardly wait to promote Evelyn Cartright. But when she reached the office the Drabs shared, she walked into a tirade. One of the Drabs was screaming at an attractive young brunette in a stunning red dress. She had to be Evelyn Cartright.

The shouting didn't stop when Coleman entered the office. She clapped her hands to attract their attention, and said in a loud voice, "Quiet, please. We can't have this kind of scene. What's the problem?"

The taller Drab—Coleman could never remember their names, thought of them as D1 (tall) and D2 (short)—was more animated than Coleman had ever seen her. She snarled, "This impertinent young woman had the gall to say that one of our wallpapers is tasteless and inappropriate!"

Coleman turned to the girl in the red dress. "You must be Evelyn Cartright?"

"Yes, Ms. Greene," she said.

"May I see the wallpaper?" Coleman said.

"Is that necessary?" D2 said. "Why do you need to see it? This is our department, and we know what the customers like."

"Show me the wallpaper right away, please," Coleman said.

The D shrugged and handed Coleman a sheet of wallpaper.

Coleman looked at it and felt her face go hot.

"You've been sending samples of this wallpaper out to readers? Recommending it?"

"Yes, for years," a D said, sounding smug and proud of herself.

"It's offensive," Coleman said.

The paper featured little black boys, clad in tiny grass skirts, each clinging to a palm tree against a cream-colored background. The pattern was repeated every few inches.

"Don't you recognize this?" Coleman asked. "It's right out of *Little Black Sambo*, the children's story."

"So what?" snapped one of the Ds, bristling with hostility.

Coleman tried to hold her temper. "It's racist, it's tacky, and it's ugly. Get rid of it immediately. I don't ever want to see it again," she said.

"Who are you to tell us what we can and can't do?" One of the women said.

Coleman lost it. "As you should know, if you paid any attention to what goes on here, I am Coleman Greene, the owner of *First Home*, and both of you are fired. Collect your belongings, and go to Human Resources. I'll call them and let them know you are coming. They'll handle the paperwork, and will arrange to see you out of the building."

"You'll be sorry," a D threatened.

"Yes, we'll tell the world how you have abused us, and you'll hear from our lawyer," the other one chimed in.

"Goodbye," Coleman said. Turning her back on the furious women, she looked at Evelyn, who'd stood silent during the storm. "Miss Cartright, please come with me to my office. We have a lot to talk about."

When they were seated in Coleman's office, Coleman said, "I'm sorry we had to meet like this. I'd meant to keep those women on a little longer, while I figured out what to do and brought in new people, but I just couldn't let this pass. May I call you Lyn?"

"Yes, ma'am. Uh—am I fired, too?"

Coleman laughed. "No, I want you to manage the department, help me do whatever needs to be done. Do you have any ideas about how to handle this mess?"

Lyn smiled. "Yes, I've been thinking about what should be done ever since I came to work here. Do you have an assistant who can help me with practical issues?"

Coleman nodded and pressed a button she rarely used, summoning her assistant. At Heyward's urging, she'd hired Mrs. Anderson, a middle-aged woman with considerable office experience, to be gatekeeper and to take care of the library. She sat in the big foyer outside her office and Heyward's. Mrs. Anderson also answered Coleman's phone and acted as Coleman's secretary on the rare occasion when she needed one. She was efficient, unobtrusive, and competent. But there was so little for her to do when Heyward wasn't around, Coleman had worried that she'd leave for a more stimulating job.

Maybe the decorating department was the challenge that would keep her interested. She would be terrific helping Lyn to handle all the details of closing the obsolete department and starting up a new one.

Half an hour later, Coleman excused herself. Mrs. Anderson and Lyn were having a wonderful time, preparing memos for distribution internally, explaining that the interior design department was temporarily closed for alterations. The head of the human resources department met with them, as did one of the company lawyers, to discuss settlements with the departed Ds. A technician appeared to deal with telephones and computers. They were getting along famously—they didn't need her. She'd leave them to it and head for home. She wanted to plan a getaway, and didn't want interruptions until the details were settled.

•••

After being confined to the office while she dealt with the problems of the decorating department, Coleman had cabin fever. She looked forward to escaping and spending a spring day in Connecticut, on her maiden field trip for *First Home*. She had invited Bethany—tired of being stuck indoors at the Greene Gallery—to join her, and hired a car and driver to take them to Merriweather. Debbi's description of the area had galvanized her.

With Dolly in her lap, and Bethany beside her, Coleman was as excited as a child playing hooky to go to the circus. She felt free after what seemed like a very long period of captivity. Running *First Home* was much more of an indoor job than *ArtSmart* had been. She missed all the outside activity *ArtSmart* required: openings, exhibitions, lunches and dinners with artists and collectors. She enjoyed the intellectual part of being in charge of *First Home*—learning about furniture and the like—but she needed to get out more often.

She looked out the car window. They were on I-95, a highway Coleman hated—so many big trucks roaring by, threatening to blow smaller cars away. There wasn't much to look at to take her mind off those trucks—signs advertising McDonald's, Dunkin' Donuts, Wendy's, no trees, no flowers. Ugly and boring.

She was grateful when they turned onto a wooded road with little traffic, leaving the trucks behind. Through the trees she caught glimpses of charming villages, church steeples, flower gardens, and, beyond them, the glitter of the sea. Oh, joy!— exactly what she'd hoped for.

Half an hour later they left the road, and turned into a tiny village called Silverdale, only a few miles from Merriweather. Coleman spotted the handsome stone railroad station for which Silverdale was famous. Early pink roses in boxes and pots surrounded the building, adding to its attractiveness.

"Look at that station, Bethany! Isn't it fabulous? I can see why people like to come up here by train. I read about the train ride in an article about the Swan Inn," Coleman said.

"It's the best lookin' train station I've ever seen," Bethany said. "But do they have good train service?"

"They must. There's an art colony near here, and the artists arrive at this station, too. Lots of people depend on it."

A few miles further on they turned again, this time onto a paved road that bordered an exquisite green. Its perfection reminded Coleman of a film set. She asked the driver to pull over so that they could look at everything. A sign on the roadside read, "You have entered Merriweather, Connecticut. Welcome!"

"How friendly! Did you ever see a prettier square? Look, that church is just like the one in Stowe, Vermont. I love New England churches," Coleman said. "The house nearest it must be the parsonage—it's the same style and, like the church, white with dark green trim. I think the building on the other side of the church has a library sign on it, and that bigger one must be a school . . . "

"Yes, the square is beautiful—picture perfect. Is the inn you want to visit near here? I don't see any cottages," Bethany said.

"According to the map, we should drive through the village and we'll eventually come to a little park. The bay should be on our right, and the inn is in front of the bay, right beside the road. I think the cottages are scattered around," Coleman said.

There was almost no traffic, and the driver was able to drive slowly through the village, which was as pretty as the square, and amazingly neat. Most of the houses and commercial buildings were shingled, grayed with age. Some had brightly colored painted doors or shutters—green, yellow, red, blue, orange. Many had low fences and hedges bordering the road, and most had small front gardens celebrating spring with daffodils, tulips, forsythia, and other flowers she couldn't identify.

The little town seemed to have everything one could need. They passed the post office, a dry cleaner, a supermarket, a delicatessen, a movie theater, a gift shop, and several restaurants, including one specializing in seafood, with a big swordfish painted over the doors. A colorful fruit and vegetable stand, backed by a shop with other kinds of food, stood next to a coffee shop. A bookstore caught Coleman's eyes, and Bethany spotted a window full of smart-looking clothes.

"I'd like to take a look in there," she said.

"We'll come back to town later, have a late lunch, and visit that shop," Coleman said.

The houses ended at the park, where more forsythia, daffodils, and a few early azaleas and dogwoods bloomed. Graveled paths and small benches invited visitors to come for a stroll, or sit down and enjoy the flowers.

Coleman could hear the pounding of the sea in the distance, and she could glimpse blue water through the trees. She was sure she'd be able to smell salt water, and she let down the window to take a big breath of the cold, clean air. Delicious, better than any air she'd breathed in a long time. It reminded her of the beach near her childhood home in North Carolina.

Just beyond the park, they arrived at a sizeable white-painted building, identified by a large black-and-gold sign as the Swan Inn. Rhododendrons not yet in bloom softened the rather stark outline of the building, and, in the background, waves crashed against a stone seawall.

Frances Forester, a tall, slender woman with straight snowy white hair cut in a style Coleman's grandmother called a "bowl" cut—about the same length all the way around, as if someone had put a bowl over her head and trimmed around it—greeted them at the door of the inn, and invited them in. She was nicely dressed in a gray wool skirt and a blue cashmere sweater set. She wore a pearl necklace and matching pearl earrings. Coleman was glad she and Bethany had decided to dress up for the trip. They might have arrived in jeans, which, seeing Mrs. Forester, would have been a faux pas.

Bethany was wearing a beige wool pantsuit, with a brown pullover, brown suede boots, and a gorgeous topaz brooch on her jacket lapel. Coleman had chosen a yellow wool dress, and its matching jacket with big black shiny buttons and black patent leather boots. Her black leather cap mostly covered her blonde curls. Dinah had sent it to her from London, with a note that it was the rage. Coleman was trying it out. If she liked it, she might buy more caps and hats. She was looking in all directions for change.

The inn was handsomely furnished, with polished wooden antique pieces among soft-looking sofas in blue and gray and white. Scattered on the sofas were pillows covered with needlepoint, featuring swans—flying, swimming, nesting, in couples, with cygnets, alone, against colored backgrounds. Paintings and prints of swans decorated the walls.

Coleman and Bethany exchanged smiles. They recognized some of the works. Dinah and Bethany had put together a swan print exhibition at the Greene Gallery last year.

Mrs. Forester didn't invite them to sit down. They were still standing in the foyer when she asked, "How can I help you? I know you want to see the inn—and here it is. Do you want to make reservations? Or entertain here? I believe you are also interested in the cottages?"

Her words were pleasant, but her voice and manner were decidedly chilly. Coleman remembered that Debbi had called her the Cranky Yankee. They'd have to tread carefully.

Coleman explained that she owned the magazine *First Home* and wanted to write an article or a series of articles about the inn and cottages. "We want to point out the wonderful ideas you have here—like the swan art in the inn. This is Bethany Byrd. She works with my cousin Dinah Greene Hathaway at the Greene Gallery. They exhibited some of the prints you have here in a swan show."

Mrs. Forester smiled. "So you're that Greene! Yes, I bought two swans by Margaret Patterson from Dinah, and the Botke. I loved that show, and Dinah is lovely. How is she? Why didn't she come with you?" she said. "Would you like a tour of the inn?"

Coleman explained that Dinah was in England, and that they'd very much like a tour.

The chill vanished. The connection with Dinah and the Greene Gallery had broken the ice: Mrs. Forester was welcoming, warm, and friendly as she showed them the house. Swans decorated all the rooms—on painted furniture, quilts, wallpaper, shower curtains, rugs, everywhere.

Back downstairs, Mrs. Forester led them to a small sitting room where only one work of art, featuring one large swan, hung. Coleman recognized it as a color lithograph by Louis Rhead. She suspected Dinah was the source. A little clutter—a newspaper, opened mail on the desk—suggested this was Mrs. Forester's private space.

"Tell me about the cottages," Coleman asked. "How many do you own?"

"Four: Flag Cottage, Flower Cottage, Shell Cottage, and Butterfly Cottage. From the outside they are all pretty much alike—gray-shingled like the houses in the village. Each has a little sign over the door with its name on it, and an emblem—a flag or a butterfly, whatever."

"Can we see them?" Coleman asked.

Mrs. Forester shook her head. "I rent them from Memorial Day through Labor Day, and close them the rest of the year. They are still sealed for winter, but I can show you pictures. You'll see some more Greene Gallery art in them—I always turn to Dinah when I'm doing up a cottage—but Butterfly is the last one I decorated. I could rent more, but I haven't been able to buy more cottages," Mrs. Forester said.

Coleman longed to see the interiors of a couple of the cottages, but she could tell Mrs. Forester wasn't about to open one. Fortunately, the photographs she showed them were of high quality.

Flag Cottage was decorated with American flag images in many different media, and the interior walls were shades of blue. The walls of Flower Cottage were painted pale green, and several rooms were papered in green and white stripes. Flower paintings and prints adorned all the walls. They recognized some of Dinah's favorites.

"Yes, I was thrilled when I asked Dinah about flower prints," Mrs. Forester said. "She had everything I needed—Edna Boies Hopkins, William Seltzer Rice. I was able to buy all the prints you see from Dinah."

The photographs of Shell Cottage and Butterfly Cottage were as attractive as the others. Coleman was beginning to get the glimmer of an idea about how she could adapt Mrs. Forester's concept for *First Home* readers when she saw Mrs. Forester glance at her watch and realized it was probably past their hostess's lunchtime.

Coleman stood up, as did Bethany. Coleman thanked Mrs. Forester and apologized for staying so long. Mrs. Forester brushed off the apology and escorted them to the door. "If I can be of further help, let me know," she said. "Please give my regards to Dinah."

Half an hour later, they were eating delectable clam chowder, and the best grilled swordfish they'd ever tasted. Stuffed after lunch, and longing for a nap in the car on the way back to New York, Bethany decided to forget about the clothes shopping.

"If you decide to come back up here, count me in," she said.

"I'll be back," Coleman said. "I want to stay in touch with Mrs. Forester. I've decided one aspect of our decorating department will be 'My Dream House Is a Theme House.' I'd like to persuade her to become a consultant to *First Home*. We'll show our readers how to change a simple little house into a flag cottage, a flower cottage, a butterfly, shell, and more. I think it will be a huge success."

Bethany woke up, and they discussed the possibilities, both for *First Home* and the Greene Gallery, all the way back to New York, bubbling with enthusiasm.

•••

Back in her office, Coleman was absorbed in the report Lyn and Mrs. Anderson had put together about the new design department when Heyward called on her private line.

"I need you to come to London for a couple of weeks. Before you start telling me all the reasons you can't come, you should know there are important business reasons for you to be here," he said.

Coleman hated leaving New York. When anyone suggested she should go out of town, her answer was always the same. "I'm too busy," she said.

"Nothing you are doing is as important as what's going on here. We have some great business opportunities, and you need to meet with Rachel Ransome to discuss the strategy for the art book publishing business."

"I'd like to get to know Rachel," Coleman said. "Maybe she could come here?"

"No, Rachel *can't* come to New York. Her gallery keeps her tied to London. She doesn't have a Bethany or a Zeke to take over while she's away. Anyway, I told you: I have business opportunities I want you to look at."

"Like what?"

"The most interesting is *Cottage & Castle*, an English magazine I think we should buy. The castle part is too grand for us, but you could change that to a kind of 'my home is my castle' feeling. And the cottage part would work well with *First Home*."

Coleman perked up. "Is *Cottage & Castle* anything like *Country Life*? I *love Country Life*."

"They have qualities in common, but *Cottage & Castle* is a monthly, not a weekly, and it doesn't include articles about animals."

"Oh, too bad. I read every word in *Country Life* about badgers and hedgehogs—I just read a great letter in *Country Life*: 'Hedgehog Breaches Contract.'"

"You don't own a magazine about animals. Stop changing the subject. I need you to come to London. I want your help."

"What about Dolly? I'm not leaving her here, and I'm not putting her in quarantine and she's not flying in the baggage compartment. Bigger dogs than Dolly have died back there," Coleman said.

"No, of course not. You'll fly to Paris with Dolly in her carrier at your feet. I'll meet the two of you at Charles de Gaulle Airport, and we'll fly to England together. Don't worry about anything—

I'll take care of it all. She'll never leave your side. Lots of dogs like Dolly have flown the way she will, comfortably and safely."

Coleman frowned. "What do you mean, 'dogs like Dolly?' There *are* no dogs like Dolly."

Heyward took a deep breath, meant for her to hear. He wanted her to know he was struggling to be patient. "Small, well-behaved dogs that can travel in carriers, that are used to being out and about, that are quiet when necessary."

"Where would we stay? Most London hotels don't take dogs, do they? And don't say I can stay with Dinah and Jonathan. I'd like to stay with Dinah, but Jonathan and I don't get along all that well when we see too much of each other."

"You and Dolly will stay with me. I designed a suite for you in my house. You'll like it, I promise."

"I hear they kidnap dogs for ransom in London. I can't risk losing Dolly," she said.

"Coleman, she's never out of your sight—how would anyone kidnap her?"

She sighed. She wasn't going to be able to avoid this trip, much as she disliked the thought of it. Still, it had bright spots. She'd see Dinah, and she'd meet the legendary Rachel Ransome. There were places in London she wanted to visit. She'd make a list, and insist on doing a few things no one else would think important, like going to Liberty, the classic department store, to look at fabrics.

"How long do I have to stay?" she asked.

"I told you: two weeks. I've already made your and Dolly's reservations—she has to go to the vet tomorrow afternoon at five for a special shot, and he'll fill out her papers, her shot record, and everything she needs. Start packing. You're leaving Thursday night."

"I can't possibly go that soon," Coleman argued.

"It's a done deal," Heyward said. "I've made appointments for you in London. See you Friday morning in Paris." He hung up.

Coleman put her elbows on her desk, and her head in her hands. Double damn. She dreaded the trip. She'd flown very little, and she didn't like it; she had a problem with heights. But she owed it to Heyward.

Her private line rang again. This time it was Dinah.

"Coleman? I've got a huge mess here. Could you come over? I need your help. I start work next week and—"

"Calm down. I'm all but on the way. I'm flying over Thursday night. Heyward's meeting Dolly and me in Paris. We'll be in London Friday morning. What's the problem?"

"I'm so glad you're coming. I hate this horrible house, and the cook and the housekeeper are monsters. I'm furious with Jonathan, and I don't know what to do. I start work at the museum next week, and I feel terrible. I simply cannot cope."

"Don't worry. We'll sort it out. I'll see you Friday. Do you want to tell me about it now?" Coleman asked.

"No. Just come."

"Is there anything you need?"

"No, no. Just come."

Coleman hung up and pondered Dinah's call. Dinah was rarely angry. She was typically calmness itself, unless she was crying over a dead bird or a stray dog. Her problems sounded like a tornado in a teacup. She'd had several conversations with Dinah about the obnoxious servants of the rented London house. Dinah should have been able to bring them into line. Or she or Jonathan should have fired them. Why was the situation upsetting Dinah so much? And why wasn't Jonathan helping her? And why in the world would servants behave the way Dinah described?

Maybe they thought they could force Jonathan and Dinah to vacate the house. Could that be what they wanted? If so, why? Dinah was sweet-tempered and agreeable to a fault. Jonathan was demanding, but willing to pay well over the market to get what he wanted, and very generous. It all sounded very odd, but easy to deal with. Before she could turn to Heyward's projects, she would deal with Dinah's problems.

CHAPTER FIVE

Dinah

Monday, May, London

The black Mercedes with the uniformed driver behind the wheel was waiting for Dinah when she left Rachel's gallery. Dinah sighed when she saw it. The sun was shining and the sky was blue. On a day like this, she would rather walk than be shut up in a car. When it wasn't pouring rain, London was a wonderful walking city, with its beautiful parks, buildings, elegant shops—but Jonathan wouldn't hear of her walking anywhere. An English business associate and his wife had recently moved to New York after being violently mugged twice near their Kensington home, and they had impressed Jonathan with their stories.

After the Hathaways's arrival in London, Jonathan, over-protective since their wedding the previous June, became obsessed with Dinah's safety. He insisted she take all sorts of inconvenient precautions. She might have found it easier to tolerate the outdoor rules he established had their living conditions been satisfactory, but they were unbearable. She felt claustrophobic in the car, and miserable in the house.

Her husband's preoccupation with the dangers of London had led him to rent, sight unseen, a house in Culross Place, near the U.S. Embassy, where the security was formidable. Large uniformed men carrying submachine guns strolled up and down the block, and Dinah had to show her passport at a checkpoint when she returned to the house, no matter how often she came and went in a single day, even after the guards knew her, her driver, and the car by sight.

Fortunately, since she spent so much time with him, Dinah liked James, the driver Jonathan had hired. James was happy to answer her questions about the buildings and parks and stores they passed, and he took her wherever she wanted to go. He was amazingly patient with the checkpoint people, and the ever-present guards. Maybe he was afraid of being shot if he didn't cooperate.

Londoners joked about the security around the U.S. Embassy, but they hated the guns and the fences and bollards that spoiled beautiful Grosvenor Square. Dinah shared their distaste, and missed the freedom she'd enjoyed in New York. In London, she had little freedom, and, except for Rachel, no friends.

Where should she go today for food? Her favorite place was Fortnum's, but she couldn't go there every day. "Let's go to Whole Foods," she said.

"Yes, madam," James said.

Dinah had been thrilled to hear there was a Whole Foods in London, and not very far away. She had found London supermarkets very different from those in New York, and Whole Foods was a store she knew well. But the Whole Foods in London was unlike those she knew in the United States. In some ways it was better: The cheese department was fabulous, as was the produce. Whole Foods offered a large selection of prepared food and a wide range of spices, reflecting London's diversity. The Kensington High Street store was multistory, and the shopper took an escalator down to the basement to reach the main floor, much like Eli's in New York. Not much in the way of frozen food or American brands, but a store that was fun and rewarding to visit.

•••

She returned to 23 Culross with her groceries, including a cold supper for Jonathan. He preferred a hot meal, but it was the best she could do. She couldn't get into the kitchen to cook, or even heat food. The women in the kitchen guarded the room. Tonight would feature another boring meal with an irritable husband, and early to bed.

CHAPTER SIX

Rachel

Tuesday, May, London

By seven, Rachel had dressed and breakfasted, and was at her desk. She planned to work on her book until Dinah and Stephanie arrived at eight thirty. When her private line rang before she had written the first word, she was annoyed. Few people would call her at this hour. She picked up the receiver, expecting a recording trying to sell her something, or a wrong number.

"Rachel? Julia here. You're not going to believe this: Princess Stephanie has discovered a man's body in her bathroom. I think it's suicide. But, of course, it could be murder. She's hysterical. The police are on their way. If you can get here before they arrive, I'll let you in as my guest. If they arrive first, they may close the building to visitors. Once you're in, you'll be in a position to know what's going on."

Rachel didn't hesitate. The death must be connected with the theft of the prints and the extortion. Surely Stephanie wasn't involved in two sinister and almost simultaneous unrelated events? Since Rachel was committed to helping to solve the first crime, she felt compelled to look into the new one. Maybe she should alert the police to the theft of Stephanie's prints and blackmail, since the crimes were almost certainly connected. If she was in the Little Palace, she might have an opportunity to speak to the police.

Her driver wouldn't arrive until ten, but she would have no difficulty hailing a taxi. She wished she had time to change into something less frivolous. The cream-colored suit she'd put on to wear to lunch with Julia at The Goring was inappropriate for visiting a death scene—too celebratory, too cheerful. Oh well, it couldn't be helped.

She slipped on the coat that completed the outfit, tossed her beige carryall over her shoulder, and hurried to the door, pausing to let her maid know where she could be reached, and to send her driver to the Little Palace as soon as he arrived, and wait for her there. She scribbled a note for Miss Manning, her assistant, who would come in at eight, asking her to call Dinah and cancel their coffee date. She would telephone Dinah later.

At the Little Palace, the doorman and the concierge were as calm as usual. The marble-paved lobby, adorned with tattered and slightly soiled oriental rugs and several enormous arrangements of fading cherry blossoms, showed no signs of disarray, or police activity. The doorman saw Rachel into the elevator to the fourth floor.

Julia had left the door of her flat ajar, probably to listen for the elevator, and she came out into the hall to greet her. Rachel was startled by Julia's appearance. Usually carefully dressed, Julia wore droopy beige slacks, a threadbare white cotton shirt, fuzzy blue bedroom slippers with yellow ducks' heads, and white cotton gloves. She put a gloved finger to her lips.

"Let me take your coat. I'll hang it in the closet. You should leave your boots here—they are rather noisy. I'll put them in the closet with your coat. Let me give you a pair of slippers. We have to be quiet. We'll slip up the stairs to the fifth floor, and I'll show you the crime scene," Julia whispered.

Rachel suppressed a smile. Julia's excitement seemed ghoulish, but Rachel could understand it. She and Julia shared a passion for mystery novels, films, and television, but neither of them had ever been close to a criminal investigation, or been near a crime scene. Julia would relish every minute of the experience, as would

Rachel. It was sad that someone had died, but the dead man was not someone she knew, and it sounded as if Julia was right—his death was his own choice. In any case, the death seemed unreal, like something out of a book.

Of course, Julia was like a character in a book. She played up her resemblance to the late Joan Hickson—the actress who had played Miss Marple in the BBC series featuring Dame Agatha Christie's elderly heroine. Rachel and Julia agreed this was the best adaptation—wearing country tweeds, ruffled silk blouses, dowdy hats, and no make up. Like Hickson, Julia was tiny. She resembled one of Beatrix Potter's small animals, just as Hickson had. Julia did her best to act like Miss Marple. She sprinkled her otherwise elegant English with expressions she picked up from her favorite books and television. Some of them probably dated back to the 1930s, when Dame Agatha's books about Miss Marple were new; others were from contemporary novels and programs, and sounded strange coming from Julia.

Rachel followed Julia up to the fifth floor, which was as quiet as the fourth floor and the lobby. The corridor was empty, but a door stood open.

"That's Stephanie's flat," Julia whispered.

"Where *is* Stephanie?" Rachel asked.

"Downstairs with her friend Izzy. When around six I heard Stephanie screaming, I ran upstairs to see what was wrong. She was crying and shaking. She said she'd just come home, and found a body in her bathroom. I escorted her to Izzy's flat on the third floor—Izzy is the girl-in-waiting I mentioned. She tags after Stephanie everywhere, and is willing to put up with her theatrics.

"After I dropped Stephanie off, I came back up here and sneaked into her bathroom to see for myself. I had no intention of calling the police on Stephanie's say-so. She tends to exaggerate and cry wolf—to do anything to get attention. But this time she was quite right. The poor man looks like a waxwork at Madame

Tussauds, before they are painted or dyed or whatever it is they do to try to make those figures look human. I'm warning you, the room is a ghastly mess—blood all over the floor—an abattoir, my dear. Would you care to take a look?" Her small, heavy-lidded eyes gleamed with excitement.

Rachel knew she should not enter that apartment. She'd learned about crime scene contamination from films and television programs. But she could not resist. If it was suicide, no criminal was involved, but the police would investigate, and they might be angry if they learned she had trespassed.

Nevertheless, she was determined to do it. She felt disoriented, as if she were someone else—perhaps Helen Mirren in *Prime Suspect*?

She walked as quietly as she could behind Julia, who tiptoed in her silly slippers through the pale pink entry and sitting room. The rooms were fragrant with the scent of the stargazer lilies in bowls on every tabletop. The pink-flowered chintz curtains were closed, but the rooms were lit by table lamps and Rachel could see that the sofa and chairs were covered in the same chintz as the curtains.

She followed Julia down a corridor to the open door of the bathroom. When Julia used her gloved hand to widen the opening, Rachel realized why she'd worn gloves: fingerprints! Smart Julia. Good thinking about the gloves and the soundless slippers, too.

The contrast of all the pink flowers with the bloody corpse was horrific. The bathroom smelled like a badly kept butcher's shop, mixed with the even worse odor of human waste. Rachel put her hand over her nose and mouth, and held her breath. She'd read that police smeared Vicks VapoRub on their upper lips to block nasty odors at death scenes. She wished she had some, but Vicks was not the sort of thing one carried in a handbag.

The man's nude body was gray and waxy, just as Julia had said. His overlong black hair made him look paler than he probably was. Except for his pallor, and the great slash across his throat from ear to ear, the man looked young and healthy. His most prominent feature was his hairiness—black hair grew on his arms, his hands, and his chest. A white towel appliquéd with pink roses covered most of his face, and another was draped across his groin. His arms were stretched out, Christ-like, and a little blood was trickling to the floor.

A straight-edge razor—it looked brand new—lay beside the body, not far from his left hand. The razor troubled Rachel.

"Where does one get that kind of razor?" she asked.

"Lots of places," Julia said. "Barbers and hairdressers use them."

"This scene reminds me of Dorothy L. Sayers's book *Have His Carcase*, when Harriet Vane finds the body on the beach."

Julia raised her eyebrows. "Well, Harriet's corpse and ours were both killed by having their throats cut. That's the only similarity I see," she said.

Cut with a straight-edge razor. Rachel thought the similarities were remarkable, but this was not the time or the place to discuss it. She'd had more than enough of this room.

"Let's go," she said.

A few minutes later they were back in Julia's sunny sitting room. Rachel glanced around, thankful for the lavender-blue walls, and that the flowers in the chintz that covered the sofa and chairs were yellow daffodils and yellow and white narcissi. The room smelled clean and fresh, with a hint of the scent from a vase of fresh narcissi. She could see through the glass doors to the tiny balcony, bright and cheerful, with pots of yellow and white tulips. Rachel had never cared for the color pink. After what she had seen this morning, she disliked it intensely.

"Inconsiderate of him to kill himself in Stephanie's bathroom," Julia said.

"Why would anyone commit suicide there?" Rachel asked.

Julia shrugged. "I can think of a number of reasons. Perhaps he asked her to marry him, and she refused him. Or he was her lover, and she broke it off. Or he found out she was two-timing him."

"Who is he? You sound as if you knew him," Rachel said.

"I don't know him, but I've seen him with Stephanie. He's a Russian, claims to be a descendant of one of the tsars—his first name is Ivan. I never heard his last name. He was one of several men courting Stephanie. All of the young men she goes out with want to marry up. They think Stephanie's a matrimonial prize, because of her distant relationship with the Windsors, even though she is not in line for a throne, nor do her relatives pay her much heed."

"How did you recognize him?" Rachel asked.

Julia raised her eyebrows. "My dear, he has a pelt, and he's very dark. I've never seen blacker hair. He has bushy black eyebrows, too, although you couldn't see them. I'd know him anywhere, even naked and dead in a bathroom not his own."

"Isn't cutting one's throat an unusual way to commit suicide?" Rachel said.

Before Julia could reply, the telephone rang. Julia answered, and after a brief conversation, turned to Rachel. "That was Izzy. She says Stephanie has calmed down, and knows you are here. She wants to talk to us. Do you mind if they come up?"

"No, not at all. I'll be interested to hear what Stephanie has to say."

•••

A few minutes later the doorbell rang. Julia admitted Stephanie, wearing a quilted pink robe and matching slippers, her hair loose and tangled, and her face bare of makeup. Her eyes were red, but she wasn't crying.

With her was one of the plainest women Rachel had ever seen, even in the orphanage in Oklahoma where she had spent her childhood. The harridans running that place had worked hard to make the girls look as ugly as possible, because many women would not hire a pretty girl to work in their homes, fearing that a son or husband would be attracted.

Stephanie's companion had mouse-brown hair pulled back tightly from her bony face. She wore orange plastic-framed glasses, held together on one side with adhesive tape. Her long tan dress—it looked as if it was made of burlap—fell to her ankles, and hung loosely over her gaunt body.

"Come in, have a seat," Julia said. "Rachel, this is Stephanie's friend Izzy."

Izzy nodded. She sat in a straight-backed chair and crossed her ankles, revealing droopy tights, and clogs.

Stephanie paced up and down the room, talking all the while. "I don't know why this is happening to me. I don't know why Ivan was in my apartment. When I came in this morning, there he was . . . yes, yes, I stayed out all night! There's no law against it; I'm an adult," she said, as if she had been accused of misbehavior.

"Where were you?" Julia asked.

"With a friend," Stephanie snapped.

Julia raised her eyebrows and looked at Rachel. "So much for Miss Congeniality," she murmured.

Rachel thought finding a dead man in one's bathroom might make anyone irritable. "Do you think this—uh—event is linked to the stolen prints?" she asked.

Stephanie shook her head. "No, of course not. I was afraid you might think that. That's why I wanted to see you. I'm certain Ivan had nothing to do with the theft. I think he was murdered."

"Who would do such a thing?" Rachel asked.

Stephanie turned to Julia. "I have enemies. You know I do. You saw the letters I received when I changed my name."

"Yes, I saw the letters. Very ugly. Rachel told me about the stolen prints. Why are you so sure the murder isn't related?" Julia said.

"Ivan was rich," Stephanie said. "He didn't need to extort money from me, and he knew I have nothing. We'd talked about marriage. He was happy."

"If it was murder, you'll need an alibi. Will the man you spent the night with give you an alibi? If he will, you have nothing to worry about," Rachel said.

"I'm not worried about being suspected of anything. I'm worried because someone out there hates me so much they would do this." Stephanie began to cry again.

Julia rose, opened the door to the corridor, and nodded at Izzy, who stood up, put her arm around Stephanie, and escorted her out.

"I still don't know how she can be so certain the body in the bathroom isn't linked to the theft of the prints," Julia said.

Rachel had an idea about that, but before she could reply, the doorbell rang. Julia looked through the peephole and whispered, "Cheese it, the cops. They're here sooner than I thought they would be. I should have changed my detective clothes for something more conventional." She opened the door to a pair of tall men in dark suits.

"Lady Fitzgerald?" the bald one asked.

"Yes, I am she. Are you here about the dead man?" Julia asked.

"Yes. May we come in?"

"May I see some identification?"

The bald man flashed a badge too fast for Rachel to see it, then handed Julia several traditional-looking calling cards. She glanced at them and said, "Please come in. Let me take your coats. Won't you sit down?"

The men sat side by side on the big sofa facing Rachel and Julia. They looked like soldiers at attention. Their features and coloring were different, but they were oddly similar—short haircuts, dark blue suits, white shirts, shiny black shoes. Like a pair of bookends. Or maybe they were in uniform?

"I've been expecting the police," Julia said.

"They'll be here soon enough," the fair one—the one with hair—said. "We're from the Palace. My name is Charles Graham, and this is David Lancaster."

"Yes, so I observed from your cards," Julia said. "This is my friend, Mrs. Ransome."

Graham glanced at Rachel, dismissed her, and turned back to Julia. "I understand you discovered the body, Lady Fitzgerald?" he said.

"No, Princess Stephanie did. I heard her cries of distress, and went upstairs to see if I could help her. If you wish to see her, she's with her friend Izzy, on the third floor."

Graham shifted his attention to Rachel. "Do you live here, too?" he asked.

"No. I am Lady Fitzgerald's guest," Rachel said.

He frowned. "This early? It must have been an urgent matter that brought you here at what? Seven? Seven thirty?"

"It *was* urgent. I am concerned about Stephanie. She has suffered a theft, and is being blackmailed. I had planned to meet with her this morning at my home to discuss the situation. Lady Fitzgerald knew this, and telephoned to explain that Stephanie could not come, and why. I am here to see if I can be of assistance to her," Rachel explained.

The men exchanged glances. "And you knew about this—uh—theft and blackmail—how?" Graham asked, not troubling to hide his skepticism.

"She called on me yesterday, and told me about it," Rachel said.

"Are you close friends? Is that why Miss Stephanie decided to tell you this improbable story?" Graham asked.

"No, I know Princess Stephanie only slightly. I, too, was surprised that she chose to confide in me," Rachel said.

Julia raised her eyebrows. "You underestimate your reputation, Rachel." She turned to the men from the Palace. "Mrs. Ransome has helped solve two important art crimes."

The men exchanged glances again. This time Lancaster spoke. "Let's start again, at the beginning. May I see your identification, Mrs. Ransome?"

Rachel sighed and reached for her shoulder bag. "Here is my passport. Here is my business card. My London attorney is George Quincy. The lawyer who dealt with my affairs in Boston before I moved to London is Bernard Gregory. You will easily find them—they are both well-known. And if, as you imply, you do not believe my account of how I learned about Stephanie's problems, you may wish to speak with an American friend who was with me at the time, and heard everything Stephanie told me. Her name is Dinah Greene Hathaway. Her London address is 23 Culross Place. But I should be careful when questioning her. You will have heard of the Boston Hathaways. Richard Madison Hathaway was the Ambassador to the Court of St. James's a few years ago."

Julia looked at her watch. "I'm rather tired, and very bored. You are wasting your time and ours. Surely you should be talking to Stephanie?"

Lancaster—the bald one—shook his head. "Excuse me, Lady Fitzgerald, but we must ask Mrs. Ransome a few more questions. Can anyone vouch for your arrival time this morning? And your actions last night from midnight onward?"

"I attended the Royal Shakespeare Theatre last night. My lawyer, Mr. Quincy, and his sister and her husband, Lord and Lady Darny, called for me at about half past seven. The play began at eight. We dined at the Ivy after the play. My friends escorted me home. My maid brought hot chocolate to my bedroom at about midnight, as she does every night. Her name is Eileen Kelly, and she can be reached at the number on my card.

"After Eileen served my chocolate, she locked up the house, set the alarms, and went to bed. Her room is directly over mine on the floor above. A red light goes on in my bedroom when all is secure, and remains on until a door or window is opened. No one left the house until I did this morning. I came in a taxi that is frequently hovering outside the gallery. You should have no difficulty finding the driver. If you cannot, telephone Miss Manning, my secretary, at the number on my card. She uses that taxi frequently, and will know the driver's name. The doorman here let me in. He and the concierge know me by sight. They can tell you precisely what time I arrived."

"And this address on your card: the Ransome Gallery. It is a business? But you claim to live there?" Lancaster seemed prepared to challenge every word she said.

Julia interrupted. "Oh, for God's sake! I've had enough of this. Do you realize you are insulting my guest? I shall report this."

Rachel intervened. "Do not worry, Julia. I want to complete this interrogation. My gallery—the Ransome Gallery—specializes in Renaissance art and jewelry, and is on the first floor—street-level—of my house. The rest of the building is my home," she explained, as if speaking to a child.

"We will need to verify everything you've told us," Lancaster warned.

"Please do. You may also wish to investigate my financial situation—taxes paid, and the like. Mr. Quincy can assist you with that, too."

Graham frowned. "You are amazingly cooperative, Mrs. Ransome. We rarely encounter anyone with such a strong desire to help us."

"I have nothing to hide. Perhaps others do. I should add that Lady Fitzgerald, Princess Stephanie, and her friend Izzy are the only people living in this building whom I have met," Rachel said.

"Uh huh," Graham said. "We'll verify that, too. I think that's all." The two men stood up. "Oh, just one more thing . . . "

Julia giggled. "You're pulling a Columbo—that detective on American TV. That's what he always does—comes back in at the last minute—asks the really important question and catches the criminal. Is that what you're about to do?"

Graham, ignoring Julia, said, "How did you meet Lady Fitzgerald?"

"We met at a bookstore called Make Mine a Mystery," Rachel said. "A writer we both admire was reading from her new book. We stood in line together, waiting for the author to sign our books, and discussed our favorite mysteries. We enjoyed the conversation so much we made a date for lunch. And we've been friends ever since."

Neither of the men commented, but Rachel thought they looked dubious, even about this innocent meeting. They thought she was guilty of something. But of what? And why?

A phone buzzed. Graham excused himself and stepped out into the corridor. A few minutes later, he came back in. "The police have arrived," he said. "I am told they wish to see you alone, Lady Fitzgerald. Shall I arrange a taxi for you, Mrs. Ransome?"

Rachel stood up. "Thank you. That will not be necessary. I am sure my driver is waiting downstairs. But I should like my passport back, please."

"I'm afraid that isn't possible. We'll need to hold it for a while. You don't plan to leave the country, do you?"

Rachel looked at Julia and raised her eyebrows. She turned back to Graham. "I do not intend to leave the country. I have tried to be cooperative, but I do not like having my passport confiscated. My lawyer will be in touch with you."

Graham shrugged. "As you wish," he said.

"May I have your cards? You gave them to Lady Fitzgerald, but I shall want my own."

He handed her two cards.

Julia, obviously annoyed, escorted Rachel to the door, collected her coat from the closet, and helped her put it on.

"I'll ring you later," Julia said. She turned back into the apartment, and spoke to the two men. "I never met any Pal Pols until today. Did no one ever tell you about the 'special relationship'? Americans are our friends. Especially when they bring a great deal of money into the country, as Mrs. Ransome does. Being rude to Mrs. Ransome was a serious mistake. Anyway, I know why you're here. It's not about the poor man who was killed. It's all about Stephanie. You guys are always after her. Why can't you leave her alone?"

Rachel, waiting for the elevator, could hear Julia berating the men until the elevator doors closed. Good for Julia. The men were obnoxious in every way.

CHAPTER SEVEN

Rachel

Tuesday, May, London

On her way home from the Little Palace, Rachel asked her driver to stop at a newsstand to pick up a copy of *Secrets*.

While she waited for him to return to the car, she tried to reach her attorney, George Quincy. His assistant said Mr. Quincy was engaged and would have to call her back. She hoped he would call soon. She could not understand the suspicion and hostility she had encountered, but she was certain she needed legal assistance. She had nothing to hide, as the offensive Palace Police would soon learn, but she had much to lose if these creatures decided to damage her reputation. She feared they had the power to do so, and perhaps the power to cause her a great deal of trouble.

The photograph of the etching was on the front page of *Secrets*. Its subject was familiar: a female nude lying with her back to the viewer, a pose used by both contemporary and ancient artists. The print closely resembled Velázquez's *Rokeby Venus*, without the mirror.

The woman could not be identified, but the caption was provocative: "*Photograph of an etching made from a drawing of a woman visiting the Little Palace, where nearly everyone is connected to the Royal Family. We'd like to hear from readers who recognize this woman.*" An e-mail address followed.

Rachel sighed. Stephanie's problems must be resolved quickly, but she could not see how to do it. She was almost certain that no one could prevent the press from printing this sort of thing. What would the blackmailer do next?

Her cell phone rang. Thank goodness, it was George Quincy. When she started to explain why she was calling, he interrupted.

"I know all about it, and it's quite serious. I want to speak with you right away, but not on the telephone," he said.

"You are worried about those officious men? I thought that it would be possible to put the whole affair to rest quickly, if we gave them the facts they asked for, and they verified them. But come immediately if you think it is necessary. I will be at home shortly," Rachel said.

A few minutes later she sat on a bench in the foyer of her house, removing her beige boots. To her astonishment, they were stained with blood. She must have walked in it, but when? She hadn't entered the room where the dead body lay, and she hadn't seen blood anywhere else. When she started to hang up her white coat, she was horrified to see blood splotches on the hem. How was it possible?

She removed her skirt and examined it. It, too, was blood-stained. The outfit was ruined, but that was the least of her worries. She needed time to think about where she could have brushed against blood, or walked in it, and what she should do about it.

But George would arrive momentarily. She took an empty garment bag out of the hall closet and shoved the entire outfit, including the boots, in it. She hurried upstairs with the bag, and hung it in the back of her off-season clothes closet, behind her summer wardrobe. She locked the closet door. She selected a gray knit suit from her active closet and dressed as fast as she could, pulling on the gray suede shoes that went with the suit, and tying a gray and wine-red scarf around her neck. She was halfway downstairs when the doorbell rang.

The maid ushered George, looking harassed, into the library. They sat in front of the fire. She sipped a cup of coffee, but the lawyer refused coffee and ginger biscuits. He must be seriously disturbed: He never turned down food. He wiped his perspiring forehead and frowned.

"The men you encountered this morning are quite strange. They called on me to question me about the information you gave them. I verified everything, of course. When they left, I tried to investigate them, but they don't have addresses or an affiliation on their business cards. Nor are they listed in any of the usual places. I asked for an address, the location of their headquarters, and the names of their supervisors, but they said everything was 'classified.'

"I asked an associate for help. He did a fair amount of research on 'Palace Police,' but found nothing. No organization called 'Palace Police' is listed anywhere," he said. "This is like something out of an American spy film."

Rachel frowned. "I did not even look at their cards. But if we do not know how to reach them, how will I recover my passport?"

"I have it," he said. He took it out of his briefcase and handed it to her.

"How did you manage to get it back?" Rachel asked.

"I told them I would telephone the American Ambassador and explain that they had seized your passport and refused to return it, so you must have a new one. They returned it by messenger. I don't think they care to be involved with a U.S. government official," said George. "That tells us something, but I'm not sure what."

"Were you able to determine why they are so hostile to me?" Rachel asked.

"All they would say is that you keep 'bad company,' and that 'birds of a feather will gather together.'"

"But that is absurd. I do not 'keep company' or 'gather.' I see few people. Hardly anyone, in fact," Rachel said.

"Yes, I know that. I explained it to them. They asked for a list of the people you see frequently. Would you be willing to put together a list?"

"I suppose so, although I cannot give them a client list. Anyway, Miss Manning sees most of the clients," Rachel said.

"Forget about your clients for the moment," George said. "Tell me whom you have seen recently."

"In the last three weeks, other than those in my household, I saw you and the others in the party that attended the play at the Royal Shakespeare Theatre Tuesday night. I have seen Julia and Dinah Greene Hathaway and Princess Stephanie. I see my publisher and my editor occasionally, and my banker once a month. I frequent various libraries and museums, so I see librarians and curators. I go to bookstores, so I know people who work in them. Once in a while, when he's in London, I see Heyward Bain. I have no family, and few friends."

George sighed. "I'll give them your list, but they must be looking for something or someone else. The associations you mention are too harmless to provoke these men. I can't imagine why they suspect you, or why they are so hostile, but I find them disturbing, even frightening," he said.

"Are they like the Ku Klux Klan in the United States?" Rachel asked. "Ignorant, but dangerous?"

"I sincerely hope they are not violent like the KKK. But like the Klan, they are anonymous, and one mistrusts those who hide behind anonymity." He stood up. "My office has queries out to many sources. I should know later today why they suspect you, and of what."

"Will you come for a drink later to tell me what you have learned?" Rachel asked.

"Yes, of course. I'll be here by six. I hope I have something useful to report."

•••

Rachel returned to her desk and her manuscript, but she couldn't concentrate. All she could think about were problems: the blood on her clothes; the death of the young man in Stephanie's bathroom; Stephanie's foolishness, and the trouble her behavior might cause; and the hostility of the Palace Police. Would George be able to help her with any of these difficulties? Should she tell him about the blood on her clothes?

She was so perturbed, she decided to turn to an old favorite that always soothed her: Jane Austen's *Pride and Prejudice*. She'd put away her papers and lose herself in the trials and troubles of Elizabeth and Darcy.

•••

George arrived promptly at six. He looked exhausted and even more worried than he had earlier.

She offered him tea or sherry, but he shook his head. "After the day I've had, I need something stronger. Whisky, I think. May I pour my own?"

"Certainly," Rachel said.

He poured himself a large drink from the bottle of Macallan on the drinks tray, and took a swallow.

"Well, I've learned why these people are suspicious of you," he said. "They believe you support a group in Northern Ireland that uses violence to sabotage the peace process—Republicans, fighting for a united Ireland."

Rachel frowned. "Where did you come by that absurd information?" she asked.

"The intelligence came from a high-level government agency. Government organizations are always watching extremists, especially those willing to kill to achieve their objectives. And other organizations watch the watchers," George said.

"Do these high-placed persons believe this nonsense about me?" Rachel asked.

"I have no idea what anyone other than the Palace Police believes. They are all that concern us for the moment. They are obsessed with a few recent episodes of violence in Northern Ireland, and are afraid that the violence will overflow into England, as it did in the 1970s," he said.

"I can understand why they might be worried, but why am I a suspect? I have never been to Ireland. I do not know anyone from Ireland. I don't have the faintest interest in Ireland, not even any Irish clients," Rachel said.

"The police concerned with Irish terrorism keep a special watch on Americans living in England, especially those with Boston connections, and most especially those with Irish relations or ancestors. Surely you know that rich Bostonians supported the IRA for decades?" George said. "As for not knowing anyone from Ireland, they claim that you know an unusually large number of people from that wretched country."

"Good heavens!" Rachel said. "How is that possible?"

"Your household is decidedly Irish. Your maid and your housekeeper are from Ireland, as are your cook and your chauffeur. And Miss Manning's mother was Irish," he said.

"I had no idea," Rachel said. "Everyone but Miss Manning came to me through the same agency. Miss Manning was recommended by the minister of my church—which is Anglican, by the way, not Catholic. I have never discussed Miss Manning's family with her. I can only suppose the agency I used has a positive bias toward the Irish, but I did not know that, and I did not inquire about their ethnic backgrounds— or their politics—or their religion before I hired them. They came with impeccable references. I trust them all, especially Miss Manning."

"How did you choose the agency you used?" George asked. "It is *very* pro-Irish, and the Palace Police think you selected that agency to make sure you hired servants with Irish backgrounds."

"I can scarcely remember how I came to use the agency, it all happened so long ago. But I'm almost sure the referral came from my banker. You know him. His English roots go back to the Norman Conquest."

George nodded. "He's definitely a Royalist. As for your friends," he continued, "Dinah Greene is married to Jonathan Hathaway, who is from Boston, as was your former partner, Simon Fanshawe-Davies. Your friend Lady Fitzgerald has an Irish name. The owner of the bookstore where you met her is David Griffith. Griffith is an Irish name associated with violence: Arthur Griffith founded Sinn Féin, which argued for total independence from Britain, and was at the heart of the early rebellions. Heyward Bain is suspect, because no one is able to learn anything about his past. What do you know about him?" George asked.

"I know that his family was from North and South Carolina. I understand that he is highly regarded by many people and organizations in the United States, including the U.S. government. Dinah says he is vouched for by Daniel Winthrop, a very influential American—a Bostonian, but one with whom I believe no one can find fault. Mr. Winthrop can also vouch for Dinah's husband, Jonathan Hathaway, whose family has been in America since the 1600s. I believe Jonathan Hathaway is a member of every aristocratic organization in the United States, and I do not believe any of his ancestors were Irish. Dinah Greene is also from North Carolina. Her family is Presbyterian. She told me her ancestors left Scotland and England in the 1700s to go to America. I understand that Mr. Bain and Mr. Hathaway are very well connected in England."

"We'll confirm all that you've told me, and pass it on to the appropriate authorities. But then there's you, Rachel. You could be what is called Black Irish, given your black hair and dark eyes. And you came to London from Boston, and they can't find out much about you," George said.

"Black Irish? What is that? I never heard the term."

"It goes back to the Spanish Armada," George said. "When the British Navy—and a big storm—defeated the Spanish fleet in 1588, some disabled Spanish ships were blown around the top of Scotland, and landed in Ireland. Many sailors stayed there. That's why a small minority of Irish folk have dark eyes and hair."

Rachel laughed. "I was left on the doorstep of an orphanage in Oklahoma when I was a newborn infant. Those in charge decided I was an American Indian because of my hair, eyes, and skin, and because Oklahoma swarms with Indians. 'American Indian' is how I am described on my earliest documents. It has never mattered, since I was indubitably born in the United States."

"I see. I'll also turn this information over to the agency watching the Palace Police."

"I hope that they will process it, and tell the wretched Pal Pols where they have erred," Rachel said.

"Are you going to tell Lady Fitzgerald about their suspicions?" George asked.

"Yes. I think she will be as surprised as I am to find that I am suspected on so little evidence. She will doubtless be equally surprised to learn that she, too, is a suspect."

"Perhaps," he said. "But Lady Fitzgerald has a colorful reputation, and may be more accustomed than you are to being suspected of crime."

Rachel waited for him to elaborate, but he stood up, as if the subject was closed.

"Excuse me," George said. "I'm due at my club to dine with an old friend. I'll call you tomorrow."

Rachel remained by the fire, thinking about all he had said, and about the blood on her clothes. She had not been this perturbed since Heyward Bain banished Simon to Australia. She had a great deal to ponder. Her last thoughts before going upstairs to bed were of the print that had appeared in *Secrets*. Such prints would continue to appear. No one would pay to have them stopped.

CHAPTER EIGHT

Dinah

Tuesday, May, London

James was waiting in the car outside as he did every morning. Dinah had looked forward to going to Rachel's, and had been disappointed when early Tuesday morning Rachel cancelled their coffee date. She was left with nothing to do and a strong desire to be out of the house. James would take her wherever she wanted to go.

Sometimes he took her to a museum or an art gallery. She'd devoted half a day to exploring Harrods. She often went to Hatchards and skimmed the books she pulled from shelves, often buying one or more. Today was especially bleak because she'd counted on hearing more from Princess Stephanie. She could at least get the paper where the print was supposed to appear.

"James, could we go to a newsstand and pick up today's *Secrets*?"

"Certainly, madam."

Five minutes later she was staring at a reclining nude, her back to the viewer. Not very revealing, and a boringly familiar image. She had expected something spicier.

Her little variation in behavior was refreshing—pathetic that going to a newsstand was an adventure—and made her want to do something else new and interesting. She didn't like eating in restaurants by herself or going to the theater alone, but today she was determined to get out of the house and out of her rut. She'd try a new place for lunch, and see a matinee—unusual for a

Tuesday in London, but some shows were so popular there were extra performances. It would be the first play she'd seen in London.

Her day out was a disaster. The highly recommended museum restaurant she chose was packed with children and so noisy she didn't stay to finish her chicken salad. Her theater choice was bad. The play was political, and composed of dialogue among a group of men, each with an incomprehensible accent. She left at intermission and decided she might as well shop for that night's dinner. She asked James to take her to Fortnum & Mason, where she treated herself to tea and chocolate cake to make up for no lunch and the disappointing play. Then she went to the food hall to shop for dinner.

An hour and a half later, her arms full of shopping bags, she opened the door of 23, and nearly fainted at the odor that enveloped her: urine. O'Hara was cooking kidneys, one of Jonathan's pet hates. Dinah had repeatedly told her not to cook kidneys because of the odor. Jonathan would be beside himself. One of his tantrums would be the end of a perfect day.

Dinah put her packages down and ran upstairs to get a dozen of the scented candles she used when the house was filled with unpleasant cooking odors. She distributed them around the rooms, lighting them as she went. After she arranged the roses and lilies and jasmine she'd bought the day before, and set the bowls in appropriate places, she hurried to the kitchen.

As usual, the witches were sitting at the table, drinking cups of tea, their all-day activity.

"Mrs. O'Hara, I've told you repeatedly—we do not eat kidneys, and we cannot abide that smell. It makes us ill. Please remove whatever you're cooking from the oven. Mr. Hathaway will be furious if he comes home to that smell."

"I'm cooking a delicious nourishing steak and kidney pie," Mrs. O'Hara snapped. "I'm serving it for dinner tonight—"

Something inside Dinah exploded. She grabbed the hot pads from the counter, opened the oven, and took out the pie. She dumped it into the sink, and turned on the water and the disposal. Mrs. O'Hara glared at her, her face scarlet with rage.

"That's a disgrace, that is, wasting good food," Mrs. O'Hara said.

"Since I pay the bills, that's no concern of yours. Have you even looked at Mr. Hathaway's list of preferences?" Dinah asked. "On it are the foods we like, and also the foods we don't like. We both detest kidneys. Why do you continue to serve these repellent foods we cannot eat?"

"Repellent, is it? I'll give you repellent," Mrs. O'Hara shouted. "This is good English cooking, and you'll eat it or nothing. I run the kitchen here, not some Yankee know-it-all!"

Dinah lost it. "You may run the kitchen, but I pay for the food—and your salary. You're fired. Get out. And get out now. We were able to rid ourselves of the butler, and we can get rid of you, too."

"We're not leaving unless Mr. Ross at the agency tells us to go," Mrs. Malone shouted. "He's our employer, not you." She picked up her teacup and turned her back on Dinah.

Dinah ran out of the kitchen, up the stairs, and into the bathroom, nauseated by the smell of kidneys. Her stomach churned with rage and the rank odor. After she'd vomited, she brushed her teeth and washed her face in cold water. She wouldn't eat chocolate cake again for a long time. She phoned Jonathan, but he was out of the office, and couldn't be reached. His secretary said he'd be home about seven.

She locked the bedroom door, lay face down on the bed, and struck the pillows with her fist, still in a rage. If Jonathan didn't fire those women, she had to move out of this house. But where would she go?

Thank goodness Coleman was on her way. She'd be at 23 Culross Friday morning.

She wished she didn't have to show Coleman the house in its present state, so crowded you couldn't move. Maybe she had time to change it. She ran downstairs, and got in the car where James waited until it was time to pick up Jonathan from his office.

"James, you know that Mrs. O'Hara and Mrs. Malone are out of the house every day from three to six?"

"Yes, madam," James said.

"And you've heard me complaining about tripping over the footstools and whatnots; the detestable oversized planters containing dirty plastic plants; yellowing, chipped, and dingy marble sculptures in every niche and corner; and far too many chairs and occasional tables. Most of the furniture on the ground floor of the house—the drawing room, the sitting room, the dining room—is neither useful nor attractive, and there's far too much of it. The paths between objects are so narrow, I can hardly walk through the rooms."

She took a deep breath, crossed her fingers, and said, "I hate living in that house. There's enough extra stuff in those rooms to furnish two more houses, and there are six bedrooms we'll never use. I want to move everything we don't use—or don't like—into those bedrooms. I want to do it while Mrs. O'Hara and Mrs. Malone are out for the afternoon, tomorrow, if possible. Can we get a mover, and do it in less than three hours? They're usually away between three and six."

He looked at her in the rearview mirror, his gray eyes twinkling. "Yes, madam. With a little help we can easily finish before O'Hara and Malone return. I have two friends who'll assist us for much less than the cost of professional movers. I'll call them straight away. They can be at the house at three P.M. Wednesday. Do you want to shop in the morning as usual?"

"Oh, yes. Let's go to Whole Foods—the Kensington High Street store. It will be quicker than Fortnum's. I always spend too much time in Fortnum's."

Dinah went back in the house, excited by her plan for moving the furniture, still annoyed by the smell throughout the house, and dreading Jonathan's arrival. She'd keep the candles burning until the last minute, spray her favorite perfume around, and hope for the best.

CHAPTER NINE

Dinah

Wednesday, May, London

Dinah completed her usual morning activities, and saw Jonathan off to work. As soon as James returned with the car, he drove her to Young Street, next to Whole Foods, where he would wait for her. She raced through her purchases and rushed back to the car, anxious to get back to 23 Culross and implement the big change.

Back at the house, she walked through the crowded rooms, looking cautiously at everything. After she had examined everything twice, especially where she planned to put the furniture she'd leave downstairs, she returned to her bedroom and tried to read. At lunchtime, she made a cup of coffee in her make-do kitchen, and took the salad she'd bought at Whole Foods out of the refrigerator. After only a bite or two, she gave up—she was too anxious to eat. She tried to read again, but after she heard the departure of the witches, she couldn't concentrate, and found herself pacing the floor, fingers crossed.

•••

At three o'clock she looked out the window. Two men in jeans and work shirts were standing near the car talking to James. She ran downstairs. James introduced the men as Franklin and Hamilton. Dinah wasn't sure whether those were first or last names, but she was delighted to see them.

She explained what she had in mind, and showed them the furniture that would remain downstairs. She photographed the rooms they were about to empty, and as soon as she'd finished, raced up to her bedroom to change into a washable denim jumpsuit and sneakers. She'd postponed changing until the last minute—she hadn't wanted to jinx the plan by changing, and having her movers fail to appear.

Back downstairs, she was delighted to see that they had already plunged into the task.

James and his friends moved the large furniture into the spare rooms, while Dinah collected vases, cushions, bric-a-brac, fake flowers, china figurines, cake stands, and dozens of doodads— anything she could carry—and took them upstairs, racing against the clock. When she had moved everything small, she threw out the dirty plastic plants and dead flower arrangements. The flowers had been stiff and ugly when several days ago Mrs. Malone had stuffed them into tacky plastic vases and scattered them around the house. They were now not only unattractive to look at, but the stale water in the vases smelled terrible. After she poured out the odorous water, she left the vases in the kitchen. Maybe a thrift shop would accept them, or the witches would take them away.

The move was completed with an hour to spare. The men helped Dinah rearrange the remaining furniture, and at her direction, removed the most depressing of the dark, old paintings that seemed to absorb the small amount of light the heavy, wine-red velvet curtains let in. The paintings joined the furniture upstairs. Once everything was in its new location, she photographed every object, and noted its exact location in a notebook.

Dinah, thrilled with the uncrowded drawing room, opened the curtains to bring more light into the room. The room looked spacious and inviting, but she was dismayed by how filthy everything was. Even the curtains were gray with dust. The rugs looked as if they hadn't been vacuumed in years. A musty smell pervaded the rooms.

The cleaning woman, who was hired by Mrs. O'Hara, probably never entered these rooms. Dinah knew she'd be unable to make the woman—whose name she didn't know—clean the place properly. If only she could replace the cleaning woman with someone who knew dirt when she saw it, and was willing to do something about it. Jonathan insisted that she accept and work with the entire group that came with the house. She couldn't budge him, even about a cleaning woman. She would clean as much as she could before Jonathan came home at seven, but she had so little time, she feared she'd only move the dust around.

Franklin, the shorter and younger of James's two helpers, apparently read her mind, and stepped forward. "I can take care of the cleaning, madam. I know where the equipment is kept." Without waiting for a response, he disappeared through the door to the kitchen.

Dinah looked at James. "How can he know where the vacuum cleaner and broom and such are kept?"

James smiled. "Franklin used to work here, madam. Hamilton, too. They're unemployed, which is why I was able to arrange for them to help us today."

Dinah frowned. "I don't understand. When did they work here? Why did they leave? Why are they unemployed?"

"It's a long story, and if you'll excuse me, madam, we don't have time to discuss it. We need to finish here. Do you have keys to the bedrooms?"

"Yes, they're in the safe upstairs, but Mrs. O'Hara has a set, too. She may also have the combination to the safe. I haven't changed it since we moved it. We'll have to figure out how to keep her out of these rooms, and the spare bedrooms, or she'll put everything back where it was."

Franklin reappeared with his arms full of cleaning material—brushes, dusters, mop, and broom—and dragging a cart crammed with even more cleaning apparatus, including a vacuum cleaner and a steamer. He'd donned one of the big white aprons Dinah had seen in the laundry room, but which none of the servants wore. With his round chubby face, and short plump body, he looked like the Pillsbury Doughboy. Grabbing a mop and a dust cloth, he appeared eager to begin his Herculean task, but he paused to show Dinah a large key ring.

"Other than those you have, these are the only keys to the bedrooms, including the one to the master suite. I took them from the kitchen drawer where O'Hara stores them. This key ring should not remain in the house, madam—O'Hara and Malone will find it. I suggest you let James keep these keys." He turned to Hamilton. "Would you go around and lock up, and give the keys to James when all the rooms are safely locked? Excuse me, madam, but you should keep everything private behind locked doors, and drawers. Nothing is sacred in this house. Those women snoop through everything. I heard you say you haven't changed the combination on the safe. You should do that immediately. Now would be a good time."

Hamilton, tall, gaunt, and silent, nodded, took the key ring, and headed up the stairs again. Franklin continued his cleaning, and Dinah ran upstairs to change the safe combination. When she came back down, James was waiting at the foot of the steps.

"We have an errand to run," he said.

"Where are we going?" Dinah felt as if she were being swept up by a tornado. Would she land in Oz?

"To the florist's, madam. You told me you want to take charge of the flowers, and from today you shall."

"But Mrs. Malone takes care of the flowers—she says they are her responsibility," Dinah said.

James handed Dinah a fat manila envelope. "Here's a copy of your lease. You should read it carefully. You need to be familiar with it to deal successfully with O'Hara and Malone. Do not believe anything they tell you. They are accomplished liars. The flowers are *not* Mrs. Malone's responsibility. She buys half-dead flowers from one of her cronies for almost nothing, and charges you top prices for them. You must tell her that from today you are buying and arranging the flowers, and you will no longer reimburse her for any she buys. You should regularly examine the house accounts, and cancel all the accounts at the places they have been buying food or household goods. There's a list of reliable and honest sources in this envelope. Malone and O'Hara cheat you on everything, and pocket the money. They will rant and rage, but you must ignore them."

Dinah cringed at the thought of confronting the harridans, but she knew James was right. "Jonathan has an assistant look at the bills, but I suppose she automatically approves everything. I'll take over the accounts right away. But Mrs. O'Hara says that Mr. Ross, the man we dealt with when we rented the house, is their boss, not us. They say they'll call him, and he'll decide what's to be done," she said.

James nodded. "Ross is responsible for the upkeep of the house—the exterior, or a plumbing or heating problem—that kind of thing. But when you read the lease, you'll see that many aspects of living here—including the flowers—are up to you and Mr. Hathaway. The flowers in the window boxes are Ross's responsibility, but he hires the florist you'll meet this afternoon to take care of them."

"I wondered about those window boxes—they're lovely. Is Mr. Ross a good person or is he one of *them*?" Dinah asked.

James hesitated. "I'm not sure," he said. "I don't know the current management. Perhaps you know better than I do. What has been your experience with Mr. Ross? Didn't Mr. Hathaway talk to him about the butler?"

One of Jonathan's first acts after they'd arrived in London had been to visit the famous wine merchant Berry Bros & Rudd, founded in 1698, where he spent a fortune on wines. Three days into their stay at 23 Culross Place, Jonathan caught Connell, the butler, swigging Jonathan's precious claret "as if it were Coca-Cola, right from the bottle," her irate husband declared. Connell was summarily ejected, with a sharp reprimand to Mr. Ross, who not only headed the agency that had rented them the house, but had also supplied the servants. Jonathan was waiting for Ross to send a new butler to replace Connell.

"Mr. Ross didn't object to dismissing Connell, but we still don't have a butler. Apparently they are hard to find. I don't care, but Jonathan is annoyed."

"I know a butler you'd like: Hamilton, who was butler here for twenty years. You couldn't do better."

"I'd love to hire him. He obviously isn't afraid of work, and I can tell he's a nice person. His knowing the house and being a friend of yours make him perfect. What was Franklin's job?" Dinah asked.

"His title was footman, but he did all the cleaning. A house this size requires a full-time cleaner," James said.

"Oh, I agree. I would hire both of them in a minute, if I could. But how can I do it? I can't do anything without major attacks from these wretched women."

James smiled. "One thing at a time. First, flowers. When these rooms are clean, and there are flower arrangements on every appropriate table, 23 Culross will come alive. Mr. Hathaway will be able to see how the house should look, how it once looked all the time. He will agree to hire both Hamilton and Franklin, when you explain that they helped you rearrange the downstairs, and show him the before and after pictures."

In the car and on their way to the florist, excited by the prospect of solving many of her domestic problems, Dinah didn't pay attention to their route, but when James turned onto an unattractive street that appeared to be a dead-end, she thought he must have made a mistake.

Before she could comment, he turned again, and they were in a delightful mews. The small houses were identical, white with green shutters and green doors, but every garden was unique. Each was a riot of spring color, with blossoming pink and white trees, and beds filled with bright flowers. The flowers were of many varieties, and every garden had an individual feature. In one, an old-fashioned swing hung from a tree branch; in another a fountain tinkled. Chirping birds clustered around a bird tray in one garden, and in still another she could see bright-colored fish in a lily pool. She longed to stroll up and down the street, and admire each garden.

"Oh, this is so lovely. I wish Jonathan had rented a sweet little house like one of these," she said.

James stopped the car in front of the house at the far end of the mews, where pink and white tulips bloomed in the green window boxes, and the flower beds were even lovelier than the others she had admired. He opened the car door for her, smiling. "We've arrived," he said.

"This can't be the florist's," she protested. "It's someone's home."

"Just wait, madam," James said, and rang the bell.

A smiling young woman in faded jeans, boots, and a raggedy blue sweater, opened the door. "James! What a nice surprise," she said. "Please come in." Her curly red hair was pulled back into a ponytail, but curls escaped on her forehead, and dirt smudged a cheek. She held garden gloves in her hand.

"Lady Jane, this is Mrs. Hathaway. She and her husband are leasing 23 Culross," James said.

"How do you do, Mrs. Hathaway," Lady Jane said. "Have you come for flowers for the house? I'm so glad. That house cries out for flowers. I have some of the vases from Number 23 in the little cottage. Come with me, and I'll show you around."

Dinah was confused. Was this lady the florist? She looked young—maybe early twenties—and despite her disreputable clothes, every inch a lady. She had a lovely lilting speaking voice. Was she English? Who was she? And how did she happen to have vases from 23 Culross Place?

They walked through the little house, decorated in delicate pastels—the palest blue lavender, yellow, and green. Floral paintings hung on the pale yellow walls, and needlepoint-covered pillows on the chairs and sofas featured flowers of all kinds. The house smelled of a delicate floral scent she didn't recognize. Dinah longed to slow down and look at everything, and to inquire about the scent, but she forgot the house when they reached the rear wall, composed of glass doors. She could see the garden that lay beyond, and could hardly wait to step outside. Lady Jane opened the doors, and Dinah followed her into the garden.

She had arrived in fairyland, not Oz. The garden, fenced and hedged to screen out nearby buildings and unattractive views, was enormous. Blossoming trees were arranged in small groves; beds of flowers in every color, alive with butterflies, dotted the field, divided by narrow gravel paths. Here and there birds bathed and drank at fountains. A small greenhouse and a smaller cottage stood near the back hedge. Dinah breathed deeply. The air smelled of the recently trimmed grass and a medley of blossoms. Birds sang and bees hummed.

Dinah, dazzled, followed Lady Jane. In no time, James was loading the car with vases full of roses and lilies from the greenhouse, and larger vases of tall branches of forsythia and apple blossoms, from the blooming trees and shrubs. Dinah barely had room in the back seat to sit among the flowers, and was drunk with their perfume.

She longed to question James about Lady Jane, but within minutes they were back at the house. Dinah was glowing with happiness when they pulled up in front of 23 Culross. James stood by her side, both of them with armfuls of flowers, when the heavy oak doors opened.

Her heart sank when she saw O'Hara and Malone. O'Hara's face was red and swollen, like a malevolent balloon. Malone wasn't as red, but she looked just as angry. They might burst with rage. They blocked the door, their bulk making it impossible to enter.

"*I* do the flowers," Mrs. O'Hara screamed. "I don't want all that dirt in the house. We'll have leaves and petals everywhere. And where'd you get them vases? They were stolen from here."

James pushed past her and set his vases down on a marble-topped table. Dinah slipped in behind him. She'd never seen Mrs. O'Hara and Mrs. Malone so angry. They terrified her. She was glad James was with her. He spoke loudly over Mrs. O'Hara's screeching.

"O'Hara, you know the flowers are not your responsibility. The mistress of the house has always selected and arranged the flowers. I gave Mrs. Hathaway a copy of the lease. She now knows exactly what your duties are. You can't lie to her anymore. As for the vases, you know very well that Lady Jane took them with her when she left the house. She's lent them to Mrs. Hathaway, and if anything happens to these vases, you and Malone will pay dearly.

"As for petals and leaves on the floor, they will be an improvement over the filth you've allowed to build up here, Malone. You call yourself a housekeeper! More like a house wrecker. Franklin was appalled when he saw how you're treating the house."

"We'll see about this," Mrs. O'Hara shouted. "Mr. Ross makes the decisions here. Not these Americans, certainly not the likes of you, James Taylor. What have you done with all the furniture? The place is empty. If you've stolen anything, we'll see how long you're here, Mrs. Hathaway. You'll find yourselves on the street."

Relying on James to keep them from attacking her, Dinah put her vases down beside his, and stood up straight. She said as firmly as she could: "Mr. Hathaway and I plan to entertain here, and the house was too cluttered and dirty to invite anyone into it. Not only was this floor crowded and fussy, neither beautiful nor comfortable, it was also filthy. Everything is upstairs. With less furniture, perhaps you and the cleaning woman can take better care of the house, Mrs. Malone.

"I've photographed every room as it was, and I've photographed each object in its new location. I've annotated the inventory with the new locations of every item, and I've commented on conditions. Some of the furniture needs restoration. I also have pictures of the filth, showing how you kept the house, and how it looks now that it's been cleaned. We'll be living here for several months, and I'm determined to make the house livable and attractive, and to see that its contents are secure. Feel free to call Mr. Ross at the agency and complain, but I assure you that nothing I have done is forbidden by the lease."

She spoke bravely, but her mouth was dry. Jonathan would think her fear of the women was irrational, but she knew they were dangerous. She was sure they would retaliate for her actions. She was terrified of what they might do. She kept wishing Coleman were in London. Coleman would know how to deal with these women.

The men were leaving, and she was feeling forlorn, frightened, and exhausted, when Hamilton approached and offered to stay for the evening and deal with dinner and after-dinner cleanup.

"I suggest you go upstairs and rest, then change for dinner. Leave everything to me."

"Oh, I'd love to," Dinah said. "Thank you."

She ran upstairs, locked herself in her bathroom, and filled a tub with warm water and the freesia-scented bath salts Jonathan had ordered for her. She was still worried about retaliation from the witches, but for the moment, she was triumphant.

She felt like a new person after her bath and rest, and when Jonathan came home, she was sitting in the drawing room, in a long blue dress he loved. He was delighted with the transformation of the drawing room, the dining room, and the sitting room, and relieved that none of the furniture in the library had been moved. That room had been cleaned, but his books and papers had not been disturbed.

He commented on the beautiful proportions of the rooms, visible now that the clutter had been removed. He admired the flowers and the vases, was interested in her description of Lady Jane and her flower garden, and was intrigued when he heard that the vases had once been at 23 Culross. He was happier to find his wife looking as she did in New York when he came home from work.

He was also pleased with dinner, as was Dinah. Hamilton had prepared a delicious mushroom soup, and brought in excellent roast chicken and spicy rice from a restaurant he'd told Dinah was Portuguese.

The main course was followed by a delicious salad of Brussels sprouts, flakes of Parmigiano-Reggiano, walnuts, and a lemon-juice dressing.

Hamilton served the meal unobtrusively. After the salad, he brought in a cheese tray, which featured some of Jonathan's favorites. He paired the appropriate wines with every course.

Jonathan was delighted by the food and service. Dinah took advantage of his good mood by telling him about Hamilton—how he had once been butler at 23 Culross Place, and that James knew him well and recommended him to replace Connell.

Jonathan looked up from his Stilton. "Is he available now? Can he come right away?"

"Oh, yes. James says he can start tomorrow."

"Hire him," Jonathan said. "I'm tired of waiting for Ross to find someone."

Dinah smiled. "I'll see to it," she said. "And I'll let Ross know we've found a butler, so he can stop his search."

Before she went upstairs, she went in the kitchen to tell Hamilton he was hired, and she'd see him tomorrow. Dinah, relieved to have found an ally, slept better than she had in weeks.

CHAPTER TEN

Rachel

Wednesday, May, London

The day of Rachel and Julia's lunch date at The Goring had arrived: Rachel called for Julia at twelve thirty. Julia looked very English in a lavender tweed suit. Rachel smiled to herself. She was wearing a purple dress. She wondered if they had chosen those clothes as homage to the royalty who often appeared at The Goring. New by English standards, The Goring—a hotel and restaurant—opened in 1910, toward the end of the Edwardian period.

In the car they chatted of nothing in particular, and when seated in the serene dining room of the elegant hotel, Julia was silent. She looked around her, smiling. Rachel knew how Julia felt. When so many restaurants reinvented themselves monthly, or disappeared completely, The Goring dining room, with its gold-colored curtains, spotless white linen tablecloths, impeccable service, and muted voices, was a dependable island of civility. The dining room seemed remote from murder, blackmail, and scandal.

Asked if they desired an aperitif, they ordered sherry, and for their lunch, lobster omelets and green salads, with a glass of Chablis for each of them.

After the sherry was served, and Julia had taken a sip, she said in a soft voice, "I have news. According to the police, Ivan was murdered. Someone else cut his throat: The razor was found near his left hand, but he was right-handed. And Stephanie was wrong about him being killed elsewhere. He was killed where we saw him, in her bathroom."

"I am not surprised that he was murdered. It was always a possibility. Rather an inept murderer, wouldn't you say? So messy, and imagine making that mistake with the razor. How do you know? Did the police tell you?" Rachel said.

"No, but the police gossip with the doormen and the concierge, and they can't resist telling people in the building what they've learned. And that's not all: They say Ivan left all his money—apparently quite a lot—to Stephanie," Julia said.

"My word!" Rachel said. "It is fortunate that she has an alibi, is it not?"

"If it stands up. She claims she was staying with an American at the Connaught. I've never seen her with an American, and I thought I knew all of her followers," Julia said.

"We always thought that if Ivan was murdered, he was probably killed by a rival. Who are the other contenders for Stephanie's hand?" Rachel asked.

"Besides the mysterious American, a tall, blond German, rather arrogant, but handsome. An Italian almost as dark as Ivan, and a Spaniard, also dark, with that unmistakable Habsburg jaw. Those are the only ones I've seen," Julia said. "I hadn't thought Ivan was murdered, but now that we know he *was*, I'd put my money on the German as the killer."

"I do not doubt that you know best. Now, let me tell you *my* news." Rachel repeated what she had learned about the Pal Pols's Irish conspiracy theory, including their belief that both she and Julia were involved in some kind of Irish rebellion.

Julia laughed so hard, heads turned. Those who lunched at the elegant Goring were unused to loud laughter.

"Why is that amusing?" Rachel asked. "My attorney is quite concerned."

"I'm sorry. It's just that my late and unlamented husband, despite his Irish name, was so English, you could barely understand a word he said. He nearly choked on his plummy accent. He worshipped all things English. He even died a very English death—broke his neck chasing a fox. Perhaps someone in his family was Irish way back, but if so, the genes didn't survive. I got to know the entire tribe, and they were all English to the bone. Remind me to show you my husband's scrapbooks, and you'll see what I mean. I don't think the Pal Pols will find satisfaction climbing *that* family tree. I hope they waste a lot of time checking on my in-laws, who will snub them mightily, given half a chance," Julia said.

"I hope they leave us alone," Rachel said. "On another topic: what is happening with Stephanie and the missing prints? I saw the etching in *Secrets*—a nude, but not very explicit. I would like to know what she is doing about her problems. The next image could be more damaging."

Julia shrugged. "She acts as if she's forgotten about the prints and the threats. She's been preoccupied with Ivan's death, and her inheritance, but you'd think she'd give some thought to the theft."

"I have doubted her story from the beginning. I have wondered if she pretended the prints were stolen, and if it was she who sent the print to *Secrets*," Rachel said.

"Why would she do that?" Julia asked.

"I suspect she needs money badly, and hopes to collect the blackmail money for her own use, although I cannot imagine who she thinks will pay it," said Rachel. "Do you think she inherited enough to make it unnecessary to go through with the extortion?"

"I haven't the foggiest," Julia said. "But I'm sure we'll hear something soon. She can't keep anything to herself. If I learn anything, I'll let you know."

The waiter arrived with their omelets, and while he was serving them, they stopped talking and finished their sherry. When the waiter left, Julia said, "I've been meaning to ask you: You know Heyward Bain, don't you?"

"Yes, he is my great benefactor, and a good friend," Rachel said. "As I think you know, my former partner, Simon, left me in a terrible financial situation. Heyward sorted it for me—took care of everything."

"My dear!" said Julia. "You are fortunate to have such a friend."

"Indeed. Why did you ask about him?"

"Well, he's famous now that he's building an empire in London, but what put him in my mind is a bit in the paper that says he's coming to London," Julia said. "He may already be here."

"He is? I am so very glad. He has been on my mind," Rachel said.

"I'm glad to bring good news. Before we leave the subject of your friends, did I hear you tell the Pal Pols that you have a friend living at 23 Culross Place?"

"Yes, do you know the house?" Rachel asked.

"Everyone knows the house. It's notorious. There always seems to be another foreigner willing to rent it because of its size and location, but they never stay long," Julia said.

"Why? What's wrong with the house?"

"It has an unhappy history, and it is said to be a bad-luck house. It's owned by Lady Jane Ross. Jane Ross comes from a line of Scots whose ancestry goes back to the twelfth century. The family was once wealthy, with a magnificent castle in Scotland, and properties all over England. But the wars took their toll, and Jane is the last of her branch of Rosses. It was important that she marry well, to a man who could help her manage what was left of the estate.

"When she married Lord Augustine, a much older man and a distant cousin, everyone thought she'd made a good choice, but the marriage was a disaster. Augustine was a drinker, a gambler, a womanizer, a cad. He went through everything she owned faster than you would think possible, and piled up huge debts. He drowned in a boating accident—drunk at the time, people say—unfortunately too late to save much of her fortune. There were rumors that Jane's governess, who lived with them even after her marriage, had managed to hide some of the estate's greatest treasures, but she died of a heart attack before Lord Augustine did, without telling Jane what she had done with the treasures, if she did anything. It could be just a silly rumor.

"Be that as it may, Jane was left very badly off. By the time everything was sold, and all the debtors paid, she had almost no money. She was left with 23 Culross Place, which she rents out, and she had enough left to establish herself as a florist. Unfortunately, she was also left with a tribe of hangers-on—all her Ross relatives—harassing her, asking for money. They're infamous—lazy, good-for-nothing layabouts. One or another of them gets picked up drunk and makes the news all the time. They see her as the senior person in the clan who should take care of them," Julia said.

"But why is the house bad luck?" Rachel asked. "And why do people leave?"

"Stephanie said the house is haunted, perhaps by Lord Augustine. She says people who have rented the house claim they hear noises in the night, and can't sleep. I don't know how she knows all that, but it's true that after a few days, the tenants leave," Julia said.

"Dinah has not mentioned ghosts nor, indeed, any problems, but I sense she is not happy there," Rachel said. "I do not believe in ghosts, but I do think some houses have an evil atmosphere. I hope she and her husband do not stay if there is anything seriously wrong with the place."

•••

Back at home, an e-mail from Stephanie awaited Rachel:

The thief gave me an extension to get the money when he heard about Ivan's death. But he called this morning to tell me he knows I inherited money, and he wants it. He says I can borrow against the legacy, and get cash right away. It's not nearly as much as he originally asked for—I think he wants my legacy as partial payment. There's another print in today's Secrets. *I don't know what to do. What do you advise?*

Rachel didn't want to talk to or meet with Stephanie. She e-mailed her reply:

Stephanie:

It is time to talk to the police. I urge you to take the whole story to them, but first hire a lawyer. The theft of the prints and the extortion scheme could be connected to Ivan's murder. You may find yourself in serious trouble if you do not tell the police.

She'd like to think that Stephanie would follow her advice, but the girl was a fool, and unpredictable. Rachel could do nothing for the moment. She sent her driver to buy a copy of *Secrets*. She wanted to see the image. She was tired of Stephanie, and wished she'd never met her. But Rachel feared the consequences if she brushed the girl off.

The second print showed a Degas-like nude stepping out of a tub. The woman was wrapped in towels, carefully draped. Like the first print, it was relatively harmless, but it was slightly more revealing than the first print.

Rachel wished she had someone to advise her. She didn't think George was up to unraveling the web in which she was entangled. His was a sheltered life.

When the maid came in to let her know Mr. Bain was on the telephone, it was as if her prayers had been answered. He had called to invite her to a dinner on Friday night to welcome his sister, Coleman, to London. He apologized for the lateness of the invitation. Rachel barely heard him. She accepted his invitation, and seized the opportunity to ask him if he could come to see her as soon as possible, explaining that she had serious problems and needed his advice. Would he come for tea this afternoon, or a drink this evening?

"Of course," he said. "I'll be with you in half an hour, unless that's too soon?"

"No, no, the sooner, the better," she said.

She was in her usual chair in the library when the maid ushered him in. She rose to greet him. He was as she remembered him: handsome, exquisitely attired, with beautiful manners, and an air of easy confidence.

When they were seated, and he'd declined sherry or tea, he said, "How can I help you?"

"It's a long story, but I'll try to make it as brief as I can. It began when Princess Stephanie came to see me. Do you know who I mean?"

He nodded, and she went on to describe Stephanie's story, Julia's telephone call, the body in Stephanie's bathroom, the Palace Police and their hostility, and the blood on her clothes.

She told him about George's discovery of why the Palace Police were hostile, the appearance in *Secrets* of the prints featuring nearly nude women, and Julia's report that the man in Stephanie's bathroom had been murdered.

When she finally stopped talking, she took a deep breath and waited for his response. Would he think she was silly or exaggerating?

His expression was serious. "I can see why you are distressed," he said. "I'm certain I can assist you with some of these issues. Let me see what I can do. I'll be in touch tomorrow and let you know what I have accomplished."

When he left, she leaned back in her chair and allowed herself to enjoy the comfort she had felt when she heard that he would help her.

CHAPTER ELEVEN

Dinah

Thursday morning, May, London

Dinah went through her usual upstairs morning ritual, but Hamilton, who had arrived at five A.M., served downstairs breakfast. It was exactly what Jonathan wanted. Even the smell of fat frying and urine, which usually lingered no matter how many scented candles she burned, was nearly absent.

Jonathan was enjoying Hamilton's excellent service, and was basking in what he saw as Dinah's capitulation about the need for servants. He was wearing an "I told you so" smile. He didn't know that 23 Culross was a battleground, and Dinah had a powerful new ally. Where *were* her enemies? The kitchen was quiet; normally she'd hear them slurping up the greasy breakfast ostensibly prepared for Jonathan and Dinah. Hamilton must be able to control them. How?

After breakfast and Jonathan's departure, Hamilton explained that he'd told them Dinah was "giving them the day off," as she had the night before, and he had added a bribe to make them take it.

"I thought you needed a holiday, madam," he said.

"Oh, wonderful! When will they be back?" Dinah asked.

"Not until after dinner tonight, madam."

"That's such good news. We can get the house ready for my cousin Coleman—she'll be here tomorrow morning at eleven."

"Will she be staying here, madam?"

"No, she'll stay at her brother's house. But I want her to see everything here. We won't clean the kitchen—just leave it the way it always is—filthy—but everywhere else should be perfect."

"Of course, madam."

"We're going out to dinner tonight, so you're on your own. Is there anything we should do about the witches?" Dinah asked

"I'm going to work on that smell. I have some things I can try," he said.

"Oh, it would be wonderful if you could make it go away," Dinah said.

With Hamilton's help, the day rushed by. By late afternoon the house looked clean and fresh, and miraculously, Hamilton had been able to subdue, if not erase, the terrible odor.

Dinah, feeling cheerful, went upstairs to bathe and dress. She decided to wear a navy blue wool suit, with a lighter blue silk shirt, dark blue Manolo Blahniks, and a gold necklace, earrings, and bracelet set that Jonathan had given her to the restaurant. She was ready to go with time to spare. She used the time to choose the dress she'd wear Friday night. She wanted to look her best at Heyward's party for Coleman, her first opportunity since the move to London to wear an evening dress.

•••

Heyward had invited Jonathan and Dinah to join him at Dinner by Heston Blumenthal in the Mandarin Oriental Hotel. It was thought by some to be the best restaurant in London, and was said to be the most interesting. Dinah was looking forward to it. It would be her first visit to a famous London restaurant. Jonathan would enjoy the evening because he liked to talk to Heyward, although he might not be wild about the food. The food was adventurous, and Jonathan preferred the tried and true.

Heyward's welcome party for Coleman would be at Scott's, another restaurant Dinah longed to visit. Scott's was famous for its seafood. Even Jonathan would like their food.

After finding their way through the hotel to the strangely named restaurant, and passing the glass-enclosed kitchen where chefs were hard at work, they were seated by a large window overlooking Hyde Park. In the early twilight—days were getting longer—Dinah could see the rose garden and a group of riders trotting on Hyde Park's famous Rotten Row. Whatever the kitchen produced didn't matter. The view was grand, and after only a quick glance at the menu, she knew she'd enjoy her meal.

While Dinah gazed across at the park and studied the menu, Heyward and Jonathan exchanged stories about their new business ventures.

"I've made several trips to Beijing. I have some plans to address their horrendous air-pollution problem," Heyward said. "I think some of the techniques I've used at home to suppress the bad odors from paper plants can help the Chinese. But it will take a large capital investment."

Jonathan interrupted. "I can get the money. I'm looking for an international project where I can raise funds from global investors. My first hire here in London was a banker who knows the Middle East and the big sovereign wealth funds. They are moving more into venture capital and private equity, and are anxious to invest in Asia."

"I was in Dubai recently. Their government may be interested," Heyward said.

"Nothing I'd like better than for my first big deal in London to be with you, Heyward."

Dinah was only half listening, but she came to attention when Heyward said, "Let me tell you about another project, in an entirely different realm. I'm trying to find a treatment for amoral people, people who can't tell right from wrong, who have no moral guideline. I've just set up a clinic in New York, and if there's any sign of success, I'll build another here. I think they can be retaught, become contributing citizens as opposed to criminals."

"Fascinating," Jonathan said. "Is this for profit, or for the good of mankind, like your anti-smoking inventions?"

"Initially, I want to see if something can be done to address destructive behavior. I don't care about an immediate financial return. I've correlated childhood behavior, like torturing helpless animals or bullying, with antisocial or criminal behavior in later life. I believe most criminals know that what they're doing is wrong. I'm not interested in them. They should be punished. I want to learn whether the person who seems innately bad, without any sense of guilt or willingness to repent, can be treated, can change. I hope to discover whether the bad behavior is genetic, or the result of upbringing, parental behavior, education. I'll try to find the causes and come up with remedies."

Jonathan and Dinah exchanged glances. They were thinking the same thing: Heyward had never failed, but this sounded impossible. The saying "the poor are always with us" might or might not be true, but Dinah and Jonathan believed that there would always be people who didn't know right from wrong, and didn't want to learn.

•••

A little after eleven, Dinah and Jonathan walked into the house, laughing. Their laughter died when they encountered the smell of urine, stronger than ever. The witches had retaliated. Jonathan was furious.

"Can't you stop this?" he said.

"I wish I could. I've told them dozens of times not to cook kidneys in this house. I've told them we don't eat them, and that we find the odor unpleasant. They ignore me," she said.

"Disgusting," he said.

"I know. I hope I can get some of the smell out before Coleman comes tomorrow."

"Well, there's nothing to be done tonight. Let's go to bed," he said.

•••

In bed, Dinah thought about Coleman in London. Life would be more fun, more interesting, with Coleman here. Going to great restaurants was an adventure. She'd like to visit more restaurants. When she was rid of O'Hara, and the smell of cooking kidneys, maybe she'd cook again.

CHAPTER TWELVE

Rachel

Thursday morning, May, London

Heyward telephoned her at nine on Thursday morning. "May I come by in half an hour for a brief visit? I've learned some things you should know, and I'm tied up most of the day."

"Of course," Rachel said. She put aside her papers, closed the door to her office, and went into the library to wait for him. He arrived a few minutes early, looking troubled and rushed.

"Please excuse the early hour. I thought I should tell you right away some of the things I've learned. First, you needn't worry about the Palace Police. They're volunteers and watched carefully to keep them from going too far. No one takes them seriously. Next: your friend Julia is under suspicion and has been frequently investigated because she's a Republican—not in the American sense of the word, meaning a member of a particular political party, but in the English meaning: She's an anti-monarchist," Heyward said.

"How odd. That does not sound like her," Rachel said.

"They are not a large group—only fifteen million Republicans in a kingdom of sixty-six million people, and there are many varieties. Some just think the Monarchy is too expensive. Others have all kinds of reasons for their position. But those who are opposed to England's beloved Queen, as you can imagine, are carefully watched," Heyward said.

"Good heavens! I had no idea. Julia has never hinted at anything like that," Rachel said.

"You should ask her why she's opposed to the Monarchy, and what she does about it. Does she write letters? Participate in demonstrations? Or is she just a talker? Your name is linked with hers, and it's in your best interest to know exactly where she stands, and whether you can afford her as a friend. You should also ask her about the blood on your clothes."

"I cannot believe she is violent, or in any way dangerous, or had anything to do with the blood," Rachel said.

"I hope you're right, but you shouldn't take chances. Meanwhile, you should stay away from the Little Palace, and from Lady Fitzgerald, at least in public.

"You should also avoid Princess Stephanie. Both of those women are too close to the murder at the Little Palace, and they both have bad reputations. I picked up another important scrap of information: The so-called "Little Palace" is run by the Remembrance Society, a charity connected to the Republicans. Most—perhaps all—of the people living in the Little Palace are anti-monarchists, of the stranger kind. They all have a grudge against the Queen, or the throne, or some member of the Royal Family, for a snub or an imagined abuse, usually something silly," Heyward said.

"I have met only two people who live there—Julia and Princess Stephanie. I would not have dreamed either of them were mixed up in what you describe. Is the murder a part of all this?" Rachel asked.

"It may be, but so far the police haven't discovered the connection. My contacts tell me the Little Palace's inhabitants have always been under observation, but they have been thought of as relatively harmless cranks, until the murder. Someone in that building killed a man, and that changes everything," he said.

"Yes, I can see that it would," Rachel said.

"The murder itself is strange. The man whose body you saw didn't die from the wound to his throat. He was dying from an overdose of heroin when his throat was slashed. In a way, he was killed twice. The police are all over the Little Palace and everyone who lives there. They are puzzled and frustrated."

"I can see why they would be, but the murder has nothing to do with me. Surely no one suspects me of murder?" Rachel said.

Heyward changed the subject. "Back to Lady Fitzgerald," he said. "I know she's your friend, but the police are interested in her for many reasons, including her association with the murdered man. She says she didn't know him, but she may not be telling the truth. As for the blood on your clothes, that must have happened while you were with her."

"Oh, I know. But if I start asking her questions, she will think I suspect her of murder, and I do not," Rachel said. "If she thinks I do, and she is innocent, she will not forgive me."

"On the other hand, if she's guilty and is trying to incriminate you, you should avoid her," Heyward said.

"I wish I had never gone to the crime scene when Julia called. In a way I am not surprised about how that poor young man died. The razor always looked like a prop. The way his body lay, the razor, everything about it looked arranged, theatrical. It reminded me of a book I read in which the murdered man also had his throat cut by a razor. Like the man in Stephanie's flat, the murdered man in the book's death was originally thought to be a suicide," Rachel said.

"Trust your instincts. If anything else about the murder occurs to you, call or e-mail me. Don't discuss it with anyone except me. Anyone could be the killer. Oh, one thing I nearly forgot: you told me Lady Fitzgerald is poor."

"Yes, she has had to be quite frugal," Rachel said. "I like to take her out when I can, as a treat."

"She's far from poor. In fact, she's quite well off," Heyward said. "She inherited money from her husband, and has invested it successfully. Why did you think she's poor?"

"I do not know. The way she acts, I suppose. She does not have many clothes, and she lives modestly. I would think if she had a lot of money she would live someplace nicer than the Little Palace. She loves flowers—she says she would like to have a garden. There is no way she can have a garden at the Little Palace."

"She could afford something else. I suspect she likes the other residents. They have a lot in common." He looked at his watch. "I must go. I'll see you Friday night. By the way, Lady Fitzgerald will be at the dinner Friday night."

"I do not understand. You tell me to stay away from her, then invite both of us to your party?" Rachel said.

"It won't hurt you to be in a group with her. But you see her on your own a lot—you're too close. As to why I invited her, I want to know what Coleman thinks of her. Coleman has unusually good judgment," he said.

And I do not, Rachel thought, when she'd walked him to the door. She didn't like to think he disapproved of her, but she was sure he did.

He was right. She had to ask Julia all those questions, no matter what the consequences. She hoped she wouldn't lose a friend. She had so few. But she'd rather lose Julia than Heyward.

CHAPTER THIRTEEN

Coleman

Thursday, May, in transit

After the plane to Paris took off, Coleman reached down and patted Dolly, nestling in her carrier on an old wool dress of Coleman's. When she was sure Dolly was comfortable, Coleman leaned back in her seat and took a deep breath. It seemed as if she'd been running for as long as she could remember.

She glanced at her watch, set for French time. The next seven and a half hours, until eight thirty Friday morning when the plane landed at Charles de Gaulle, were free and clear. There was nothing she must do, and no one could reach her by phone, or drop by her desk for a chat.

She turned down the dinner the flight attendant offered, and got out her Kindle, but she was too tired to read. She should get some rest, but she was too keyed up to sleep.

She found herself thinking about her nonexistent social life. Not long ago, two eligible men were vying to take her out to dinner, lunch, the theater, films. She'd enjoyed their company, and their rivalry for her attention.

Unfortunately, while she was working night and day on *First Home*, her suitors had vanished, and she hadn't even realized they were gone until after she'd made the decision about the decorating department, and had time to think about something other than *First Home*.

The first suitor to depart was Hunt Austin Frederick, Managing Director of Davidson, Douglas, Danbury & Weeks, or DDD&W, the consulting firm where Dinah had been art consultant, suspected of murder, and cleared.

After the scandals that made headlines in the *New York Times* and the *Wall Street Journal* and decimated his staff, Hunt had decided DDD&W couldn't survive in New York. He'd laid off more people—including Mrs. Anderson, who had been his assistant and now worked for Coleman—and moved the firm to Dallas. Hunt's family had lived in Dallas for generations, and was well-known and respected. DDD&W, rechristened Davidson, Frederick & Weeks—DFW—now occupied two floors in a new skyscraper instead of the four floors that had housed the firm in New York. DFW was said to be thriving, and Hunt was as happy as a lark.

Hunt would probably come to New York occasionally on business, and phone Coleman once in a while, but she bet that within a year, he'd marry a Texas beauty half his age, not unlike the first—unfaithful—wife he'd divorced. Oh, well. Coleman liked Hunt—he was fun—but not even her pride was wounded by his defection. They'd never been close enough for any commitment on her part. So much for Hunt.

Jeb Middleton, the attractive superstar investment banker from Charleston, was working seven days a week for Heyward, closing deals, vetting acquisition possibilities, and probably dating a girl in every port and bayou. She hadn't heard from him in weeks. That stung. She'd been smitten, although their relationship hadn't had time to develop, even for a brief fling. She sighed. It had been far too long between flings.

In March she had ended her relationship with Rob, a nice man who was obsessed with marrying her. She'd told him on their first date that she would never marry him or anyone else, but he had refused to believe her. He'd hung around looking hangdog, and begging her to reconsider, but she had no interest in Rob except as a friend, and his moaning and groaning annoyed her. Still, she'd been disconcerted when only two months after their breakup, he had a new girlfriend, and, according to gossip, was wildly happy. So much for the everlasting love and wounded heart that would never heal that Rob claimed he suffered.

Maybe this trip was coming at the perfect time. She might meet someone interesting in London. She knew that most women would be reluctant to become involved with someone who lived so far away, but she wouldn't mind. A part-time lover would suit her better than one who wanted all of her attention all the time. New love or not, she'd help Dinah, work with Heyward, meet Rachel Ransome, and visit a list of places in London she longed to see. Like Liberty, the department store with all the beautiful fabrics . . .

She must have drifted off to sleep. She was awakened by the stir of the crew serving breakfast. She asked for black coffee and a croissant, and an ice cube for Dolly. She gave Dolly a biscuit, and the ice cube, and promised that they were nearly there. Dolly wagged her tail, licked the ice, and settled down to crunch her biscuit. Coleman had nothing to do but wait. They would land in France in less than an hour. Heyward would meet her, and they'd board another plane for the short flight to England. She'd be glad to be on the ground.

•••

Coleman didn't relax until the plane landed at de Gaulle, and even then she was edgy. She felt better when she saw the van that would take her to the part of the airport where smaller planes waited. She knew the van was for her, because several people standing near it were waving to her. She smiled when she saw that one of them was holding a sign: "Welcome, Ms. Greene and Miss Dolly."

Her bags were removed from the Air France plane and quickly transferred to the waiting smaller plane. One of the people standing by the van asked for her passport, disappeared for a moment or two, returned, and gave it back to her. He patted Dolly, and disappeared again.

She and Dolly were whisked into the cozy back seat of the van, where Heyward waited. The van conveyed them to the plane in minutes, and it took off immediately. When they were settled, Coleman released Dolly from her carrier, and let the little dog climb into her lap. Coleman took a deep breath, relaxed, and looked around at the wood-paneled walls, and the soft chairs and sofa, covered in what appeared to be gray velvet. If it was a synthetic, it was a good one.

"Pretty fancy plane," she said.

Heyward laughed. "Nothing but the best for you and Dolly," he said.

"This is great, and they didn't even look at Dolly's papers," she said.

"No, I told you there was no problem. The French love dogs. I wish we could stay a few days—dogs go everywhere in France. Dolly would have a great time. Anyway, you're almost in England at last. Welcome!" Heyward said.

"Yes, and I confess, I'm excited. The flight to Paris was comfortable, although I didn't sleep much—journey proud, I guess. What happens now?" Coleman asked.

"In a few minutes we'll land in England on the private airstrip on the estate of the Duke of Omnium. He's a business associate, and a good friend. An official will meet us to check your passport and Dolly's papers. When you've been cleared, my driver will take us to my house in London. I know you want to go to Dinah's as soon as possible, but do you want to change first? Freshen up?

Have breakfast? You can have something light now, or something more substantial after we arrive, or both."

"I had coffee and a croissant on the plane, and the croissant was so good, I wish I'd asked for two. I'm still hungry, and I need to feed Dolly," Coleman said.

"We can take care of your breakfast and Dolly's immediately," he said, and nodded at the young woman in a dark blue pantsuit hovering nearby. A few minutes later, Dolly was on the floor eating her favorite kibble, and Coleman was served a basket of miniature croissants, a tray of butter and jam, and a small pot of black coffee.

She took a bite of the croissant, and a sip of coffee. "Delicious," she said. "This ought to keep me till lunch. And to answer your other question, I do want to clean up and change at your house."

"Fine. Speaking of lunch, Dinah is taking you to lunch at The Fountain Restaurant in Fortnum & Mason at one o'clock. She's expecting you at 23 Culross at eleven. I thought she sounded miserable when I spoke to her. What's bothering her? Anything I can do to help?"

"She's having a bad time with the servants in the house they rented. They sound as if they should be fired, but Jonathan won't fire them," Coleman said.

"What kind of problems does she have?" Heyward asked.

"From what she's told me, I think the servants are trying to force Dinah and Jonathan out of the house. If they are, it's because they have something to hide. I'm guessing they're doing something illegal, like selling drugs or storing stolen goods— could be anything, like furniture or art—until they can get it out of the country, or sell it. They want no witnesses."

Heyward nodded. "Both could be true. Thefts of art and antiques in England total more than three hundred million pounds a year, second only to the proceeds of crime from drug dealing. What do you want to do about it?"

"I don't know what to look for if they're selling drugs, but I've been studying furniture for *First Home*, and I think I can spot antiques that look too good to be in a rental house. I'll certainly be able to tell whether the house is overstuffed with good furniture. Either could be a sign that the house is being used for stolen antiques. I've read that there are special police assigned to that type of theft in England. How can I reach them?" Coleman asked.

"As soon as you have a hint there's anything illegal going on in that house, call me on my mobile, or let me know if you don't find anything wrong. I'll be waiting for your call. If they're needed, I'll get the right people to the house immediately. Be cautious. Criminals won't hesitate to use violence against a person interfering with their profitable activities." Heyward said.

"I'll be careful," Coleman promised.

"Good. Now fasten your seatbelt. We've started the descent to the Duke's landing strip."

•••

Coleman stared down at the narrow concrete landing strip running through acres of grass surrounded by woodlands. A large hangar and a small stone building were the only buildings in sight. She wanted to ask Heyward how big the Omnium estate was. If the Duke owned a private landing strip, surely he owned a castle, or at least a very large house. It wasn't visible. Could the property be so immense that the castle was too far away to be seen?

The plane landed, and she grabbed her purse, which held her passport and Dolly's papers, and with Dolly under her arm, followed Heyward off the plane. She put Dolly down on the grass, and the little dog vanished behind a nearby shrub. Coleman took a deep breath of fresh air—cool and scented with evergreen and other woodsy smells. After being enclosed in planes and a car for hours, air had never smelled better. She smiled to herself: her first smell of England. She'd make a note in her diary.

Dolly returned and the heavyset man in a khaki uniform who had been waiting outside the plane led them into the stone house. It was sparsely furnished with a desk, a file cabinet, a desk chair, and two metal chairs piled against the wall, presumably for guests. The man didn't suggest that they sit down, but he offered Dolly a bowl of water. The little dog took a big drink, and wagged her tail in thanks.

He asked for their papers, glanced through them, stamped several, smiled, and handed Coleman her passport and Dolly's papers.

"Welcome to England," he said. "Your car is approaching."

Coleman turned to look. Sure enough, a Bentley emerged from the woods and rolled up to the plane. The driver got out, and with the help of the man in the khaki uniform, removed her bags from the plane and stowed them in the car's boot. Coleman smiled—she'd never heard an automobile trunk called "the boot"—a new word. Dinah had told her it would take a while to understand English. She'd start a collection of new words.

She looked out the windows on the drive to London, but the car was moving so fast she didn't take in much. The hedges—she'd read that they were called hedgerows in England—were glowing with white blossoms. She'd have liked to stop and look at them, and see if the flowers were scented, but before she knew it, they had arrived at Heyward's house.

•••

Coleman fell in love with Heyward's house as soon as she saw it. The white marble half-circular porch, or portico, supported by white columns, stood out proudly against the rosy brick façade. A white-painted metal railing on the porch roof created a balcony on the second floor. The central window on the third floor gently echoed the curves of the portico.

Evergreen trees in large containers flanked the massive double doors. Shrubbery on both sides of the porch and the brick steps that led up to the little porch would lead the visitor to think Heyward had lived there for years. A semicircular drive allowed the car to pull up in front of the house.

Heyward went ahead to the doors, which had been opened when the car drove up. He ushered Coleman in, followed by Dolly, while what seemed like a crowd of people clustered on the porch, collecting her bags and carrying them up the stairs.

"You can take the elevator up, if you don't want to walk up all those stairs," Heyward called.

"No, I've been sitting all night. I'd rather walk," Coleman said.

"Fine. My housekeeper, Mrs. Carter, will show you to your suite."

Her bedroom was a dream, decorated in shades of green, taken from the hues of the exquisite green-striped wallpaper. The stripes hinted at a trellis, covered with creamy white roses in full blossom. A vase of white tulips stood on the bedside table, and she could smell a faintly spicy scent. She looked for the source, and spotted a silver bowl filled with potpourri on the dressing table. The wool carpet, also green, was softer than the grass it resembled. A white-painted door opened to a sparkling white bathroom, brightened with green towels and green glass accessories.

After Mrs. Carter opened the door to a cedar-lined closet where her clothes would hang, she escorted Coleman back into the hall, and opened another door, revealing a perfectly arranged office in the same shades of green, white, and cream as the bedroom.

"Mr. Bain thought you would prefer an office separated from your bedroom," Mrs. Carter said.

"He's right," Coleman said. "Everything is perfect."

She was reluctant to leave the beautiful suite, but Dinah was waiting. She took a quick shower, changed, grabbed Dolly, and hurried downstairs, where William, Heyward's driver, stood by the Bentley, ready to drive her to 23 Culross.

CHAPTER FOURTEEN

Rachel

Friday, May, London

When Julia called to tell her about the second murder, Rachel had a horrible feeling of déjà vu. Everything was the same, except today rain was pouring down, and the air was colder than it had been on Tuesday. She wore a dark red wool suit—she couldn't help thinking blood probably wouldn't show on it, although she would make sure she didn't touch anything—her Burberry raincoat, and Wellingtons. The taxi ride to the Little Palace, the serenity of the building, and Julia's greeting were all exactly as they had been for the first death. Julia was even wearing the same strange apparel— she described it as her detective outfit.

The corpse, another swarthy young man, lay fully clothed on Stephanie's balcony, which was twice as large as Julia's and featured chairs and small metal tables, but no plants or flowers. His clothes—khaki trousers, a white shirt, and loafers—were soaked with rain, and diluted blood had spread all over the tiled floor of the balcony. Like the first man, his throat had been cut— the head nearly severed from the body—and the razor, a twin to the first one—lay near the corpse.

"Who is he?" Rachel asked.

"The Italian lover. His first name is Roberto or Robert. I'll be interested to hear whether he, too, left Stephanie money," Julia said. "If he did, I'd guess she'll be arrested."

"I hope Stephanie has an alibi. I think she is a self-centered little fool, but I cannot believe she is a murderer," Rachel said.

Julia shrugged. "Who knows? Someone killed these men and she knew them both. One of them left her a small fortune. Are you going to stay to talk to the police and the Pal Pols, if they turn up?"

"No, I'm going to go home, sit by the fire, and try to get some work done. Wait a second, there's some trash on the tiles near the body. I hope it didn't come in on my boots."

Rachel leaned over and, with a Kleenex, picked up what looked like a clump of hair or fur. She put it, wrapped in the Kleenex, in her raincoat pocket.

"You don't think it's a clue, do you?" Julia asked.

"No, I think it's something I tracked in, probably picked up from the taxi floor. I'm in trouble enough without polluting a crime scene."

"Where will you be the rest of the day in case the police or the Pal Pols ask?"

"I'll be home all day. Why don't you join me for lunch? I'll be ready for a break, and you can update me on anything you learn between now and then."

Julia accepted with alacrity, as Rachel was sure she would. She planned to confront Julia, as Heyward had suggested. This would be the perfect time. She felt guilty, as if she had set a trap for an innocent animal. But was Julia innocent? She had been quick to blame Stephanie for the murders.

She nearly ran out of the building to her waiting car. She berated herself all the way home. She was furious with herself for having come at Julia's call, after Heyward's warnings about Julia and the Little Palace. She'd have to tell him about the second murder, and what she had done. She'd also tell him about her theory about the crime scenes, which was the reason why she had gone to see the second crime scene. But was her suspicion a good enough reason for ignoring Heyward's advice? She was afraid it wasn't. From now on, she'd do what he told her to do.

Back at home, she called Heyward. She confessed that she had been at the Little Palace. Just as she feared, he was disapproving. He knew about the second murder. He had already heard she had been in the Little Palace and at the crime scene. But when she told him about her thoughts on the murders and the crime scenes, he was interested, and asked her to repeat what she had said.

"As I've told you, I've always thought the first murder looked staged, theatrical. The scene looked arranged. I still think that. I think the use of the razor is a clumsy attempt to make the murder look like suicide. I think someone arranged the scene to look like one in Dorothy L. Sayers's *Have His Carcase*, in which the murdered man also had his throat cut. That murder was also originally thought to be a suicide.

"I knew I was right when I saw the second murder scene. It, too, looked arranged, theatrical. At first, I couldn't think what book it reminded me of. Then I saw a bit of trash on the tiles—I thought I'd tracked it in, so I picked it up, and put it in my coat pocket. When it dried I realized it was gray hair. It was a clue: Whoever is arranging the murder scenes wants us to know what he's doing. This scene was meant to remind us of Edgar Allan Poe's "The Murders in the Rue Morgue." The throat of one of the victims in that book was cut by a razor although the victim had been strangled to death—twice-murdered like the first man at the Little Palace. I'm guessing this second murder is the same: The poor man died of an overdose before he was 'killed' with the razor. It was the tuft of gray hair that convinced me. There were locks of gray hair near one of the bodies Poe's story," she explained.

"What do you think it means? Why would someone do this?" Heyward asked.

"Everyone is aware that both Julia and I are mystery fans, and would probably recognize these scenes. I think the killer is hinting that one or both of us is involved in the deaths," Rachel said.

"You may be on to something," Heyward said. "Have you mentioned your theory to anyone else?"

"No, just you," Rachel said.

"Keep it that way. I'll talk to the appropriate people, and let you know what they say."

CHAPTER FIFTEEN

Coleman and Dinah

Friday, May, London

Coleman, in a new tangerine wool suit she had designed, a beige silk shirt, and beige suede boots with three-inch heels, her sheared mink coat draped over her shoulders and Dolly in her arms, arrived at 23 Culross at exactly 11 A.M.

"Welcome!" Dinah said. "I am so glad to see you."

Coleman hugged Dinah and looked around the foyer, where a magnificent vase of long-stemmed apple blossoms stood on a round table. An oriental rug in faded shades of red and blue covered the polished floor. "This is lovely," she said.

Dinah led Coleman upstairs to the master bedroom, served her coffee, and showed her the makeshift kitchen she had designed for serving Jonathan breakfast in bed. She invited Coleman to sit in one of the two large overstuffed chairs near the fireplace, sat down opposite her cousin, and started talking. She told Coleman everything, much of which Coleman had already heard. Coleman listened attentively, recognizing Dinah's need to go over it all.

When Dinah finally stopped talking, Coleman nodded.

"I think I understand the situation. We'll take care of it today. But why is it so cold in here? And what *is* that dreadful smell?" she said.

Dinah sighed. "I turn the heat up, and they turn it down. The smell is some of the disgusting stuff they cook."

"Why doesn't Jonathan fire them?" Coleman asked.

"Ever since we got married, he's wanted to buy a big fancy house, with a butler, a cook, a housekeeper, and probably more people, all live-in. It's what he grew up with, what he's used to. I love to cook and shop for groceries, and I like having a house to myself, or to be alone with him. He doesn't want me to cook or do anything related to housekeeping. I believe he thinks it lowers his status for me to cook and buy groceries, and not depend on a house full of servants. He thought this house was the perfect place for me to learn how wonderful it is to be able to sit around and have someone wait on me. If only. He's sure the reason this place isn't working out is because I can't manage the cook and the housekeeper properly, or worse, that I'm deliberately sabotaging them to get my way," Dinah said.

"I see. Well, let's go down and take a look at the rest of the house. Where will we find the enemy?" Coleman said.

"Probably in the kitchen," Dinah said. "They spend the day there, eating."

"Don't they cook and serve lunch?"

"No, just breakfast and dinner, and they are the only people who eat the food they serve. In fact, I prepare our breakfast, eat lunch out, and shop for the take-out we have for dinner. Jonathan has lunch with people from his office. At this point we're not eating anything Mrs. O'Hara prepares."

"All right. Let's tour the house first, then we'll evict the witches."

"I know you're making fun, but I think they *are* witches, or at least they're evil. They frighten me," Dinah said.

Coleman shook her head. "I'm not making fun of you. This house has a bad feeling. I think ugly things have happened here. The women are a part of it. The sooner we get rid of them, the better. It's good that the outside of the house hasn't been infected with whatever is wrong inside. I like the exterior—the blue shutters and the purple flowers in the window boxes against the white façade are very attractive. The foyer is nice, too. That big vase is beautiful, and the little table is a very handsome piece."

"I agree. I think Jane Ross, the owner of the house, must have designed the exterior. And that's her vase in the foyer," Dinah said.

"What about this beautiful antique furniture? Surely it isn't hers. Didn't you tell me she was poor?"

"Yes. James, our driver, who's known her for a long time, says she has very little money. I have no idea who owns the furniture. I've never thought about it, or even looked at the furniture except to dust it. I don't know anything about antiques. I didn't know you did, either. It's not like we grew up with them," Dinah said.

Coleman smiled, remembering the empty rooms in their childhood home. Four Oaks, the big old house in North Carolina where they lived as children with their grandmother and aunt, was almost empty of furniture. The old ladies had been forced to sell nearly everything they owned. Most of the rooms held only dust bunnies. Coleman and Dinah had loved their grandmother and aunt, and had worked with them to support their little family. They had never missed the antiques that once decorated the house.

"We certainly didn't. I've been studying furniture for *First Home*, both antiques and reproductions. I don't know a lot yet, but some of these pieces are rare. I've seen museum pictures of furniture like them. I think all the furniture in here is valuable," Coleman said.

She strolled through the drawing room and dining room, pausing occasionally to examine a chair or a table, bookcase or desk. "Didn't you tell me these rooms were crammed with furniture, and filthy dirty? Everything looks look clean to me, and the amount of furniture is just right," Coleman said.

"Yes, but we removed all the excess furniture, and cleaned these rooms to get ready for you," Dinah said.

"What did you do with the extra furniture?" Coleman asked.

"It's upstairs. Why do you ask?"

"I'd like to look at the rest of the furniture—see if it is as good as the pieces downstairs. But before we go upstairs, what do you know about this painting?" Coleman stopped in front of one of the few paintings she had seen in her stroll through the house.

Dinah shrugged. "It's dark and dull. I kept a few paintings downstairs, because the walls are so bare without them, but I dislike all of them, and most of them are upstairs with the furniture."

"I think this dull and dark painting is hiding another very valuable painting. Come here: Look at the paint curling back here. Do you have a flashlight?"

"I have a torch," Dinah said. "I tried for a while to buy a flashlight and was unable to find one until someone told me to ask for a torch. I'll get it for you, but first tell me how you knew to look for that peeling paint."

Coleman smiled. "Is that what they call it? A flashlight is a torch? Live and learn. Another word for my English collection. As to how I knew to look for the peeling paint, I read an article about thieves disguising stolen paintings by painting over them with easily removable paint. I need the flashlight to try to see the picture underneath."

Dinah left the room, returned with the flashlight, and handed it to Coleman, who focused the light on the curling paint.

"See? Where the paint has curled back, you can see another painting under this one," Coleman said.

"But you can't see it very well. It might be as bad as the top one. Why do you think it's valuable?" Dinah asked.

"Because the frame is valuable. It's made of tortoiseshell, and it's in very good shape. Tortoiseshell is no longer used for frames—its trade was banned worldwide in 1973. When it *was* used, it was expensive and fragile. This frame has been cared for. I'm sure there's a treasured painting under the top picture. And this isn't the only painting with an expensive frame. I've looked at the other three paintings on this floor and they're all in valuable frames. Come look at them with the torch."

They moved across the room, where Coleman again used the flashlight to point out details. "I'm pretty sure these are Pre-Raphaelite designs. The frame manufacturer incorporated geometric forms—triangles, circles, and squares in the design on this one. I'd guess the frame was made about 1855. This one is in Rossetti's 'thumb-mark pattern.' And this one, carved in wood, looks like whoever made the frame was trying to imitate Grinling Gibbons. Hard to do, time consuming, and expensive. These frames are amazing. How many paintings are upstairs?" Coleman asked.

"Maybe twenty. How do you know so much about frames?" Dinah said.

"The same answer: I studied them for *First Home*. It's a fascinating specialty in the art world. Could you have someone bring the paintings down here, where they can be easily examined?"

"Sure. James and Franklin can do it. Where do you want them?"

"On the floor in the dining room, leaning against the wall," Coleman said. "Let's go upstairs and take a look at the furniture before you have the paintings brought down."

Dinah led the way, and with only a glance in each of the rooms, Coleman knew that the furniture was valuable. None of the paintings was accessible, so she couldn't get a good look at them, but even from a distance the frames were impressive. She should call Heyward. He'd be waiting to hear from her. She reached him immediately.

"Heyward, it's just as we thought—this place is full of valuable antiques. They must be stolen: Dinah says the woman who owns the house has financial problems. I'm sure she'd have sold the furniture if she owned it. In addition to the furniture, I think there may be more than twenty valuable paintings here. This is a big find, much bigger than I anticipated. I think it's time for you to send in the art and antiques cops. Send a painting specialist, too. I've had all the pictures put in the dining room to make it easy to look at them. I'd like to examine them myself, but I think it should be done by an expert.

"Please urge the police to come right away. The news that we've discovered stolen goods in this house will spread fast. Dinah and I are on the way to the kitchen to dismiss the servants. They'll soon be in touch with their masters. I'll call you again after we're rid of them, and before we leave here."

CHAPTER SIXTEEN

Coleman and Dinah

Friday, May, London

Coleman, with Dolly under her left arm and Dinah beside her, walked into the kitchen and looked around.

Mrs. O'Hara, Mrs. Malone, and two other women were sitting at the table slurping up their elevenses, which appeared to be a huge assortment of sweets. Coleman spotted a fruitcake, cookies, and two pies, as well as bowls full of something topped with mountains of whipped cream.

Mrs. O'Hara stood up when she saw Coleman. "Get that dog out of my kitchen," she ordered.

"I certainly will. She's a very valuable animal, and she could sicken from the filth in this room. I've never seen anything so disgusting." Coleman was taking pictures of the kitchen and its occupants with her iPhone while she spoke. When she had finished, she stood still, staring at the women. Mrs. O'Hara had turned purple, and looked as if she were about to scream at Coleman, or physically attack her. But before she could make a sound, or move, Coleman transformed herself into a different person. She stood up tall, deepened and sharpened her soft voice, and radiated authority.

"Stand up, both of you, and remain standing, as you should when the mistress of the house enters the room," she ordered. "Now that you are on your feet, listen to me carefully. Go upstairs, pack your things, and leave this house immediately. I do not want to have to repeat myself: Go! You will be very sorry if you don't."

She held up her right hand. "And don't bother telling me that you report only to Mr. Ross. We are on the way to see Mr. Ross, with photographs of this filthy kitchen, and 'before' pictures of the drawing room and living room, when they were so dirty, because you weren't doing your jobs. We'll show him pictures of you sitting around stuffing yourselves—as you are today—rather than working. When he has heard all we have to say, he will apologize for burdening the Hathaways with the likes of you, especially when he's told that the house is full of stolen antique furniture and paintings, and that you are a part of the criminal ring that brought them here.

"After we see Mr. Ross, we are going out for lunch. When we return, you will have left this house. Do not take anything with you that isn't yours. We have an inventory of every item. I am sure crimes have been committed here—theft, at the very least, but possibly far worse. The police will be here in minutes. They will search this house and fingerprint everything in it. You will be arrested if they find you here."

Coleman turned and strolled out of the kitchen. Dinah, with a big smile on her face, followed her.

"How'd you get so big and bossy?" Dinah asked.

"Practice. I've had to fire a fair number of people in the last year or so," Coleman said.

"How can you be sure the police will come so quickly?" Dinah asked.

"On the plane from Paris, I told Heyward I thought there had to be a reason the servants were behaving as they were. The logical explanation was that they wanted you to move out. I thought they might be doing something they needed to hide: drugs? Stolen goods? Now that I've seen the furniture and the picture frames, I'm sure they're hiding stolen antique furniture and art. I just spoke to Heyward—you heard what I said. He'll do the rest. I promised to call him again when we were leaving the house. I should do that now," Coleman said. She took out her cell phone.

"Heyward? The witches have been evicted, and Dinah and I are headed to see Mr. Ross, and then to lunch. Please call Jonathan, let him know what's going on. Tell him Dinah and I are going out to lunch to celebrate. Make sure he knows the women working here are criminals." She smiled at Dinah, who smiled back, and pretended to clap her hands.

"I'm sending your car and driver back to your house. We're using Dinah's car. James, her driver, will take care of Dolly while we eat. After lunch, I'm coming home to take a nap. I need some beauty sleep before the party."

Coleman hung up, and turned to Dinah. "Now that I've told the old bats to pack up and get out, you should call James and ask him to rehire—what was his name?"

"Franklin," said Dinah.

"Yes, Franklin, to join your butler—Hamilton?"

Dinah nodded.

"They can watch the women leave, and make sure they don't try to steal the paintings or other portable items," Coleman said. "James can call Franklin while he is driving us to meet with Mr. Ross. You should also ask James how many other people are needed to run his house. Obviously, you need a cook."

"I'd rather do it myself," Dinah protested.

Coleman shook her head. "No, Jonathan's right. You should have a cook—a *good* English cook. You're going to be very busy when you start work. Anyway, I want to talk to you about a project I have in mind. You'll need a cook."

Dinah looked mystified, but cheerful.

"I'm ready to go, but I want you to change clothes," Coleman said. "I bet you've been wearing black every day. Am I right?"

Dinah nodded. "I've been too miserable to care what I wore. Black suited my mood."

"Well, it's time to change into something more cheerful."

Dinah laughed. "Okay. I'll be back in fifteen minutes."

She reappeared in a lemon-yellow dress with a matching jacket, looking like a ray of sunshine. "Will this do?" she asked.

"Perfect!" Coleman clapped her hands. "Let's call on Mr. Ross."

Dinah, smiling, climbed into the Mercedes, where she was joined by Dolly and Coleman. James was smiling, too, as he closed the door. Fifteen minutes later they parked in front of Ross & Ross, located in an attractive small building on the west side of Berkeley Square.

"Nice digs," Coleman said.

"Yes, very," Dinah agreed.

•••

The exterior of the Ross office was misleading. The civility it implied was false. Inside they encountered pandemonium. A number of men with red hair were wandering around a large room. They had similar features, were obviously related.

"Did you know there were so many?" Coleman asked.

"I heard they were a big clan, but I didn't expect to see so many of them here," Dinah said.

The room smelled of tobacco, smoke, sweat, and burnt coffee. The men seemed to be talking all at once. The noise level was deafening.

An older man approached them. He was tall and gaunt, and his red hair was graying, as was the ferocious mustache that drooped beneath his enormous nose, which was redder than his hair. "Can

I help you?" he said. His expression suggested he did not intend to be helpful.

"We wish to speak with the Mr. Ross who oversees 23 Culross," Coleman said.

"Do you have an appointment?" the man asked.

"No, but our business with him is urgent."

"You should tell me," the large man said.

"We will, but I'm sure he'll want to hear what we have to say, and we don't have a lot of time. This is Mrs. Hathaway. She and her husband are the current tenants of 23 Culross. I am a member of the family. We have fired the servants employed by Mr. Ross—"

"You canna do that," the large man shouted. "They are not yours to fire. They are Ross employees. I've heard about you: You will na eat good English food. If you want American food, you should have stayed in America. You Yankees are ig'nrant."

Coleman smiled. "The women you hired—and I cannot say anything good about them—have told us repeatedly that they report to you. Nevertheless, under certain circumstances, we are entitled to rid ourselves of them."

"No, you cannot. They are valued servants. They come with the house—live there, work there. You canna make them move out. *You* can leave, and good riddance to you, but you will not get your money back. You canna stay in the house without Mrs. O'Hara and Mrs. Malone. They keep the place clean, and keep the tenants like you from stealing."

The tall man—who was undoubtedly the Mr. Ross who employed the witches—was shouting. His younger relatives—Coleman had counted nine of them—were silent, but they had gathered around him, and nodded in agreement.

Coleman laughed out loud. "You poor old man. You must have never left England, nor even visited London's wonderful restaurants, where one can find delicious food, unlike the garbage Mrs. O'Hara cooks. We live in New York, where every food in the world is served and enjoyed. I pity you if you think Mrs. O'Hara is a good cook.

"I did not come here to discuss food with you. I've brought you photographs showing you how clean your servants keep the house. The kitchen is a pigpen. When were you there last? What kind of landlord or manager are you?"

The old man was making odd noises—mumbles and grumbles and probably foul words. Coleman hoped he didn't have a stroke until after she and Dinah left.

"The Hathaways's contract with you has a malfeasance clause that allows them to terminate anyone who is guilty of a crime. Your beloved servants are being arrested as we speak. I suggest you go to the house and take the responsibility for hiring them— although, if you do, you, too, will probably be arrested. Now you must excuse us. We are on our way to lunch. We stopped by to let you know what we have discovered, and what we have done, as the contract required us to do."

When they turned to leave, the men deliberately blocked their exit. They moved closer and closer to her and Dinah. Coleman didn't care for their manners, or the way they smelled.

"You lie," the old man shouted.

He and his young supporters were making Coleman angry. She knew Dinah must be frightened. How dare he call her a liar? She raised her right hand as she had when she'd fired the witches in the kitchen. She'd been taught that it was an effective gesture when chastising the guilty. It had never failed her.

"If you doubt what I have said, call 23 Culross. The police will answer the telephone. My brother, Heyward Bain, is overseeing the arrests, and the removal of the stolen furniture and art. He will not be pleased to learn how you have treated us."

She looked at the crowd, and noticed that several of the men were drifting away. They must have recognized Heyward's name. But not all of them were moving. She'd take care of that.

"Stand back immediately. Our driver, who is also our bodyguard, is outside the door and armed. If I scream—and I will in a moment—he will come in to escort us out, and if I say 'shoot,' he will. *NOW MOVE!*"

Everyone except the raving old man moved out of the way, and Coleman and Dinah departed. The old man continued to make strange noises. They could still hear him when they reached the car.

When they were inside the car, Coleman asked James if he carried a gun. When he said he didn't, she laughed. "I didn't think so. It's just as well some people think you do, including some of those we just left. I'm ready for lunch!" she said.

"Excuse me, madam. Did the meeting with Mr. Ross go badly?"

Coleman laughed again. "You could say that."

"He was horrible, and so were all the other Rosses. He was rude and obnoxious, and so were his younger relatives," Dinah said.

"They were like a roomful of roosters—all crow and no brains," Coleman said.

"You've always had the confidence and strength and certainty to do what you just did. I've seen it before. I remember someone saying about you, when we were young, 'Coleman walks in where angels fear to tread,'" Dinah said.

Coleman laughed. "Angels aren't afraid to tread anywhere. We should all remember that, and try to be like them. Let's go have lunch. I'm starved," she said.

•••

Dinah asked James to let them out on Duke Street, so they could walk through the side door to the ground floor of Fortnum & Mason, the fabulous store in Piccadilly. They strolled through the aisles, looking at the displays of chocolates and confections, preserves and honey, biscuits and patisserie, and in the rear, a short staircase down to the Fountain Restaurant.

"Looking at and smelling all this candy is making me even hungrier," Coleman complained.

"Yes, I know—I'm always tempted when I'm here. We could have entered the restaurant by the Jermyn Street door, but I wanted you to see the array of goodies you can buy. Another day I'll take you to the lower ground floor and you can see where I shop for some of the food I've been giving Jonathan for dinner. That floor is where the cheese and wine and meat is."

"Now that you've tempted and tortured me with candy, where's the restaurant?" Coleman said.

"We're here," Dinah said, and gave her name to the young woman standing at the bottom of the stairs.

The waitress led them to a snug table for two by the windows, which were decorated with carved wooden birds painted white. She handed them menus, and asked what they'd like to drink.

"Still water and iced tea," Dinah said.

"I'm really hungry," Coleman said. "The menu looks great."

"This is one of my favorite places to eat. Of course, I haven't eaten in many restaurants since we came to London. I could have—I had the time—but I don't like eating alone. I feel comfortable here. As you can see, there are several women eating alone," Dinah said.

"What do you suggest I order?" Coleman said.

"The Welsh rarebit, with tomato, no bacon, and only one slice of bread," Dinah said.

"That doesn't sound like much. I'm starved," Coleman said.

"It's a lot of food, but if you're feeling the absence of greens, order the rocket and parmesan salad, in addition to the rarebit," Dinah said.

"I'll do as you say, but what is 'rocket'?"

"It's what we call arugula," Dinah said.

"While I'm asking, what exactly is a rarebit? I've heard the term for years, but what's in it?"

"There's a waiter taking a rarebit order to that table—look at it on that tray," Dinah said.

"It looks like a toasted cheese sandwich without the top slice of toast. Is that what it is? If so, forget it. I want something more exciting. I can make a toasted cheese sandwich in my own kitchen. Is there more to Welsh rarebit than bread and cheese?" Coleman asked.

"Oh, yes. The Fountain Welsh rarebit recipe calls for butter, flour, milk, cheddar cheese, Worcestershire sauce, paprika, and English mustard, which is very strong. It has a subtle bite— not enough to make you think you're eating hot peppers, but interesting."

"Sounds great, I'll go for it," Coleman said. "But why did you tell me not to order bacon? Bacon, tomato, and cheese sounds delicious."

"Because you would be disappointed. It's almost impossible to get American bacon here. What they call bacon resembles Canadian bacon or ham, and there's often a lot of fat on it," Dinah said.

"Oh, okay, I'll go with the rarebit and the salad you recommended. I hope they hurry. Tell me about the restaurant where you ate last night. It's very special, isn't it?" Coleman said.

Dinah lit up. "Oh, yes. The restaurant is called Dinner by Heston Blumenthal. Most of the food is based on ancient English recipes—they put the date next to the dish. I had grilled octopus. The recipe goes back to 1390! It was delicious."

"How did Jonathan like it?" Coleman asked. Jonathan was a plain meat-and-potatoes man. He wouldn't go near grilled octopus.

Dinah laughed. "He had the filet of Aberdeen Angus and chips, which are fried potatoes—there's another word for your

English collection—and he was in heaven. Steak and potatoes are his favorite foods. He didn't care that the dish was dated 1830."

"And Heyward?" Coleman asked.

"Heyward had chicken cooked with lettuces, circa 1670. He said it was excellent. Then came dessert. We ordered an assortment of desserts. I tasted everything, but Heyward and Jonathan had the cheese and oatcakes. So unadventurous," Dinah said.

"How do you remember all that? What everybody ate and the dates?" Coleman asked.

"Like you did about the furniture and frames. I'm interested in food and cooking," Dinah said.

"I know that," Coleman said. "I remember you standing on a stool in the kitchen at Slocumb Corners, helping Miss Ida cook."

"I still love cooking," Dinah said. "Oh, here's our lunch. I ordered iced tea for both of us. I hope that's all right?"

"Please. Iced tea available in the land of hot tea–drinkers? Wonderful! I know you're interested in food and cooking, and you're a marvelous cook, and you're always coming up with new recipes. And that's what I want to talk to you about," Coleman said. "That's my idea."

"The idea that forces me to hire a cook?" Dinah asked.

"Yes," said Coleman. "I want you to write a column or a series of articles on 'Food and London' for *First Home*. You're going to be here for months, and I'm sure your job at the museum won't take up all your time. You can get to know a lot about the food and the restaurants—you already know the take-out world, you already know there are dishes Americans aren't used to eating, including some they won't eat. If you have a good cook, she will be able to teach you recipes for things you like. You can come up with travelers' tips about where and what to eat in London. I think you'd be a great addition to the magazine."

Dinah flushed. "Are you serious? You really think I can do it?"

"Absolutely," Coleman said. "I'll give you a formal proposal in writing with suggested compensation in the next day or two. Will you do it?"

"Oh, yes," Dinah said. "I'd love to! Now tell me what you think of my first recommendation—your first restaurant in London?"

Coleman took a bite of the rarebit. "Perfect! Let's eat. I need to get home to rest up for tonight."

When they were in the car again, James said, "I have a message for you, Mrs. Hathaway and Miss Coleman. Lady Jane has heard of your reception at the Ross office, and apologizes for the bad manners of her family. She was appalled to learn about the servants' behavior towards you, and astonished by their criminal activities. She will be at the party at Scott's tonight, and wants to apologize in person."

Coleman and Dinah exchanged glances.

"How very nice," Dinah said.

"I don't see how she failed to know about her house being used by criminals," Coleman said.

"I hope she isn't guilty of anything," Dinah said.

•••

In her lovely suite in Heyward's house, Coleman took a long soak in the large bathtub, dried off, put on a nightgown, picked up Dolly, and settled down in the oversized bed with its smoothly ironed white sheets and several white coverlets. She set the alarm for six. She wanted plenty of time to dress for the party. Within minutes Dolly fell asleep, and Coleman soon followed.

When the alarm sounded, she got up and took a wake-up shower. Dolly followed her into the bathroom, and cocked her head.

"Yes, I'm going out," Coleman told Dolly. "Don't worry, that nice Mrs. Carter has invited you to spend the evening with her.

She's taking your Kitty Kup to her apartment, right above this one. She'll give you supper and a walk—maybe two. Now, let me show you what I'm wearing tonight." Dolly watched Coleman's every move, and looked only a little sad when Coleman took her to Mrs. Carter's, and left for the party.

CHAPTER SEVENTEEN

Rachel and Julia

Friday, lunchtime, London

The roast chicken and apple tart had been served and devoured, and they were drinking coffee, when Rachel took a deep breath and went straight to the point.

"Julia, someone told me you're a Republican. Is it true? Are you one of those people who wants to abolish the Monarchy? I've read all the literature that group produces, and I can't understand their arguments. I can't believe you are a part of that crowd."

Julia, who was looking like a contented cat after her lunch, answered without hesitation. "Yes, I belong to a splinter group of Republicans. I don't like most of the people one meets in the larger group—they're concerned with issues that don't interest me. My group is made up of people who have legitimate grievances against the throne," Julia said.

Rachel frowned. "Against Queen Elizabeth? Surely not," she said.

"No, my dear, not our present Queen. My problems—and those of all of my group—are with Queen Victoria. My dislike of her goes back to the Crimean War."

Rachel, stunned, couldn't believe it. As unthinkable as it was that Julia could dislike Queen Elizabeth, hating the long-dead Queen Victoria seemed even more bizarre. "How can that be? What could Queen Victoria have done that makes you angry today? Didn't she die in 1900?"

"1901. But after Prince Albert died in 1861, Queen Victoria was so wrapped up in her mourning, she didn't seem to care about anything. She abused my family by sins of both commission and omission. Those of us who are angry with her thought she was a terrible queen. Many bad things happened under her reign, and she couldn't be bothered to rectify them. She ruined my family."

"How?" Rachel asked.

"Do you know anything about the Crimean War? If you don't, you aren't alone. It's been forgotten by most people. If they know anything about it, it's the Charge of the Light Brigade, because of the poem by Tennyson, and because of Florence Nightingale, who won lasting fame for her bravery and hard work during that ghastly war."

"I know about Florence Nightingale. The Charge of the Light Brigade sounds vaguely familiar, but I do not know the poem you're speaking of," Rachel said.

"It's a heartbreaking poem about a suicidal attack by the Light Brigade, ordered by the incompetents managing that war. I'll recite a little of it for you," she said.

To Rachel's astonishment, Julia stood up and began to recite the poem with great passion.

Half a league, half a league,

Half a league onward,

All in the valley of Death,

Rode the six hundred.

'Forward, the Light Brigade!

Charge for the guns!' he said:

Into the valley of Death

Rode the six hundred.

'Forward, the Light Brigade!'

Was there a man dismay'd?

Not tho' the soldiers knew

Some one had blunder'd:

Theirs not to make reply,

Theirs not to reason why,

Theirs but to do and die:

Into the valley of Death

Rode the six hundred.

Cannon to right of them,

Cannon to left of them,

Cannon in front of them

Volley'd and thunder'd;

Storm'd at with shot and shell,

Boldly they rode and well,

Into the jaws of Death,

Into the mouth of Hell

Rode the six hundred.

Julia sat down. "That's about half of it," she said, through her tears. "I can't help crying when I read that poem. All those men dying so unnecessarily. Back to the history of the war: it lasted for three years—1853 to '56—and is usually described as disastrous. Nearly one hundred thousand British soldiers and sailors were sent to Crimea. More than twenty thousand died, eighty percent of them from sickness or disease.

"The war was led by inept aristocrats, mostly old men. Their mismanagement was to blame for most of the deaths, whether the men were killed by the enemy or by disease. There were few heroes among the generals, but one of the few was my ancestor General Ward. He was my great-great-great-great-great grandfather— yes, confusing; so many 'greats,' so I refer to him as my great-grandfather. He was killed in the war and so were his two sons. That war ruined my family."

"That is a very sad story," Rachel said.

"That's only part of the story," Julia said. "After the war, death duties crippled the estate, and no one was left alive to manage it. General Ward's widow—I call her my great-grandmother— was left with almost nothing. She sold everything sellable and moved to a tiny cottage, not far from the great house she had once owned. Friends tried to help her obtain something more suitable, and they finally found a place for her.

"In the 1840s, Queen Victoria arranged the restoration of Tudor Gardens, a beautiful building in near ruins not far from

Oxford. She had it divided into a labyrinth of apartments, which were given to grace-and-favor residents. Widows whose husbands had been killed in the Crimean War occupied most of them, and General Ward's widow was given one. Tudor Gardens was not unlike Hampton Court in how it was used, and like Hampton Court, which burned in 1986, it was destroyed in a terrible fire. When our present Queen was told of the Hampton Court fire she immediately sent a message inquiring about Lady Gale, the occupant of the apartment where the fire started. Lady Gale's body was found and Queen Elizabeth visited the site. Since the fire had started in Lady Gale's apartment, there was no possibility of her being saved, or her furniture and valuables being rescued.

In the Tudor Gardens fire, my ancestor was killed, and her few belongings were destroyed. Her body was never recovered. She was the last of my family. Queen Victoria didn't seem to care. She certainly didn't visit the ruins. She showed none of the compassion that Queen Elizabeth did.

"Meanwhile, people who knew about General Ward's bravery were trying to get recognition for his heroism. The Victoria Cross was created in 1856 and was awarded retrospectively to heroes of the Crimean War. Posthumous awards were forbidden until 1902, after Queen Victoria died. It was given for 'valor' or 'conspicuous gallantry,' but only for the living. Until 1902, there was no award to honor those who had fought valiantly, and died while they were fighting.

"The Queen could have changed this rule, but she didn't. Brave men like my ancestor died in the performance of supreme acts of valor, and their acts weren't even reported because those who knew all about their heroism knew it was futile. Nothing would be done. My ancestor, and all the men like him, were never recognized.

"But the word got out. Men wrote letters to their families. The people learned who was brave and able, and who was incompetent, which was most of the big generals. People continued to try unsuccessfully to get recognition of people like my ancestor. Thousands of British soldiers lie in unmarked graves in Crimea. My ancestor lies in a grave identified with his name and regiment. No one knows where his sons are buried. They are lost forever," Julia said bitterly.

"That is very sad, but it was long ago. I cannot imagine anything being so terrible that it's still a sore point so many years after the person responsible is dead," Rachel said.

"Oh, can you not? What about the American Civil War? Wasn't it fought in 1865, more than a hundred and fifty years ago? Isn't it still a hot topic in some circles? And aren't there Americans who moved to Canada because they think your country shouldn't have declared its independence from England? Those who still believe the United States would be better off if it was part of the UK?" Julia said.

Rachel was startled by Julia's passion. This was a side of her friend she had never seen. This woman *could* be dangerous. "But, Julia, what do you want? How can restitution be made after all this time?" she asked.

"I want to move General Ward's body to England. I'm saving money to buy a small house near where the Wards lived before the Crimean War. I'll see him buried in the cemetery near the church where my family worshipped, with a ceremony acknowledging his bravery. I'll arrange to have empty graves with stones marked with the names and ranks of his sons, and another empty grave with a tombstone for the general's wife, my great-great-great-great-great-grandmother. It would be impossible to get my ancestor the Victoria Cross, but I don't care. I don't want that for him. That medal is neither honorable nor fair. But I'll get something for him. That I promise," she said.

Rachel now understood why Julia called herself a Republican. She did not seem to have any animosity toward the present

Royal Family, and she did not seem to be a danger to anyone. Nothing she'd said connected to the deaths in the Little Palace. Was Stephanie more dangerous than Julia? Put another way, was Stephanie angry with the living? Or with the long dead?

"Does Stephanie share your feelings? Is she a Republican?" she asked.

Julia laughed. "No, Stephanie is a rebel without a cause. She's only interested in herself. But Izzy is a Republican. We share a similar grudge. She, too, hates Queen Victoria."

"Are you referring to that plain little woman who follows Stephanie around? What is her name again?" Julia said.

"Isobel Strange. Can you believe it? Did a name ever match anyone any better? She's a spooky little creature," Julia said.

"What is her problem?"

"She claims her family was ruined by Queen Victoria and Prince Albert. Her ancestor, William Strange, was a nineteenth century London bookseller and publisher. He published fifty-one or more copies of a catalogue of stolen prints made by Queen Victoria and Prince Albert, which he planned to sell. In 1849, Prince Albert sued Strange and won, to no one's surprise. The Prince had the catalogues destroyed or returned to him. Strange's case was not helped by his record. He had been sued by Charles Dickens in 1844 for literary piracy; Dickens won. In 1848, Strange published a book attacking the Monarchy, which offended many people.

"Izzy believes William Strange was ruined by Prince Albert, with Queen Victoria backing him up. She thought that it was unfair of them to sue her ancestor. Strange could never have won a suit brought by Prince Albert, even if he had been innocent. Her family was impoverished after the lawsuit, and they hated Queen Victoria and Prince Albert. They still hate them.

"You now have the complete stories of why both Izzy and I are Republicans—we think that the power of the Monarchy was used unjustly against us," Julia said.

"Do you think Strange was guilty of the charges against him?" Rachel asked.

"Oh, yes, I'm sure he was guilty. But it wasn't a fair trial. Everyone knew Prince Albert would win. And William Strange had returned the prints. So why ruin him?"

"How did it ruin him? Surely Prince Albert didn't ask for costs?"

"I don't think so. But people were afraid to deal with Strange after they knew Prince Albert was against him. His business never recovered, and he became desperate. He began to sell obscene literature. In 1857, he was prosecuted for selling *Paul Pry* and *Women of London*, a case that led to the passing of the Obscene Publications Act. The Strange family still sells books of a kind, and tries to get printing assignments, but they're at the bottom of the barrel in their field. Izzy blames her family's downfall on Prince Albert and Queen Victoria."

"Why is Isobel so devoted to Princess Stephanie?"

"They've known each other a long time. I don't know how or why. They help each other. Izzy helped Stephanie make those prints, and Stephanie tells Izzy when 'she gets what's coming to her,' she'll help Izzy's family get back on their feet. I have no idea what she means by 'getting what's coming to her,' except I know she wants to marry money."

"Good luck to her," Rachel said. "Speaking of luck and marrying money: someone told me you inherited a fortune from your husband."

"I inherited some money, but nothing like what I need to buy a house, and bring my ancestor's body home from Crimea, bury him, and his sons and wife, and arrange the ceremony I'd like to have following the burials. I'll get there. I *will* make it happen," she declared.

"I'm thrifty. I'm lucky that I could get a place in the Little Palace. The Remembrance Society will admit everyone who is a Republican; no matter which royal we're against. Izzy and I aren't the only people with grudges again Queen Victoria. Living in the Little Palace is a good deal. It allows me to save money to finance my plans."

"What do you do to press your cause?" Rachel asked.

"Write letters. Write stories and articles about the Crimean War, and the people who died there, and those who are to blame. My articles sell pretty well and every little bit helps," Julia said.

"And Isobel?"

"She's lucky to be in the Little Palace, too, and she's always trying to raise money."

Rachel had one last question. "When I got home after seeing poor dead Ivan, I found blood on my boots and the clothes I was wearing. I didn't go in that bathroom. Do you know how I came into contact with blood?"

"After you left, I found bloody rags on the floor of my closet. I got blood on my shoes before I knew the rags were there. There were bloody rags on a hanger, too. Blood was all over my coat. I didn't know you'd brushed against it too. I'm so sorry.'"

"Who would have done that?" Rachel said.

"Someone who doesn't like me. Some of the people living in the Little Palace are spiteful and vicious. I guess that kind of behavior goes with unhappiness. Nearly everyone in the Little Palace is unhappy, dissatisfied, miserable. The bloody rags were a nasty trick, but not the first one."

"Thank you for explaining," Rachel said. "On a happier note, I hear you are coming to Heyward's party tonight?"

"Yes. I'm so excited! I never get to go to a party. I'm sure I have you to thank for the invitation—you're a good friend. But speaking of the party, I must go home. I have an appropriate dress, but I need to air it, make sure it's in decent shape."

She stood up and Rachel walked her to the door. "I will see you tonight," Rachel said.

She returned to the library and sat down. She didn't know what to think. She'd pass all this on to Heyward. Maybe he would find it useful. The mystery of her bloody clothes was explained. Julia was amazingly calm about it. Just another nasty trick by someone who hated her. Living in the Little Palace must be terrible.

CHAPTER EIGHTEEN

Coleman

Friday night, May, London

When Heyward's car pulled up in front of Scott's, Coleman was startled to see great torches on the front of the building, and a doorman wearing a tailcoat and a black bowler. When they stepped out of the car, lights flashed around them. Did the lights go on when they walked on the pavement that led to the doors?

She turned to Heyward. "I don't think we're in Kansas anymore."

He laughed. "I thought you New Yorkers were used to bright lights."

"Not like this," she said. "Somehow this is more exciting, more glamorous than a party in New York."

•••

Coleman looked around at the private room. "It's perfect," she said.

The Art Deco room, hung with bright-colored art, was spacious and inviting. A long table, arranged to seat fourteen people, was covered in a pale yellow tablecloth. Bowls of mixed yellow and white spring flowers, and low enough not to block the view of any guest, decorated the table. The amount of space around the table and chairs was exactly right—perfect for the group to circulate, but not too roomy.

She stood by Heyward to greet the guests as they came in. She was glad he had declared the evening to be black tie. All men looked their best in black tie, including Heyward. She had packed several evening dresses, and might buy more while she was in London, if many events called for them. Tonight she wore her new green satin dress, with a matching green satin cap, adorned with a few green feathers, inspired by an outfit she'd seen in the magazine *Majesty*. She also wore the emerald necklace and earrings Heyward had given her for her last birthday.

Dinah and Jonathan were the first to arrive. Dinah usually wore blue evening dresses to show off her blue eyes, so startling with her black hair, but tonight she wore a form-fitting white satin dress, glittering with opalescent sequins, and a spectacular diamond necklace and earrings. Coleman smiled to herself. No one would outshine Dinah tonight. Jonathan was looking at her as if he'd never seen her before. He doted on Dinah, and loved seeing her dressed up. She rarely dressed up as much as she had tonight.

After Dinah and Jonathan's arrival, the other guests poured in. Coleman met Rachel, magnificent in wine-colored velvet and the fabulous antique gold jewelry Dinah had told Coleman about, escorted by her lawyer, George Quincy. They chatted a few minutes and Rachel invited her to lunch to talk about their book publishing project. Coleman was pleased to accept. Rachel was likable, as well as intelligent and friendly.

The older couple who came in with Rachel and Quincy had to be Quincy's sister and her husband, Lord and Lady Darny. Lady Darny, in gray satin the color of her hair, and silver jewelry, looked elegant and dignified—perfectly dressed for her age. The Darnys and George Quincy seemed somewhat stiff, but very nice. Rachel's friend Lady Fitzgerald, a tiny, fragile-looking woman, wore lavender velvet, and a cluster of violets on her shoulder. She puzzled Coleman—she seemed skittish, and rather silly, but her pale blue eyes were intelligent, and she was observing everything and everyone around her. Jane Ross, in an exquisite pink dress, had piled her hair high on her head and topped it with a pink veil, and a sprig of pink feathers. All the women were wearing the fashionable long, slim look that the Duchess of Cambridge had appeared in more than once.

A stunningly handsome man arrived alone. Who could he be? He was well over six feet tall, and slender—the kind of slender that suggested he played tennis and other fast games. His tuxedo included the slim trousers that all the well-dressed men in London seemed to wear. His dark brown hair tended to flop onto his forehead. His face was craggy, and his profile and golden eyes reminded Coleman of an angry hawk. But when he smiled, as he did when Heyward introduced him, his ferocity melted away, and he looked warm and friendly.

"Coleman, this is Anthony, the Duke of Omnium's son. You should thank him for letting us use the family airstrip yesterday," Heyward said.

Coleman smiled up at him. "Are you like Lord Peter Death Bredon Wimsey, with a long string of names?"

He laughed. "Guilty, I fear. But please call me Tony."

"Do you solve crimes as a hobby, like Lord Peter?" she asked.

He laughed again. "Far from it. I always thought Lord Peter should get a real job."

"Then maybe you work for Scotland Yard, like Thomas Lynley, eighth Earl of Asherton?" she said.

"You know your English detective novels, don't you? No, I don't work for Scotland Yard, but I do have a crime-related job, and thanks to you, it's just become easier," he said.

"I can't imagine how. What do you do?" Coleman asked.

"I work for an agency that specializes in the recovery of stolen art and antiques," Tony said. "I understand I have a lot to thank you for. Thanks to you, a long list of stolen art and antiques has been recovered, and a number of criminals arrested. Your discovery at 23

Culross Place is terribly important. We arrested people who're going to turn on their bosses. We're also going to make some antique and art owners very happy when we return what they lost."

"I'm so glad," Coleman said.

"You'll be the toast of England. Let me be the first to drink to you." He lifted his champagne glass and said, "To Coleman, with congratulations and gratitude!"

Coleman smiled, and was about to thank him when the animated conversation in the room stopped, replaced by silence. She turned to see what had caused it.

She was astonished to see a fair-haired young woman in an enormous blue taffeta ball gown over petticoats and a hoop. She was holding up her skirt with both hands, revealing long white pantalets, authentically frilled at the bottom—very antebellum South, although no Southern belle would have held her skirt that high. She wore a tiara, earrings, and a necklace of what appeared to be real sapphires. Coleman raised her eyebrows and looked at Dinah, standing next to her.

"I'm pretty sure the sapphires are real, but borrowed from a jeweler. As for her dress, I can't imagine where she got it," Dinah murmured.

Jeb Middleton walked in behind the woman's hoop skirt. He wore traditional black tie, a gardenia on his lapel, and an atypically sheepish expression.

"Who's the woman?" Coleman asked Dinah.

"Princess Stephanie—I wrote you about her. An idiot, and a crybaby. She's the one who made etchings that were stolen, and the thief is trying to extort money from her. She told Rachel she borrowed jewelry for grand occasions. This is a grand occasion, but it's not a costume party," Dinah said.

"I remember all you told me about her. She and Jeb are an odd couple. I can't imagine why he let her dress up like that. This isn't a United Daughters of the Confederacy party," Coleman said.

"I've heard that Princess Stephanie is telling people she's staying at the Connaught with an American lover. Her lover must be Jeb," Dinah said.

"I liked him when I met him in New York, but if she's his kind of woman, he's definitely not my kind of man," Coleman said.

"Nor mine," Dinah said.

Heyward, normally imperturbable, seemed taken aback by the newest arrivals. "Jeb, welcome. Everyone, this is Jeb Middleton from Charleston, South Carolina. Jeb is in London assisting me with some of my projects.

"Jeb, I haven't met your companion. Please introduce her—but first, tell me, did you have her outfit sent over from Charleston? I know you're a loyal southerner, but making your companion wear a hoop skirt is a bit extreme," Heyward said.

Jeb laughed. "Not my idea. This is my friend Princess Stephanie. Stephanie, this is your host, Heyward Bain, and this is Coleman Greene, Heyward's sister and the guest of honor. I think you've met Dinah Greene Hathaway—"

"Oh, I know Dinah," Stephanie said. "We're old friends. I know Rachel, too. No, Heyward—you don't mind me calling you Heyward, do you? Jeb didn't give me this dress. I had it made for the occasion. I know you and Ms. Greene are from the South—I wanted to make y'all feel at home, so I'm wearing your native dress. Do you like it?"

Coleman could see Heyward struggling for a polite answer. She knew Heyward was annoyed with Jeb for bringing Stephanie to the party. Heyward must know all about her. He wouldn't like her calling him by his first name, either. She took him off the hook.

"Thank you for the thought," Coleman said. "I've never worn a hoop skirt, but Dinah has. She was a beauty queen in high school and wore a dress very like the one you have on."

"Yes, and it was a terrible nuisance. I couldn't get into a car, and when I sat at a table, I took up three spaces," Dinah said.

"Incidentally, you don't have to drawl when you talk to us. I think Jeb is the only one of us who has that Deep South accent."

"Really? I thought all southerners talked like that," Stephanie said.

"No, and hardly any of us wear hoop skirts," Coleman said.

"I suggest you remove the hoop," Dinah said. "It's not like you'll be naked. You have on all those petticoats and those pantalets."

"Oh, I can't do that," Princess Stephanie said. "I can't remove the hoop—the dress will droop. I'll look terrible!"

"I'm afraid Dinah is right," Heyward said. "You will have to dispense with the hoop. The table is set for fourteen people, and there's no way to rearrange it to accommodate the hoop."

"Oh, no," Princess Stephanie cried. "Please don't make me remove the hoop."

"Speaking for the southerners you're honoring, there's no choice. We can't sit down to dinner until you get rid of the hoop," Coleman said.

"Maybe I should just leave," Princess Stephanie said. Tears began to stream down her cheeks.

"There goes the crybaby act," Dinah said into Coleman's ear. "She can weep for hours."

Jeb stepped in. "Don't be silly. The restrooms are just down the hall. Run down there and get rid of the hoop so we can have dinner. The food here is delicious."

He was echoed by a murmur of agreement from the group, and everyone began to move toward the table. Coleman was pleased to be seated by Tony, but not so happy to see Charles Ross, who had accompanied Lady Jane—and who looked a lot like her—on her other side. Coleman was sure she'd seen him in the menacing crowd at the Ross office. Would he be as surly and rude as his relatives had been? Why had Heyward seated him next to her?

Before she had a chance to speak to either Charles Ross or Tony, Stephanie returned, and all eyes focused on her.

She had scooped up the blue dress and all the petticoats, and was holding them over her arm. She marched in, with the pantalets in full view. She was in no way exposed, since the pantalets were made of thick cotton, but she had set out to make people look at her. The effect was vulgar and crude. "I want to make sure I don't crowd any of you," she said crossly.

Coleman and Dinah exchanged glances of disapproval. Stephanie was a disagreeable little thing. She needed lessons on manners.

Heyward had placed Stephanie between Jeb and George Quincy. Jeb pulled out her chair and seated her. She looked around, spotted Tony, and batted her eyelashes. "Are you southern, too?" she asked.

Coleman saw him stiffen. She could tell he didn't want to meet Stephanie or introduce himself to her. "No, Tony is an old friend from the North," she said, her fingers crossed. "Jeb and Heyward are the only southern men here tonight. But you should get to know George Quincy, who's sitting beside you. He's a well-known lawyer who lives here in London. You never know when you might need a good lawyer," Coleman said.

She heard Dinah swallow laughter and Tony sigh with relief. Charles Ross looked at her suspiciously.

Coleman smiled at him and at Stephanie, and turned to the waiter, who was asking if she wanted oysters, smoked salmon, or razor clams as a first course. She chose razor clams because she'd never tasted them, and didn't even know what they looked like. When they came, she was thrilled with her choice. They were grilled with garlic and a dab of spicy sausage and served in their own six-inch-long shells. Delicious!

The main course was Heyward's favorite: grilled Dover sole, with new potatoes, tiny green beans, and creamed spinach. Coleman had heard that seafood in England was the best in the world, and after she'd tasted the sole, she believed it. She looked up and down the table. Everyone seemed to be enjoying their food and their companions except for Charles Ross and Stephanie. Both were silent and sulking.

She turned to Tony and said, "Are you enjoying the evening?"

"Only when you talk to me," he said. "Tell me all the things you want to do while you're in England."

"I will, if you promise not to laugh."

"I promise," he said.

"First, ride the London Eye. I want to see bluebells in bloom— they're in bloom now, aren't they? I really want to see them. I have friends in New York who come to England in February to see snowdrops—I'd like to do that someday. I want to see and touch a hedgehog."

"Okay. What else?"

"We don't have wild hedgehogs in the USA," Coleman said. "I only know them in books. I want to see a badger, I guess at night—isn't that the only time you can see them?"

"Yes, they're night creatures," Tony said.

"Again, I only know them in books. Most of all, I want to see and hear a nightingale."

"You are not like any woman I've ever met," Tony said.

"How so? What makes me so different?" Coleman said.

"Most women want to meet members of the Royal Family, or they ask me to take them to certain clubs, or to the most expensive places in London," he said.

"Oh, well, maybe I'll be interested in doing those things on another trip. My love for England grew out of books. I want to see animals and flowers and other things I've read about—because I already love them," Coleman said.

"I figured that out. I'm pretty sure I can handle the badger and the bluebells and the hedgehog. The nightingale might be tough."

Coleman laughed. "I'm confident you can do it," she said.

"Are you sure you don't want me to take you to the Fat Duck? Three hours, a fixed menu, and £300? It's quite an experience."

"Fat Duck?" Coleman asked.

"Yes," said Tony. "Most people want to go because the food is good, but it may also be the most expensive restaurant in England."

"No, I don't want to go there," Coleman said firmly.

He laughed. "I didn't think so," he said.

•••

When the party was breaking up, and she was standing by the door saying goodnight to the guests, Tony approached her again.

"Would you like to go to Claridge's for a nightcap?" he asked.

Coleman smiled. "Thank you, but I'm exhausted. May I have a rain check?"

"That must be an American expression. If it means you'll go out with me another night, what about tomorrow?"

She hesitated. "What I'd like more than anything tomorrow night is to ride the London Eye. Can we do that?"

"Of course we can, but we still have to eat. Where would you like to go, or put another way, what would you like to eat?"

"I'd like something very English," Coleman said. "I know, let's have a picnic with tea sandwiches. I think of tea sandwiches as very English. Smoked salmon, cucumber, egg salad, watercress— and lemonade or hot chocolate?"

"That's fine. I'll pick you up at Heyward's at seven. Dress warmly."

•••

In the car on the way home, Heyward said, "I overheard you turn down a nightcap with Tony. Are you too tired to have a cup of hot chocolate in the library with me before bed?"

"No, I'd love it," Coleman said. "I'll run upstairs and take off this dress first."

She removed her formal clothes and reappeared a few minutes later in the white robe and slippers she'd found in her room.

In front of the fire in the library, with a cup of hot chocolate in her hand and Dolly on her lap, Coleman thanked Heyward for the party.

"I had the best time," she said. "It was a fabulous party. Interesting people, marvelous food."

"Dinah looked lovely tonight, and seemed to be in the best of spirits. I assume that's your doing?" Heyward said.

Coleman smiled. "Yes, I've helped a little. But before I leave London, I'd like to see Dinah truly happy. Being here should be a great experience for her, and the criminals in the house ruined all of her time here so far. A good cook and the new assignment with *First Home* will help. She says the people at the Art Museum of Great Britain are unfriendly. I can't imagine why, but I'd like to do something about it. Do you have any ideas?" Coleman said.

"Mrs. Carter can easily find her a good English cook. I'll talk to her about it tomorrow. Your idea for Dinah's column is great. She'll enjoy it, and meet a lot of people doing it. I also think it will be very successful," Heyward said. "I'll take care of the museum. I've been asked to join their board. I think they'll be nice to her when they learn we are connected."

"That's great," Coleman said. "Thanks."

"Now let's talk about the party. I want to know what you think of all the guests," he said.

"Rachel is very nice—I feel as if I've always known her. We'll get along fine on the art publishing project. Her lawyer is as Dinah described—slow, but sound. Not a lot of fun. His relatives are very like him. Decent, reliable people, not very interesting.

"Lady Fitzgerald puzzled me. She comes across like a flibbertigibbet, but her eyes are sharp. I think she's very smart underneath all that fluttering."

"You seemed to get along very well with Tony," Heyward said.

"Yes, I like him a lot. He's taking me out tomorrow night to ride the London Eye. I can hardly wait."

Heyward smiled. "I bet that was your idea."

"Yes, it's on my list of must-dos while I'm here," she said.

"I noticed you didn't speak to Jeb?"

Coleman smiled. "Put another way, he didn't speak to me. He had his hands full with Princess Stephanie, but I thought he'd at least have the courtesy to say 'Welcome to London' or something."

"Jeb has a lot on his mind," Heyward said. "What did you think of Lady Jane?"

"She's another puzzle. I liked her, but I'm uneasy about her. I enjoyed hearing about her garden, and I plan to visit it. Someday I'd like to have a garden of my own. We have a common interest: She designs and makes her own clothes, too. She asked about my dress, and I told her it was inspired by a picture I saw in *Majesty*—do you know the magazine? About the Royal Family? I get it for the pictures of the clothes, and so does she! She's going to e-mail me a list of shops I should visit while I'm in London. She's lovely, but she's got some awful relatives! It's hard to trust her, having met them. Her companion was one of them. I saw him in the Ross office yesterday. He barely spoke to me tonight. He was jumpy and uncomfortable. I haven't had a chance to tell you about our meeting with the Ross men—"

"I know all about it," Heyward said.

"Who told you?" Coleman asked.

"The Ross clan has been under suspicion for a long time, for all sorts of crimes. We don't know whether Lady Jane is involved," Heyward said.

"Who is 'we'? You seem to know a great deal about crime in England," Coleman said.

"I'm spending most of my time here these days, and I have major investments here. I've met some very intelligent and interesting people. The UK is a wonderful country, but criminals have invaded it. I encountered a criminal organization here having to do with art fraud, with roots in New York, and I helped expose it. I've continued to help where I can. I can't tell you any more than that, but that's how I got to know Tony."

"Do *you* think Lady Jane is a criminal?" Coleman asked.

"I really don't know. Tell me more about the man she brought with her—a cousin?"

"He barely spoke to me—I don't have much to report. As I said, he was in that office yesterday. That crowd was threatening. I'm sure they're guilty of something."

"What about Stephanie?" Heyward said.

"She's a pathetic little fool," Coleman said.

"Yes, I fear you're right. It's hard to know what to do about the Stephanies of the world. Well, she's a good place to end our evening. Are you ready to get some sleep?"

"Oh, yes," Coleman said. "Thanks again for a wonderful party. Goodnight."

•••

Coleman went to bed as soon as she was in her room, but she couldn't sleep. She thought about the evening: what people had said, her impressions of everyone, mostly about Jeb and his new companion.

She was glad her back had been to the door when Jeb arrived. Her face might have revealed her feelings. She had thought they might meet in London, and pick up where they'd left off in New York. After she saw him with Stephanie, though, she'd dismissed that idea. In any case, he hadn't shown the slightest interest in her, even though she was the guest of honor, and good manners demanded that he at least exchange a few words with her. That had stung, but her feelings had been soothed by Tony's attentions.

When Jeb arrived, she was talking to Tony, and had, for the moment, forgotten Jeb was coming to the party. That was a sign she was over Jeb. The other good news: Tony was attractive and seemed interested in her.

"Out with the old and in with the new," she told Dolly. But Dolly was making little snoring noises, and didn't open her eyes. Coleman closed her own eyes, and drifted off to sleep a few minutes later.

CHAPTER NINETEEN

Dinah

Friday night, after the party, London

The house had been stripped of most of its furniture, but the master bedroom was nearly intact. The stuffed chairs, the big bed, and the bedside tables were reproductions, owned by Lady Jane, so Dinah and Jonathan had a place to sleep, and a place to sit and discuss the party.

Dinah removed the glittery white dress and matching shoes, and huddled by the fire in her cashmere robe and warm slippers.

"It's not that cold in here anymore, since no one is turning back the thermostat, but I'm used to my robe," she said.

Jonathan, still in his tuxedo, had paused downstairs to pour himself a glass of brandy, and Dinah a glass of sherry.

He handed her the drink, and said, "This will help you get warm." He took a deep breath, and let it out. "That was a great party, but it's nice to be alone with you," he said.

"I loved the party, except for Princess Stephanie—she was such a spectacle in that hoop skirt. I'm sure Heyward would never have invited her. Jeb is crazy to be involved with her."

"I doubt it's serious," Jonathan said.

"Oh, I know, but he shouldn't have brought her to Coleman's party. Coleman really liked him when they went out in New York."

"No! How could she? He strikes me as a lounge lizard, good with women like Stephanie, but not good for much else," Jonathan said.

"I think you're wrong. Jeb is good-looking and smart and he works for Coleman's brother, who's a genius, who trusts him. I didn't have anything against him until I learned he was living with Stephanie. Then I lost all respect for him. Coleman's well off without him. Tony may be the perfect man for Coleman."

"Yes, Tony is impressive. But let's talk about you. I've never seen you more beautiful than you were tonight. The dress and the diamonds glittered, but you were glittering, too. I haven't seen you this happy in a long time," he said.

"Yes, Coleman slayed the dragons, rid my house of vermin, and gave me a wonderful way to enjoy my spare time in London, while meeting new and interesting people and learning more about food. If I can do a good job at the museum, and make friends there, too—well, I'll be happy as a lark. But even if the museum job isn't fun, I'll be fine."

"What are you doing about replacing the servants for the house?" he asked.

"We have James, Hamilton, and Franklin, and Heyward's housekeeper is finding a cook for us. That ought to be enough, but if it isn't, I'll hire someone else. Maybe I'll want a secretary, or an assistant for my writing. Anyway, don't worry about it. I'll take care of it."

"You sound very confident," he said.

"I feel confident. I know my life in London is going to be a lot better. I'm even looking forward to dealing with the furniture issues, which are huge. A week ago I would have said I couldn't do it. Right now, however, I'm looking forward to bed. I'm exhausted."

Jonathan laughed, got up, and went into his dressing room. Dinah hung her robe on its hanger, and slipped into bed. She was asleep when Jonathan turned off the lights and climbed into bed beside her.

•••

Dinah woke an hour later, and couldn't go back to sleep. She was still high on the day and night she'd just experienced. Just as Dinah knew she would, Coleman had rid the house of the horrible women who had destroyed her happiness ever since she came to London.

Everything had changed. She had three dependable allies in James, Franklin, and Hamilton. They had arranged for a cleaning service to come in and clean the rooms the women had occupied, and the rooms where the antiques and paintings had been stored. She would soon have a good English cook. It would be fun to have a cook to help with her column for *First Home*. She shivered with excitement at the thought of her column.

Jonathan, contrite when he heard from Coleman just how bad the witches were, had apologized to Dinah. He told her that she should buy furniture for the house, with the thought that they would probably want antiques in New York eventually. If not, they could sell them. Coleman would help her shop, and Rachel said she'd help, too, as would Lady Darny. Meanwhile, they still had a few pieces in the house—all of the beds belonged to Lady Jane, as did some of the dining room furniture, and a few other large, heavy pieces.

Maybe they could rent some items until she found what she wanted to buy. Coleman had ordered books about antiques for her, some of which Coleman had read. If Coleman could learn about antiques, she could, too.

Dinah felt like a new person: invigorated, charged up. As she'd told Jonathan, she was excited about furnishing 23 Culross, when once she would have thought it was an insurmountable burden.

She would start her job at the museum on Monday, and she rather dreaded it—the people she'd met had been so unfriendly when she'd dropped in to introduce herself. Well, if they were cold, so what? She had an interesting and challenging task, and was eager to get on with it. She'd absorb herself in her work at the museum, and make sure she did it well. That's what mattered.

She'd had a wonderful time at Heyward's party. She knew she had looked her best, and she loved seeing all the other beautiful dresses. She enjoyed talking to Jane Ross about flowers and clothes. Jane had again apologized for the behavior of her relatives. She was horrified to hear about the cook and housekeeper at 23 Culross, and interested to hear that Hamilton and Franklin were back at the house. She said she had been sorry when they left. She seemed to think they had resigned. Dinah knew Mr. Ross had fired them.

Coleman seemed to have made a new conquest. That was good. Someone to show her London, see that she had a good time. Coleman deserved to have a good time, and to be happy. Dinah wanted the best for Coleman. She prayed for Coleman's good health and well-being, and drifted back to sleep.

CHAPTER TWENTY

Dinah

Saturday morning, May, London

Dinah was awakened by Hamilton standing by the bed, offering her a tray identical to Jonathan's. She didn't have to leap out of bed to serve Jonathan's coffee and juice, and, joy of joys, Hamilton had brought her the newspapers, including *Secrets*. For the first time she understood what it was like to have someone working for her who anticipated what she wanted. She thanked him, and he handed her a clipping from a paper they didn't normally see. It was a picture of Coleman outside Scott's and a nice paragraph about her discovery of the stolen art and antiques at 23 Culross. Good for Coleman.

She looked at the bedside clock. Hamilton must have turned off her alarm, but Jonathan's had rung, and he already had his tray. Perfect. They were awake at the same time, and could lie in bed sipping juice and coffee and enjoying the papers, like they used to in New York. True luxury. She pushed aside the *International New York Times* and picked up *Secrets*. Uh oh, Stephanie's latest print was on the front page and it was much more revealing than the last one: a female nude, standing, facing the viewer. Her head was turned away, obscuring her face, and anatomical details had been deliberately blurred, but an ogling man, obviously spying on the woman, had been introduced. It was pornographic, or close to it. Rachel would be upset. She'd have to call her later.

It was time to get up to arrange Jonathan's breakfast, and remove the smelly buffet to the kitchen. Then she remembered: The wicked witches had been banished, and she had no downstairs duties. She could shower and join Jonathan in the dining room knowing that his breakfast and her own would be perfect. Hamilton would see to it.

After her shower, she put on jeans and a blue turtleneck. She'd work at home today, selecting the room that would be her office, making sure there were bookshelves in it for the cookbooks she would acquire, and for the reference books she'd use for her job at the museum. She'd order office furniture and a fax machine, get Internet installed, set up a computer, and get all the office supplies she needed.

She'd discuss menus with Hamilton. He would handle the shopping and simple cooking, augmented with take-out, until the new cook arrived.

She was as happy as a bee—maybe a queen bee?—having rid herself of useless drones, and ready to put the hive in order.

She skipped down the stairs, and was thrilled to see a brightly colored wrapped package at her place at the table. She tore off the wrapping: a much coveted copy of *Gordon Ramsay's Great British Pub Food*. What a marvelous gift! The card read, "Good luck with your food column. James, Hamilton, and Franklin." She was turning the first pages when Hamilton brought the telephone to the table.

"It's Mrs. Carter at Mr. Bain's."

Mrs. Carter, sounding distressed, said, "Mrs. Hathaway, Mr. Bain wants you to come to his house right away. Miss Coleman needs you. Dolly vanished. She may have been stolen."

Dinah gasped. Oh, poor Coleman.

"Please tell Coleman I'll be there as soon as I can."

Hamilton said, "James is waiting for you. I put your dark blue coat in the car."

Jonathan was descending the stairs as she ran for the door. "Hamilton will explain," she called, and ran out the door.

CHAPTER TWENTY-ONE

Coleman

Saturday morning, May, London

When Coleman awoke, she felt wonderful. She pulled back the curtains to see what kind of day it was. Oh, joy! The sun was shining. It was a perfect day. She still felt the glow of the party, and the excitement of meeting Tony. She was looking forward to seeing him tonight.

She pulled on her green tracksuit and sneakers. She'd take Dolly for a long, brisk walk before breakfast. Dolly had explored Heyward's tiny garden, but she needed more exercise, and so did Coleman. Coleman attached Dolly's pink leash to the matching pink collar, while the little dog danced and pranced with excitement, telling Coleman she was eager to go. Coleman was about to head downstairs, when someone slipped a newspaper clipping under the door. Good grief, there was her picture outside Scott's! That's why the lights had been flashing! A photographer had been taking pictures of her. The picture was flattering, and a nice paragraph covered her discovery at 23 Culross. That's why Tony said she'd be the toast of London. He must have known about the article.

She was already down the steps and on the sidewalk when she realized she didn't have the house keys Heyward had given her. She told Dolly to wait, she'd be right back. To save time, she decided to take the little elevator up to her suite instead of walking. The elevator worked like a charm, and she quickly found the keys. But when she was in the elevator ready to go back down, the doors closed, and she couldn't open them. The elevator wouldn't budge. She rang the emergency bell. She could hear people tinkering with the controls, and talking to each other, but nearly half an hour passed before the elevator delivered her to the main floor. When she reached the steps where Dolly had been waiting, she was horrified to see that the little dog was not where Coleman had left her. She called her, but Dolly didn't come. Could one of the servants have taken her somewhere? Was she in the house? Coleman went inside and knocked on the library door.

"Come in," Heyward called.

She entered the room, and asked him to check with everyone in the house. Had anyone seen Dolly?

Heyward, looking as worried as she felt, used the intercom to deal with his inquiries about Dolly. No one in the house had seen the little dog. She wasn't in the house.

Coleman was frightened, and angry.

"You must call the police! Someone must have stolen her," she said.

"I'll call them, but they won't come. The police will refuse to investigate a missing dog, unless we can prove there's been a crime. They'll say she ran away—"

"Dolly would not run away," Coleman said, furious.

"I know she wouldn't, but the police don't. I'm on the phone with my office. We'll put everybody we have on this—we'll put posters everywhere, starting in this neighborhood. Give me all Dolly's information—height, weight, microchip, pictures. We'll offer a thousand pounds' reward to anyone who'll see that we get her back today. We'll ask everyone on the square if they've seen her."

"If you think Dolly's in the neighborhood, maybe I should go look for her," she said. "I can't stand here doing nothing while someone hurts her."

"Coleman, you must stay calm. I need you to make this search work. Listen to me: It's only eight thirty in the morning. She's been gone half an hour at the most. Even if someone did take her, we have no reason to believe they knew she belonged to you, or that you were a target."

"But they might have," said Coleman. "The house must have been watched. She was alone so briefly, they must have been waiting for a chance to get her. It could have been the ring connected with the house on Culross, or maybe someone who saw the article in the paper about me this morning."

"Or it could have been someone who thought Dolly belonged to me," said Heyward.

Coleman closed her mouth abruptly at the thought, which worried her even more. Of course Heyward might have enemies of his own. He was far better known in London than she was, despite the photo in this morning's paper.

"Dolly is almost certainly near this house," Heyward said. "Whoever has her, for whatever reason, they won't hurt her. If they've kidnapped her, they'll want money. They'll probably call here asking for a ransom." He turned toward Mrs. Carter, who was standing in the doorway. "Please telephone Dinah Hathaway. Tell her I want her here as soon as possible—Coleman needs her. Make sure that everyone here knows what we're doing, and that no one has seen anything suspicious."

Coleman stood like a statue, still and cold, her face as white as marble. "This is all my fault. I knew this kind of thing happened in London. I read about a dog being left alone for only thirty minutes, and stolen. I shouldn't have left Dolly alone," Coleman said. "You said before I came that she could never be dognapped because she was always with me. But I left her alone. She's too small and too sweet to fight. She's never bitten anyone. She's friendly to everyone; she's defenseless. She'll be so scared. I can't think what to do."

Coleman and Heyward were standing outside on the house's front steps when Dinah arrived. "How can I help?" she said.

Coleman shook her head. "I don't know. I'll never forgive myself. I shouldn't have brought Dolly to London. I've never known anyone in New York who's had a dog stolen," she said.

Coleman looked and sounded terrible, and Dinah didn't know what to say or do to help her. If whoever took the dog wanted money in exchange for her, it would not be a problem. Coleman had money, and Heyward was a billionaire. But suppose it wasn't about money? Suppose the 23 Culross witches or their masters had stolen Dolly to get back at Coleman for destroying their racket? Would they kill the little dog? God forbid. She prayed for Dolly and Coleman.

A red Ferrari pulled into the driveway. Coleman glanced at it but continued her monologue, blaming herself, lamenting that she had left Dolly alone, swearing that if she got the little dog back, she'd never leave her alone again.

Tony got out of the car and ran up the steps. He handed Coleman a Starbucks cup and a blueberry muffin. She didn't seem to register it, or him, but she sipped the coffee, and nibbled the muffin.

"How did you hear?" Dinah asked.

"It's on the radio," he said.

Heyward looked at him. "Police radio?"

Tony nodded.

Mrs. Carter returned with a tea cart loaded with a coffee pot, a teapot, a pitcher of orange juice, and a basket of pastries. She spoke to Heyward. "I don't think Miss Coleman wants to come inside."

"Maybe not, but she doesn't look warm enough. Would you bring her a coat?" Heyward asked.

"Yes, right away. All the telephones are ringing. It's people who want to help, or the press."

"Yes, I hear the phones. Thank the callers, tell them we'll announce any news, but for now we're trying to keep the lines clear in case whoever has the dog is trying to reach us."

Mrs. Carter hurried upstairs, returned with Coleman's fur coat, and draped it over her shoulders. Coleman slipped her arms into the sleeves, and pulled the coat closed.

One of the maids came to the door carrying a telephone. "Mr. Bain, there's a man on the phone who says he has your dog. He wants to speak to you."

Heyward took the phone and pressed the button to put it on speaker. A gravelly voice with a heavy Scottish accent spoke. "You want your dog? How much will you pay?" Heyward exchanged glances with Tony.

"A Ross," Tony whispered. "Keep him on the line. I'll make some calls, see if the police can locate him." He went inside. Coleman could hear him talking on the phone.

Coleman stared at Heyward. Were they saying it was that nasty old Ross man who'd taken Dolly? What a fiend. She'd like to go after him, but it was impossible. If she were a man, she'd beat him up. Someone should.

Heyward moved into the house and joined Tony. Coleman could hear the two of them speaking, in separate conversations. She started to follow them inside so she could hear better, but when she tried to move, her coat caught on something, maybe one of the evergreens in the big pots on the porch? She pulled hard, but she couldn't get it loose. She reached down to untangle it, and a wet tongue licked her hand.

"Dolly!" she said, "Oh, I'm so glad to see you. How'd you get here? Look, Dinah, Dolly chewed through her leash. Look at her leash—only a short bit left. That's how she got away. Smart Dolly."

Coleman picked up the little dog and cuddled her, but Dolly wriggled and was impatient to get back down.

"What is it? Are you hungry?" Back on the ground, Dolly grabbed the hem of Coleman's coat in her mouth again and pulled it—and Coleman—toward the street.

"She wants to go somewhere," Coleman said.

Heyward, who'd hung up on the foul-mouthed Scot when he heard Coleman cry "Dolly," was the first to understand. "She wants to take you to the people who abducted her."

"Of course. I should have known," Coleman said. "What should we do?"

"She must have been held very nearby, probably in one of the houses in the square," Heyward said.

"There are a lot of police in the area," Tony said. "It will be easy to have all the nearby houses watched while she takes us to the right one. But Coleman, you can't walk alone with her. James and William should walk with you and Dolly. They're both big men, and can protect you if necessary. We'll follow you in my car. I want to stay in touch with the police—I can do that best from the car."

"I'm going with Coleman and Dolly," Dinah said.

"Okay, let's go," Coleman said.

When Coleman picked up what was left of Dolly's leash, the little dog looked at her approvingly, and dropped the coat. She trotted out to the street, and turned left on the sidewalk. She led them to a house only four houses away. She sat down in front of it, stared at it, and then up at Coleman. Her attitude was clearly "I've done my part. Now it's up to you."

Within minutes the house was surrounded by police. One of them knocked on the front door, which was answered by the old Ross man who had screamed at Coleman and Dinah the day before. An argument ensued, while Coleman, Dinah, James, and William watched. Heyward and Tony got out of the car and joined them for a better view.

One of the officers came out to speak to them. "This man's house is full of dogs and drugs, and red-headed men who all look alike," he said.

"Are the dogs all right?" Coleman asked anxiously.

"They're not happy. They're in small cages, and some are big dogs. They miss their families. Some of them have ID tags. We'll try to get all of them back to their owners as fast as possible." He leaned over to pat Dolly, and Coleman saw a light flash—a photographer? "You've made some dogs and their families mighty happy, Miss Dolly. You ought to get a medal." Coleman saw more lights flashing. The London reporters had arrived.

"Is it a major drug discovery?" Heyward asked.

"Yes, and it's all heroin. Quite a haul."

"Thanks for the update. You can find us at my house, if you need us for anything. Here's my card," Heyward said.

"Let's go home," Coleman said. It seemed as if weeks had gone by since she got up this morning. She wanted to sit down and cuddle Dolly.

Heyward looked at her and smiled. "Ride with Tony," he said. "I'll walk. When you get to the house, go inside and sit down in the dining room. Mrs. Carter and the kitchen have prepared a feast. I'm hungry, and I suspect you are, too, Coleman."

"Starved," she said. She turned to Tony. "That bite of blueberry muffin and the coffee you bought me probably kept me from fainting. Thank you! I'm ready for a huge meal now."

The dining room table was loaded with food: smoked salmon, prosciutto, sausages, and, Coleman saw . . . American bacon?

Scrambled eggs, boiled eggs, and deviled eggs. Several kinds of bread. Jams, jellies, peanut butter, marmalade. Pastries. A big bowl of fruit—orange pieces, melon balls. Sautéed mushrooms, grilled tomatoes. Yogurt, cream, milk of several kinds. Coffee, tea. Halved grapefruit, baked apples. And on the nearby buffet, a waffle iron and an electric griddle for pancakes stood ready.

Dinah went into the corridor to telephone Jonathan, asking him to come join the celebration. When she returned, she was big-eyed at the sight of the table. "Heyward, where did you get that bacon? I've been craving crisp bacon."

"I have it sent from New York," he said. "Help yourself."

Dinah whipped out her iPhone again and took pictures of Coleman, with Dolly, who was sitting between Heyward and Tony, in front of the mountains of food.

Mrs. Carter came in. "Excuse me, Mr. Bain. There are reporters on the porch who want to talk to Miss Coleman and get a picture of her and Dolly."

"Oh, heavens," Coleman said. "Must I change clothes?"

Heyward looked at her. "No, don't. That kelly green tracksuit is becoming, and they'll want Dolly with the broken leash and you in the clothes you were wearing during the recent events. We'll invite some of them in shortly to share our feast, and take pictures, and ask questions, but first, while we're just family, I want to ask for your help."

The group at the table stopped eating and looked at him. "What is it?" Coleman asked.

"You've all met Rachel Ransome, and you know she's a good person who's had a lot of bad things happen to her. She's in trouble again, and I'd like your help in getting her out of it."

Heyward went on to explain Rachel's association with Lady Fitzgerald and Princess Stephanie, the murders, and the police suspicion of her.

"The police seem to think the murderer is Stephanie, Lady Fitzgerald, or Rachel, or maybe Jane Ross," said Heyward. "They have no proof that it's any of them, but they're not giving up. I've put together a package of all the background for you, Coleman, and you, Dinah. Put your minds to these murders. The police have narrowed their investigation in a way that may be keeping them from seeing all the evidence. If you can see something they haven't, it may help remove the cloud that's hanging over Rachel. You can tell Jonathan about it, Dinah, but no one else. Tony, if you'd help, too, I'd be grateful. Will all of you help?" he said, looking at them.

"Of course," Coleman said.

"Oh, yes," Dinah said. "I know what it's like to be suspected of murder."

"Yes, sir," Tony said.

"Great. The sooner we can clear Rachel, the better for her. Now, how many people are waiting outside? Would you take a look, Tony?"

Tony left for a few minutes and came back. "Only five," he said. "I know them all by sight, two of them well. They're okay. Shall I invite them in?"

A few minutes later three men and two women joined them, and the noise in the room rose. They questioned Coleman, petted Dolly, photographed everyone, and ate hugely.

Jonathan arrived and Dinah filled him in. Tony managed to have a private word with Coleman. "Are we still on for tonight?" he asked.

"Oh, yes," she said. "I can hardly wait. A good evening is what I need to get over how I felt when Dolly was gone."

"I'll see you at seven," he said.

The room grew hot and noisy, and he slipped away, followed by Dinah and Jonathan, and the reporters. Only Coleman, with Dolly on her lap, and Heyward were left.

"I can't believe all that food is gone," Coleman said.

Heyward smiled. "The reporters were hungry," he said.

"That was nice of you, inviting the reporters in," Coleman said.

"It's always good to be friendly with the press whenever possible. They can be very helpful," he said. "What are you going to do today?"

"Have a quiet day," she said. "I want to go see Jane Ross's garden, if I can have the car. When I come back I want to go over these papers on poor Rachel's problems. Write in my diary. Enjoy my beautiful office."

"The car is yours. If you want or need anything else, let me know."

"Before we part, you said the police wouldn't come, because they didn't investigate missing dogs unless you could prove a crime has been committed, but they were here. What happened?"

"Your friend Tony happened."

"Wow! He has that kind of influence?"

"Oh, yes, and far more," Heyward said. "He's the next Duke of Omnium—that makes him a big deal. In addition, he's served the Kingdom in many ways. He's a truly remarkable man."

"I can see that," Coleman said.

•••

Coleman felt drained after the emotional sweeps of the morning: Dolly's disappearance and Dolly's return. She had no desire to do anything rigorous, but she wanted a little fresh air. This was a good time to visit Jane Ross's garden. Jane had invited her to come, and the car was available.

Jane looked different in her work clothes, and she seemed troubled by Coleman's arrival.

"Am I here at a bad time?" Coleman asked.

"No, it's fine," she said, not very convincingly. She must be concerned about her relatives' arrests, but did those arrests affect her? She couldn't believe Jane was involved in drug trafficking or dog stealing.

"I want to see your garden, of course, but I also want to buy some flowers for Heyward's library, which I think you know is also his office. What would he like?"

"He likes blue hyacinths for that room. Come in and I'll get you some," Jane said.

Jane did not offer her a place to sit, nor did she suggest a tour of the house or the garden. Jane was a different person today—not exactly hostile, but definitely unfriendly. So be it. Coleman paid for the hyacinths, thanked Jane, and said, "Perhaps another time?"

"Oh, yes, of course," Jane said. She was quick to close the door behind Coleman.

Coleman was puzzled, but she put aside Jane's attitude, while she turned to the material Heyward had given her about Rachel.

An hour later, Coleman had been through all the material Heyward had given her. She was deeply puzzled. She could find no reason why Rachel should be suspected of anything, let alone murder. She had put the material in table form, but there was little to list:

- **Background:** No known criminal activity or offenses.
- **Motive for murder:** None that I can see. Rachel claims she never met the victims. No reason to doubt her.
- **Suspicious behavior:** She went to the Little Palace to view the bodies and crime scenes. Strange, and perhaps unwise, but not criminal.
- **Why do they suspect her?** It can't be about her playing detective.
- **Why do they suspect Princess Stephanie?** The first murdered man left her money. What about the second one?
- **Alibis:** Rachel has a very good alibi for the first murder. What about the second one?

•••

She called Heyward. "Do you have any new information about the second murder?"

"Yes. The man—Roberto—was dying of an overdose of heroin, just like the first one, when he was 'killed' with the razor. He didn't leave a will, or if he did, no one has found it. They don't have a time of death yet—sometime Thursday night or early Friday morning. I talked to Rachel several times on Thursday, but I might have been her only contact that day, except for her employees."

"The police's suspicion of her is ridiculous. Why do you think they're after her?"

"I think most of it has to do with her friendship with Lady Fitzgerald and her association with Princess Stephanie."

"Absurd," Coleman said. "How are we going to clear her?"

"I don't know," Heyward said. "I hoped you'd have some ideas."

"I'll keep thinking," Coleman said.

"On another topic, I went to Lady Jane's to see the place and to get some flowers—your flowers are in the library—and she seemed rather stressed—almost unfriendly."

"Yes, her villainous relatives are trying to make her sell 23 Culross and the nursery—they're desperate for money, and they say since she's the head of their clan, she should give them hers. She's very worried. We've had someone watching her trying to figure out whether she's been a part of her relatives' criminal activities. She's clean—but they'll destroy her if she lets them. We're trying to figure out how to help her."

"Okay, good—I'm glad she's not like her cousins, and I'm glad you're trying to help her."

CHAPTER TWENTY-TWO

Dinah and Jonathan

Saturday morning, May, London

On the way home from Heyward's, Jonathan said, "You look pale and tired, too—almost as bad as Coleman."

"I know. I felt so bad for her. Now I feel bad for Rachel. We have to help her."

"I agree. We'll do all we can."

"As soon as we get home, I'm going through the papers Heyward gave us. I'm sure Rachel's innocent. I wonder why they think she's guilty."

•••

Dinah settled in the bedroom in one of the big soft chairs, with a kitchen tray on her lap substituting for a table, with the papers Heyward had given her, and studied them carefully. By the time she finished, she was furious. The police had nothing. Why did they think Rachel had anything to do with those two men?

The most interesting information in the folder was Rachel's summary about the murder scenes resembling the two books, and her belief that the structured scenes were designed to implicate her or Lady Fitzpatrick.

Dinah picked up the latest of Stephanie's prints, planning to put it away. She looked at it again, staring at the picture. A female nude, standing, facing the viewer; her head turned, obscuring her face. Deliberately blurred anatomical details, saving it from total pornography. But Stephanie had stepped up the heat with the introduction of an ogling male, obviously spying on the woman. The image was familiar. But how could that be?

Suddenly it came to her: She'd first seen the image when she was a student. Stephanie had copied a lithograph by the American artist Arnold Rönnebeck, made about 1930. Rönnebeck had died in 1947, and had never been famous. Stephanie must have thought she could safely copy it, but a friend of Dinah's had used it as an illustration in a book. It was Stephanie's bad luck that Dinah knew the image so well. She couldn't wait to call Rachel—but first, Coleman.

"Have you been through the Rachel papers?" she asked.

"I have," Coleman said. "The police have nothing. I can't imagine what they're doing. Her notes on the murder scenes are interesting. I bet the police haven't even looked at them. I'm trying to figure out what we should do. I'm going to call Heyward to discuss it," Coleman said.

"Good! Meanwhile, I have a bomb to drop. The latest etching in *Secrets* is a copy of a lithograph by an obscure American artist, Arnold Rönnebeck. Our friend Susan Davis used it as an illustration—you've seen it in her book. I'll call Bethany and have her fax the page from Susan's book to Jonathan.

"I have the newspaper in front of me—I do recognize it," Coleman said. "What are you going to do?"

"Call Rachel. Go to see her with the evidence. She'll be livid, and will want to confront Stephanie. I want to be there. Want to come with me?"

"Absolutely! I wouldn't miss it," Coleman said. "Will you pick me up?"

"Yes. I'll call Rachel—she'll drop everything for this. Pick you up in half an hour."

CHAPTER TWENTY-THREE

Rachel

Saturday morning, May, London

Rachel had enjoyed Heyward's party, which was marred only by Stephanie's appalling behavior. Stephanie weighed heavily on her mind. What could be done about the outrageous young woman? Once again, she wished she had never met Stephanie. The problem of the young woman's wretched prints still troubled Rachel, and seemed unsolvable.

She sent her maid out to buy *Secrets* so she could look at the latest etching. She was appalled to see the image of a voluptuous female nude facing the viewer. Her face and hair were covered, so the woman wasn't recognizable, but a male face peered at the nude, like a peeping Tom, giving the work a lascivious look. In her opinion, the work was pornographic. The caption repeated the first message: *Photograph of an etching made from a drawing of a woman visiting the Little Palace, where nearly everyone is connected to the Royal Family. We'd like to hear from readers who recognize this woman.* The same e-mail address followed.

What next? Something had to be done. But what? She had been over and over the problem to no avail. She was still worrying about it when Dinah called.

"I got *Secrets* this morning and I recognized the image!" Dinah said. "May I come over and show you what I saw? And Coleman's with me—she recognized it, too. We'd like to discuss it with you."

"Oh, yes, please come right away," Rachel said. Had they recognized the woman in the picture? If so, did that mean the woman was famous? Would fame make the image even more damaging?

•••

Dinah and Coleman came in together, bubbling over with information. Dinah started talking before she sat down.

"This work is a copy of a lithograph by an American artist, Arnold Rönnebeck, made in about 1930. He died in 1947. He wasn't famous, and she might have gotten away with it, but a friend of ours used it as an illustration in a book she wrote. Both Coleman and I recognize it."

Rachel looked bewildered. "What does it mean?"

"It means she copied it, and pretended it was her work—it's a forgery. And it certainly isn't a portrait of anyone connected to the Palace."

"How could she have done it?" Rachel asked.

"Copying another print is easy. Trace the original, using a pencil and very thin paper. Once that's done, place the traced image on a prepared etching plate. Go over the traced drawing with a very sharp pencil, so the lines are impressed onto the waxed surface of the plate. Then take an etching needle and score the lines impressed in the wax all the way to the plate, exposing the copper. Pop it into the usual acid bath—the acid does its work, biting the plate. Neutralize, clean off the wax, and you've got an etched plate," Dinah said.

"Do we think the earlier works were forgeries, too?" Rachel asked.

"Almost certainly. They were probably taken from cheap reproductions that were inspired by the real thing," Coleman said.

"Why did she do it?"

"She probably had no ideas, no talent to originate art, so she stole someone else's work," Coleman said.

"We think all of her prints are copies," Dinah said. "We could probably prove it, but it would be time-consuming. If we confront her, I'm sure she'll confess."

"I've always suspected everything about those wretched prints was a racket. It's time I called her and confronted her. We'll try to get the truth from her, although sometimes I wonder if she knows what truth is," Rachel said. "Excuse me while I go into my office, phone her, and send my car to get her—she won't be able to resist that."

The three women sat down, chatted desultorily, and sipped coffee while they waited. Twenty minutes later, Stephanie pranced in. She was in powder blue again, a dress with a matching coat, and appeared to be in fine spirits.

"I enjoyed riding in your car," she said to Rachel. "You should lend it to me. You can't need it all the time, and I get tired of taxis."

Rachel ignored her remarks, and held up *Secrets*. "Have you seen this?"

"Oh, yes, it's too bad, isn't it? The Royals will be so upset." She shrugged. "As you know, I couldn't get the money the thieves wanted."

"Stephanie, we know this is a copy, a forgery of an American lithograph. Coleman and Dinah have seen the original."

Stephanie broke into tears. "I didn't think anyone would recognize it. Just my luck—American art experts see it," she said through her tears. "I hate these damned prints. I wish I'd never seen Queen Victoria's. I wish I'd never seen the bloody prints. They're ugly and boring."

"Of course someone recognized it. Maybe a lot of people have. You have not heard from them yet. But why are you doing this? To hurt the Queen?"

"No. I'm related to the Royal Family, and I'm very fond of them. I had to pretend to be a Republican to get the flat in the

Little Palace. It was the only way I knew to get a decent place to live," Stephanie said, tears still pouring down her face.

"But if not to hurt the Palace, why did you tell all these lies? Put those pictures in the paper?"

"I need money. I thought this would be an easy way to get it," Stephanie said.

Rachel frowned. "Who did you think was going to pay you to stop printing these images?" she asked.

"I thought *you* would. That's why I came to see you, to tell you about the stolen prints. Everyone knows you love the Queen, and that you're rich. And you have that rich American friend, Heyward Bain. I thought he would help, if you asked him. If you'd paid up when the first print appeared in *Secrets*, I wouldn't be in this mess. Why didn't you? You can afford it," Stephanie said. She was still crying, but her tone was angry.

Rachel, exasperated, shook her head. "Intelligent, law-abiding people do not pay off blackmailers or kidnappers or other criminals. It may be illegal to do so. It is certainly illegal to try to extort money as you have done," Rachel said.

Stephanie cried harder. "Are you going to have me arrested? Will I have to go to jail?" she whimpered.

"I do not know," Rachel said. "Why are you so desperate for money that you would forge art and extort money?"

"I've done bad things. I'm being blackmailed. If I don't pay the blackmailer I'll be exposed, and all sorts of awful things will be in the papers, and I'll go to prison." She was crying louder, so loud the others could barely understand her words.

"I'd like to smack her the way people in films do when they want to shut up a hysterical woman," Coleman murmured to Dinah.

"I know," Dinah said. "I can't stand crybabies."

"Stephanie, please compose yourself," said Rachel. "I will see about getting you some tea. Dinah, Coleman, will you help me carry this tray back to the kitchen?" She stood and moved across the room, not looking to see whether Dinah and Coleman followed.

In the hallway to the kitchen she said softly, "What are we going to do with her? She is not ashamed or repentant. She seems to be totally lacking in morals, ethics. She is swamped in entitlement. You heard her. She thinks I should give her my money, my car, just because I have it, and she does not. I do not understand that kind of mentality."

"She's becoming hysterical," Coleman said. "I think we ought to try to get her to calm down. Do you have a room where she can rest, while we try to figure out what to do with her? I have to leave soon. I have an early date this evening, and I need to get some sleep this afternoon. I'm still jet-lagged."

"Yes," Rachel said. "I will ask Eileen, my maid, to take her up to the guest room, and stay with her. I do not want Stephanie alone while she is here, or making phone calls. She is too disturbed. Who knows what she will say or do?"

"Coleman, go ahead and have James take you home. I'll stay with Rachel," Dinah said.

"Thanks. I'll send James back with the car when I get home. I'll talk to you tomorrow," Coleman said.

Before Rachel and Dinah returned to the sitting room, Dinah said, "I think Stephanie's a candidate for Heyward's new clinic."

"What clinic?" Rachel asked.

"It's a new project of his. He has this idea about helping people who can't understand the difference between right and wrong. They're not exactly insane, and putting them in jail solves nothing—they learn how to become even worse. He and some other people who share his ideas think maybe they can be saved. They've opened special clinics to treat them—one in London, another in New York."

"Would he get her in the clinic?" Rachel asked.

"I'm sure he would. I'll call him in a few minutes, but I doubt anything can be done today. Where can she go for tonight, or maybe for a day or two?" Dinah asked.

"I will call her friend Isobel Strange to come and get her. I am sure she can stay with Isobel overnight, if Heyward can get her in the clinic tomorrow," Rachel said.

Rachel waited while Dinah called Heyward, who promised to find Stephanie a spot in the new clinic by Sunday morning.

"What is the name of the clinic?" Rachel asked.

"The New Eden. Heyward says it's where people can learn about right and wrong and learn to make better choices: Think about Eve and the original Eden. He says it's designed to help the Stephanies of the world. He'll have a car and a nurse collect Stephanie from the Little Palace Sunday morning at ten," Dinah said.

Rachel called Isobel Strange, who hadn't known where Stephanie was, and sounded frantic about her disappearance. She was relieved to learn that Stephanie was with Rachel, and accepted Rachel's offer of the car to pick her up. She was with Rachel and Dinah twenty minutes later.

Rachel thought Isobel looked worse than ever. She wore the same tattered and ugly clothes she'd had on when Rachel saw her at the Little Palace. Was it necessary to look that bad? She would talk to Julia about Isobel's situation, try to find out more about her. She looked as if she deliberately tried to be a fright. But why would anyone be deliberately repulsive?

Isobel—Rachel refused to use her ugly nickname—started talking as soon as she knew Stephanie was upstairs and safe. "I know what everyone thinks of her. She can't help the way she is. Her parents were killed in an automobile accident when she was a baby. She was put in foster care, where she was sexually abused. She wasn't removed until she was five, when she was put into another foster home, where her caregivers rented her out. She was very pretty and they took many photos of her and sold them. Some went to decent magazines and papers, others to pornographers. When she was twelve and too old for the men who had used her, she was sent to a children's home. She was too old for it, but no one knew what to do with her. That's where I met her. She didn't know what was true and what was false. She told me she was a princess, and she named herself Stephanie after a real princess. She still doesn't know what is real and what is not real. She talks about people connected to the Royal Family who come to the Little Palace. No royal visitors have been anywhere near the place. She talks about being close to the Royal Family. It isn't true. She has never had any connection with them. She is not descended from Queen Victoria.

"She ran away from the children's home, and when I next saw her she was living with an old man who shared her with his friends. He'd found her on the streets, and, bad as her life was with him, it was the best she ever knew. What little education she had, she got in that man's house. When he died, she was lost again. I took her with me to the Remembrance Society. They'll help anyone who'll say they're anti-Royal. That's how we have flats at the Little Palace.

"Stephanie's not very bright, but she can be very sweet, and she's still pretty. I think Ivan would have married her if he hadn't been killed."

"Who do you think killed him?" Rachel asked.

"I don't know. I heard that the police think Stephanie did it, but I don't believe it. She had no reason to," Isobel said.

"Well, we think we have found a good place for her." Dinah explained about the clinic and Isobel seemed satisfied with the idea of Stephanie entering The New Eden.

"I'll visit her as soon as they say I can," Isobel said. "May I take her back with me now? I'll have her ready tomorrow morning."

"Yes, my maid—her name is Eileen—will show you upstairs to her room, and help you bring her downstairs, if she is too upset to walk by herself. My driver will take you both back to the Little Palace."

Rachel summoned Eileen, and introduced Miss Strange to the maid, who escorted Stephanie's friend up the stairs.

Rachel returned to the library, and Dinah stood up. "I have to go, too," Dinah said. "What a horrible story about Stephanie. I disliked her so much. I still do, but now I'm also sorry for her. How does she seem? I'm ashamed of how I've thought of her."

"I didn't see her with Isobel, but the woman is said to be her best friend. I think she'll be glad to see her, but who knows? I know she'll be thrilled to ride back to the Little Palace in my car."

After Rachel walked Dinah to the door, she returned to the library to settle down and think about all she'd learned today.

When she heard the story of Stephanie's life, Rachel had flinched. It was not her story, but it could have been. Like Isobel, she had been plain. Her plainness had saved her from many of the terrible things that had happened to Stephanie. Also, as bad as the Oklahoma William Brown Home for Orphans had been, the places where Stephanie spent her childhood were apparently far worse.

No one seemed to have helped Stephanie. Several people had befriended Rachel along the way: Luna in the orphanage had helped her—why had she never called Luna or written to her? She could have made the wretched woman's life better. Mrs. Watson in Chicago had been nice to her, had tried to be her friend. Rachel had never written to thank her, or to tell Mrs. Watson how she was doing.

When she moved to Cambridge, Gregory had been wonderful to her, and she hadn't spoken to him in months. How could she have been so rude, so ungrateful, so forgetful of all he had done for her? Angela Fox, Ransome's secretary, had also been helpful and friendly. Where was she now? Rachel had never even sent her so much as a Christmas card. Clara the hairdresser—she should have sent her a card, too.

She berated herself for what she had become—selfish, self-involved. She had expressed her gratitude to Ransome and to Heyward, her great patrons, but not to the people who had helped her along the way. Worse still, she could have helped so many others, especially children who had been abandoned or neglected as she had been. She might have been able to save some children. She might have made a few children's homes better places.

Rachel stood up and paced the room. It wasn't too late. Thanks to Heyward, she had plenty of money. Maybe Heyward would know how she could find a way to help unfortunate children. It was time to give back. Time to rethink, rearrange her life. Every morning she set aside time to be thankful. She would still do so, but she would also make sure that every day she did something for someone else.

Maybe she should start with Stephanie. Heyward's clinic was bound to be expensive. Maybe Heyward would let her pay Stephanie's way? There had to be something she could do for the poor girl. Like Dinah, she was ashamed of the way she had thought about Stephanie. She'd discuss her with Heyward tomorrow. Between them, they would come up with a plan to help Stephanie.

CHAPTER TWENTY-FOUR

Coleman

Saturday night, May, the London Eye
When Tony arrived at seven to pick up Coleman, the first question he asked was about Dolly.

"How is she?"

"Fine," Coleman said. "Heyward volunteered to keep her tonight. She knows him well. Dolly and I share an office with him in New York."

"Good. I don't want you worrying about her tonight. Let's go."

Tony introduced the young man sitting in the back seat as Paul, who, he said, helped him with all kinds of things. "He'll be our butler on the London Eye," he explained.

"Do we need a butler?" Coleman said.

Tony laughed. "Yes, we do. The management of the London Eye insists. If we don't take our own, they'll give us a stranger. Now, let me tell you what's going to happen. When we get to the Eye, we're going first to the 4D experience."

"What is it?" Coleman asked.

"You pick up 3D glasses on entry and you see a film."

"What makes it 4D?" she asked. "I've never even heard of 4D."

"This is what management says: 'The following special effects are used in the 4D Cinema Experience: fog, bubbles, wind, snow, strobe lighting, and vibrating flooring. There are no words, and the images are set to the music of two popular bands, Coldplay and Goldfrapp.'"

"The film is about a little girl who visits London with her father. She wants to be higher to get a better view, so they come to the London Eye. She imagines what it would be like to see London from a bird's eye view, so the film gives us 3D aerial footage of London at different times of year—Chinese New Year, New Year's Eve, and so on."

"I know about 3D," Coleman said. "What makes it 4D?"

"Stimulation for your other senses, not just your eyesight," said Tony. "They put dry ice around the seats so you feel cold when the screen shows scenes of winter. It snows and rains in the theater when it snows and rains on the screen. When the fireworks go off, you can smell them."

"I'm not sure I want to be rained on," said Coleman.

"We have a private capsule, and I've brought shawls and sweaters," Tony said. "The Eye won't let you bring food, but they'll supply it. Here's your picnic." He read from a card: "Tiny elegant sandwiches on specialty breads, including tomato and herb, spinach, brioche, and wholemeal. Fillings include lobster salad, truffled chicken, burrata, with heirloom tomato and pesto, Cornish crab with watercress mousseline, and classic cucumber and cream cheese. A special order of lemonade and hot chocolate for you, and champagne for me and Paul."

"Goodness! I must be dreaming," Coleman said.

"I'm doing my best to make your London dreams come true," he said.

"So far, you're doing better than my dreams," she said.

•••

In fact, the experience was far more delightful than she had imagined: high up in the air, the dark blue sky scattered with stars, the blue lights of the Eye, the lights of London below. Tony pointed out sights, saw that she was thoroughly wrapped in cashmere, and served her tea sandwiches and hot chocolate.

•••

Back at Heyward's late that night, Coleman and Tony stood in the foyer to say goodnight.

"It was a perfect evening. I didn't want it to end," Coleman said.

"Good," he said. He kissed her hand, then very lightly, her mouth.

"I've arranged the hedgehogs and the badgers for tomorrow night," he said. "You'll see some bluebells, but not very well—it will be too dark. We'll make a daytime trip to another place to give you a better bluebell view. I'm working on the nightingale. We'll have to go out of London to get it. We'll go on Tuesday, if that suits you?"

"Of course. I can hardly wait." Coleman, still dazzled by the London Eye experience, couldn't believe it. "No! Really? You'll have to tell me how you arranged the hedgehogs and the badgers. Didn't they object?"

He laughed. "No, not when I told them it was for you. Dress warmly, wear walking shoes, take gloves. I'll pick you up at six. We'll have an hour's drive to the place where we'll see the animals. We'll go to a pub for a meal later—I think you told me you've never been to one? There's a very good one near where we'll see the animals."

"Sounds like a great evening," she said.

"What are you going to do all day tomorrow?" he asked.

"Maybe shop a little. Buy some books. Write in my diary everything about the Eye. Worry about poor Rachel's problems," she said.

"Be careful," he said. "I'll see you tomorrow at six. When I come I'll have a surprise for Dolly."

•••

Coleman knocked on Heyward's door. "It's me," she said.

Dolly made a small hello noise, and Heyward said, "Come in."

Dolly ran to greet her, and Coleman leaned over to pick her up.

"I don't have to ask whether you had a good time. You're glowing."

"It was the best night of my life," Coleman said.

"I bet you'll have even better nights," he said. "Sleep well."

•••

Coleman lay in bed, reliving the evening. Tony had said she was an unusual woman. He was unique in her experience. He seemed to think only of her wishes, her comfort, making sure she had a wonderful time. No grabs, no pushiness, no demands. She was sure he'd had more than enough of the Eye long before he met her, but he hadn't ruined the experience for her by acting bored, or talking about something else when she was trying to absorb everything.

Would he be as considerate, kind, and gentle as a lover? Or if they became lovers, would he turn possessive and demanding, like all the other men she had known?

"Dolly, I'm thinking like a schoolgirl. One date and I'm worrying about what kind of lover he would be. He hasn't even hinted that he feels that way about me. Rob was always all over me, wanting to possess me, send me to the suburbs . . . so much so I had to break off our relationship. I knew as soon as I met Jeb that we'd be in bed that night if I didn't put on the brakes."

She sighed. "Tony is the nicest man I ever met, and one of the best-looking. Could he be gay? Or is he just being nice to me because he's a friend of Heyward's? What a fool I am, lying here fretting. What will be, will be. I'll know soon enough."

CHAPTER TWENTY-FIVE

Rachel

Sunday, May, London

The telephone woke Rachel a little before seven. Who would call her so early? She reached for the phone, and was not altogether surprised to hear Julia. She was talking so fast Rachel at first couldn't understand a word she said.

"Slow down," Rachel said. "Say it again?"

"Stephanie," Julia said. "She's been murdered."

"What?" Rachel said. "How—why? Where?"

Julia couldn't seem to explain. She sounded rattled, couldn't pull herself together.

"Shall I come over there?" Rachel asked.

"No," Julia said. "No, it's chaos. Don't come, but I had to let you know. I expect the police will want to ask you some questions. You saw her yesterday, didn't you?"

"I did," Rachel said, not asking how Julia knew this. The Little Palace was a gossip center. "I sent her home with Isobel Strange. She was upset, but she seemed glad to go. Are they sure it's murder? Who would want to kill that poor creature?"

Julia said, "I don't know, I don't *know*! I don't—I can't—I'll call you later."

It was too early for Rachel to call Heyward, or her solicitor. But going back to sleep was impossible. The girl she had sworn to help was dead. Rachel could do nothing for her now. Rachel's guilt would never vanish.

CHAPTER TWENTY-SIX

Coleman

Sunday morning, May, London

Coleman was deeply asleep and dreaming about Tony and the Eye when she heard knocking on her bedroom door. She was slow to wake, until she heard Heyward's voice: "Coleman, I need to speak to you right away."

She called, "Come in," and he entered, followed by Mrs. Carter with a tray of coffee and orange juice. The housekeeper set the tray down on the table near the door, and disappeared. Heyward poured Coleman a cup of coffee and handed it to her.

"I have to tell you something terrible. I thought it best to tell you right away: Princess Stephanie was murdered last night."

Coleman sat up, and took a swallow of coffee. She had to wake up, she had to give Heyward her full attention. This was awful news. Heyward, normally so calm and cheerful, looked distressed. "What happened?" she asked.

"The usual: heroin overdose at the Little Palace. It's time for me to give you some background. We—a number of us concerned with the drug problem in London—have known for some time that Stephanie sold drugs. She had a very active social life, and knew many drug users. She went everywhere, and she was very successful at what she did, but she couldn't have been the brains of the outfit. Someone was telling her what to do.

"We hoped to learn from her who her boss or bosses were, but she wouldn't talk to us. We think she was too afraid of the people she reported to to tell us anything. Jeb was in London assisting me with some of my projects. I suggested he would be a good person to get information from her: attractive, charming, unknown in London, and able to pose as a wealthy catch. I couldn't tell you about it; we were all sworn to secrecy. I'm sorry the subterfuge made you think badly of Jeb. His association with Stephanie was very hard work."

Coleman listened attentively, but she didn't comment. She wasn't sure Jeb saw his time with Stephanie as work. She had seen the way he looked at Stephanie. He had looked at Coleman that way during their brief association.

"Stephanie wasn't about to confess, nor was she telling Jeb anything useful," Heyward continued. "Her behavior became more and more erratic. We feared her bosses might see her as a loose cannon and kill her to prevent their exposure. We saw her breakdown as an opportunity to put her in the clinic where we could help and protect her. As you know, she was to go to the clinic this morning, but someone made sure she didn't get there."

"How terrible," Coleman said. "What now?"

"Only a few people knew she was going to the clinic. Unfortunately, one of them was Rachel. I'm afraid poor Rachel will continue to be a suspect. I'd hoped we could get her off the list, but that was not to be. There's a lot to cover, and I want to discuss everything with you. Why don't you get dressed and come downstairs? We'll have some breakfast and decide what to do next."

Coleman took a shower, and pulled on her black jeans, a black turtleneck, and flats. She'd considered a brighter outfit, which might lift her dark mood, but rejected it. She felt the need for some kind of mourning for that poor foolish girl. She took Dolly downstairs and let her out in the garden.

Heyward was waiting for her at the dining room door. They went into the room together, and sat down at the table in their usual places: Heyward at the head, Coleman on his right. A maid whose name Coleman didn't know came in and poured coffee, and waited silently by the table for their orders.

"What would you like?" Heyward asked Coleman.

"Just a muffin, blueberry if there are any, but anything will do," she said.

Heyward ordered dry toast and scrambled eggs. When the maid left the room, he turned to Coleman. "Tony called early this morning with messages for you: He said he'd hoped to see you today—to take you to lunch, or tea, but something has come up and he may not be able to, but he'll call later. I suspect that what came up is Stephanie's death. He left a package for you. I brought it in here—here it is." He handed her a small package wrapped in green paper.

"He also said he'll pick you up tonight at six. It's 'hedgehogs and badgers'—does that make sense to you? And the nightingale is set for Tuesday."

"Oh, yes, that's all great news—things I'm really looking forward to. They'll cheer me up," Coleman said. "That poor girl's death is so depressing. How old was she?"

"I don't think anyone knows. She may not have known her own age. Maybe twenty-something? About her death: as I said, only a few people knew she was going to the clinic today. I'm sure that's why she was killed. Once she was in there, we could protect her. They'd have no control over her, and she'd probably talk to us. You, Dinah, and Rachel knew she was going to the clinic, and— what's her name?" Heyward asked.

"Isobel Strange. She says she's known Stephanie since she was a child. They were in a group home together. She accompanied Stephanie to the Little Palace yesterday. Rachel said Isobel was devoted to Stephanie—that's why Rachel called her to come over when Stephanie was hysterical. It's hard to believe she would harm Stephanie. Anyway, I'd bet everyone in the Little Palace knew Stephanie was there. She was making such a fuss at Rachel's. I'm sure she was still making a scene when she arrived at her destination," Coleman said. "Where was she killed?"

"Her body was on her bed. The policemen I spoke to said she looked as if she was asleep. The police have interviewed everyone in the Little Palace, and they have no suspects except Julia—Lady Fitzgerald—and Rachel. The only new information they've discovered is Roberto what's-his-name's will. He, too, left everything to Stephanie. She died well-to-do," he said.

"That's sad in a way—she was so poor all her life, when she could have enjoyed the money. Who inherits it?" Coleman asked.

"I don't know. It's probably too soon to have found her will, if she has one. I don't even know if she had a lawyer."

"Has anybody searched her apartment?" Coleman asked.

"I don't think so. I don't know who found the body either. I'll call the police officer I'm dealing with, and try to get more details."

Coleman went to the garden door to let Dolly in. When she came back Heyward had put aside his cell phone.

"I learned a little," he said. "The concierge found her. He had flowers for her. When he took them upstairs to deliver them, the door to her apartment was ajar. She didn't come to the door when he rang the bell, so he went in to check on her, found her body, and called the police. A police officer accompanied Julia and Isobel all through the apartment to see if anything was disturbed or missing, but they said all was as it should be. The police say there was no paper, no books in the flat."

"That's not surprising," Coleman said. "Isobel told us she could barely read or write."

"The concierge told the police that Julia and Isobel were in Stephanie's flat constantly. She was hardly ever out of their sight."

"I suppose they felt she was helpless and they had to watch over her," Coleman said.

CHAPTER TWENTY-SEVEN

Coleman

Sunday night, May, London

Tony arrived at exactly six o'clock, carrying a package wrapped in pink paper and pink ribbons.

"This is for Dolly. Where is she? Who's taking care of her tonight?" he asked.

"Heyward again. They settle down in the library and he works while she naps," Coleman said. "Come on in, you can give it to her yourself. She likes to unwrap packages."

Coleman knocked on the library door, and asked Heyward if she and Tony could come in. He opened the door for them, and Dolly rushed to greet Coleman. Tony handed Dolly the package. She took it in her mouth, but looked at Coleman for approval. When Coleman nodded, she ripped off the ribbons and paper. She began to gnaw the box, and Coleman rescued it. Inside was a new pink leash and a new pink collar. Attached to the collar was a gold medallion. Coleman held it up. "My goodness," she said. "Dolly, you got a medal!"

"Let me see it," Heyward said, and reached out to take it. "For Dolly, with thanks from a grateful nation, including all its dogs," he read aloud.

Coleman saw Heyward and Tony exchange glances.

"Approved at the highest level," Tony said. "If Dolly was a corgi, I suspect the Palace would have adopted her, or given her a title."

•••

The car flew along the highway in the cool night air. Coleman was glad she had worn her black wool pantsuit. She'd worn it with the thought that the night would be cold, and that night creatures might be frightened by bright-colored clothes. She'd read that in Africa one shouldn't wear bright colors or white—the animals would be startled and run away. Her walking shoes were black, too, as were the heavy socks she wore with them. Even her gloves were made of black wool, and she had pulled a black knit cap over her blonde curls.

Tony laughed when he saw her, but when she told him why she was dressed as she was, he said she was probably right.

The car turned sharply into deep, thick woods. In minutes they were in complete darkness. He drove further into the woods, and stopped by a small clearing, where a little light broke through the trees. When he helped her out of the car, she was standing on closely cut grass. She could smell it, and the evergreen and other woodsy scents she'd noticed when the plane from France landed on the Duke of Omnium's property. Was that where she was?

"Where are we?" she asked.

"A putting green on my father's land. Hedgehogs like it. I see them here often. It's very dark tonight. You may have a hard time seeing them, but that's good for the hedgehogs. If the moon comes out from behind the clouds, they're in danger of predators. I've brought you a torch. Keep it pointed towards the grass, and you should see one or maybe more. You said you don't have hedgehogs in the United States?"

"No, although my friend Susan told me there's a South American hedgehog that people can keep in a cage as a pet. She said they're unpleasant. The one she'd seen slept all day and hissed all night, so they'd named it Hiss. It hated captivity, I guess."

"That doesn't sound at all like our hedgehogs. How do you even know about them?" Tony asked.

"All I know is from Beatrix Potter's stories," she said.

She saw a dark spot in the grass and leaned over to look at it. "Is that a hedgehog?" she whispered.

"Yes, it is. Since you have on gloves, you can pick it up. Just slip your hand under it. It won't mind."

The little creature lay in her hand, perfectly still, apparently unafraid. Coleman could have stood looking at him all night, but she spotted a much smaller one. She pointed it out to Tony.

"Is that a baby?" she asked.

"Yes, you can pick it up, too. Put the one you're holding down carefully. It will go about its business. Pick up as many as you like one at a time, but always from underneath. I'm going into the woods to the place where we'll see the badgers, just to make sure they're there. I'll be right back."

Coleman leaned over to put the hedgehog in the grass, and was about to pick up the smaller one when a strong arm grabbed her from behind. She tried to stand up, but the man holding her was forcing her body down. He had a hand over her mouth, and the arm that was holding and pushing her had encircled her body, including both of her arms. He knocked the flashlight out of her hand. The man smelled horrible, of unwashed body odor, pigs, chicken pens, horse manure, tobacco, and beer. He was mumbling to her, but she couldn't understand him. She wasn't sure he was speaking English. Her mind was all over the place as she tried to think of a way to escape his grasp. She was wearing sneakers, so stamping on his feet was useless, but she tried it anyway. She tried and failed to bite the hand he held over her mouth. He was trying to push her to the ground and rape her, and she was helpless to stop him.

Without warning, Tony was beside her. He didn't hesitate, but hit her attacker on the head with the heavy torch he was carrying.

The sound of the blow was horrifying, but the man didn't cry out or fall. The man's head must be made of stone.

"You know you're not supposed to be here," Tony said to the man. "You're off limits. Get off this property, and if you've set traps in this area, take them with you. If I ever see you here again, you're going to jail. I'll send someone to see you tomorrow. You'll have to be punished." The man disappeared into the woods and Tony pulled Coleman into his arms.

"Are you hurt?" he said.

"No, but I think it was a near miss. Who was that?"

"A traveler—some people call them gypsies. His name is Fred. My father allows the travelers to camp not too far from here, but they aren't allowed in this part of the grounds. Fred would not have touched you if he'd known you were with me. He's backward— has the mental capacity of a six-year-old, but the sexual desires of an adult. He saw a woman alone and struck. No wonder you were frightened. He'll be appropriately punished. We'll report him to the elders in his family who are supposed to see that he behaves. Forget him, if you can. Are you sure you're okay? Are you still up for badger watching? We can do that another night, if you'd rather?"

"Oh, no, I want to see the badgers," Coleman said. "I wish I could wash up, though. That man was filthy. He smelled so bad, I was nearly sick. I want to try to get his dirt off my face and hands."

"There's a hut near where the badgers live. You can clean up in there. Come on, let's go." He put his arm around her shoulders, and pulled her close. "We shouldn't talk anymore," he said softly. "We must be very quiet. They have excellent hearing."

Coleman had been genuinely frightened by the gypsy's attack, and was glad of Tony's support. If Tony had not appeared, she was sure the man would have raped her. She wondered what would happen to her attacker. She hoped he would be put in jail, so he couldn't attack anyone else.

•••

"We'll go in the hut the back way," Tony said. "After you clean up, we'll sit in the chairs inside the hut, and look out through the windows at them. We can't talk in the hut—the badgers would hear us. Save your questions. I'll explain everything later when we go to the pub."

They tiptoed into a small room, with a bathroom near the back door. Coleman darted in and scrubbed her face, her hands, and the bare skin she could reach with a minty soap she found on a nearby shelf. There was also a bottle of germicide. She used it to wash her hands again and again. She could still feel his hand over her mouth. She wished she had mouthwash or mints, but no such luck. She rinsed her mouth with cold water, and tiptoed back into the little room.

Tony pointed to a chair facing the window, and she sat down. Soft lights were scattered among the trees, illuminating a clearing. A large black-and-white badger, looking as handsome as in the pictures she'd seen—sort of like a panda cousin—was eating something on the ground. Several smaller badgers were munching near the big one, a little closer to the woods, as if they were shy.

What glorious animals! Seeing hedgehogs—holding them—and watching badgers, all on the same night. What a marvelous experience.

She turned, beaming at Tony. He asked softly, "Had enough? Ready to go?"

She nodded and they slipped out the way they had entered.

•••

Tony drove up to the pub with a prominent gold-and-red sign: "Duke's Inn."

"Picture-postcard perfect! Both quaint and inviting," Coleman said.

Exterior lights revealed an appealing mixture of stone, dark wood beam, and white plaster building—two or three buildings connected—crowned with a thatched roof. The interior was charming, with low ceilings, exposed wood beams, and a worn wood floor. Ancient farming implements—wood and rusted iron—hung on the white walls. She looked at Tony, a question in her eyes.

Tony said, "The pub is very old. It's named for an ancestor, and the decorations reflect my family's forever interest in agriculture."

He steered them to a small table near a fireplace, where a few lumps of coal and a couple of logs smoldered, radiating heat. Coleman warmed her hands, and glancing around, asked, "Why is this place empty? It's so attractive, I'd think it would be packed."

"It's Sunday night," Tony explained. "Sunday lunch is the big meal here, and the Duke's Inn is always overflowing midday Sunday until early afternoon. Everyone nearby and even people from far away turn up for roast beef, roast potatoes, Yorkshire pudding, and a delectable sweet. After that heavy lunch, people stay home Sunday night, eat lightly, and go to bed early. There'll be a limited menu tonight, but they always have their signature cottage pie, which is what we came for," he said.

"Dinah has raved about cottage pie. I'm dying to try it. I've never tasted one. I think the only kind of main-dish pie I've ever eaten is chicken pie."

"You have a treat in store, but first, refreshment. Come to the bar with me," he said.

The pub keeper touched his forehead, and offered a friendly, "What'll it be, Gov?"

"A half pint of Duke's, and a cider for my guest, please," Tony said.

Coleman gave him a quizzical look, and Tony admitted, "Yes, we have a local ale named for the family. It's the patriotic thing for me to order. The cider is nonalcoholic. And, yes, that gesture is traditional, and somewhat embarrassing."

When they returned to the table, and smelled the freshly baked bread the waitress had just put on the table, Coleman realized she was starving. Split pea soup, garnished with bacon bits—ideal for a chilly evening—arrived as soon as they sat down. It was delicious, and warm. The cottage pie was even better, with mashed potatoes—browned on top, making a light crust—piled on top of a small casserole dish of hot beef chunks, chopped carrots, and onions, swimming in thick gravy.

"Just as Dinah told me: it is fabulous," Coleman said, after her last bite. "Why don't we have this in New York? There's nothing special about the ingredients."

"I don't know," Tony said. "Cooking isn't one of my skills."

"I've eaten every bite," Coleman said.

"In England, you haven't finished a meal here without a sweet or cheese. Which do you want?" Tony said.

"I don't think I could eat either," she said.

"How about some coffee?"

"How about a cup of hot chocolate?" she asked.

"As you wish. Tell me, has the hedgehog and badger experience been what you expected?" he asked.

"Oh, yes, wonderful. I have a lot of questions, though."

"Please, ask anything you want."

"I read hedgehogs were like porcupines, covered with spines that would hurt anyone who touched the creatures. I've been puzzled because Beatrix Potter's hedgehog was a pet, and liked to sleep on her knee."

"Yes, a hedgehog has six or seven thousand spines all over its back. The spines are everywhere except underneath. That's why you have to pick them up the way you did," he explained.

"Do most people have hedgehogs in their gardens?" Coleman asked.

"No, but a lot do. They're gardeners' friends because they eat slugs and caterpillars and other threats to plants. People will say 'my hedgehog,' but hedgehogs don't belong to anyone—they are free spirits. I've read that a hedgehog might visit as many as seven gardens in a single night."

"They're so cute. I'd love to have one or more. I don't have a garden, but I plan to have one, and it would be fun to have hedgehogs in it," she said.

"You could do that, if you stay in England. You can't take one to the States, but it's fairly easy to attract them here," Tony said.

Coleman looked at him, startled.

"I can't stay longer than two weeks," she said.

"Why?" Tony asked. "Dinah's here and Heyward's here. Aren't they your family?"

"Yes, but I have a business to run. That's why I'm in London—to look into buying another magazine. Heyward and I have an appointment with the owner. I'm also supposed to be working with Rachel Ransome on a project, but as you know, she's been caught in a web of suspicion, and we haven't spent as much time together as I'd planned."

"I still don't see why you can't live here. You could manage the magazines from here. Others have done it," Tony said.

Coleman shook her head. "I couldn't."

"This conversation is not over," he said. "Do you have any other questions?"

"No more on hedgehogs, but a lot about badgers," she said.

He laughed. "Go ahead. You have badgers in the States, don't you?"

"I guess so: Wisconsin is called the Badger State. I've never seen one, but I don't think they're like yours."

"I think you're right," Tony said. "I don't think you have our badger problem. We have a real conflict. Farmers—cattle raisers—are convinced badgers carry a disease that causes bovine tuberculosis. Last year thirty-seven thousand cattle were slaughtered, at a cost of one hundred million pounds, to prevent the spread of the plague. Farmers want the badgers removed, permanently. Environmentalists want the badger protected as a native animal. It's hard to know what's right."

"But what about your badgers, or should I say the Duke's badgers? Are they in danger of being killed?" Coleman asked.

Tony said, "They're our badgers—they are a family charge. They're protected. All of our land is posted. Our badgers have been in the family for generations, always in the same area. They're territorial; they typically live in social groups of four to seven animals, in defined territorial boundaries. We protect them and supplement their natural diet—moles and mice and voles and such—with corn and sunflower seeds."

"But what about your cattle?"

"This may sound extreme, but we vaccinate our badgers. It's not easy, and it's expensive. Catching shy creatures that live in holes in the ground, and only come out at night, is difficult, and as you can imagine, they have no desire to be vaccinated. But we, and others dedicated to the preservation of this lovely animal, do it."

"How?" Coleman asked.

"You saw tonight how they all came out? They knew we were offering them a treat—peanuts. They could smell them. They love peanuts. We use peanuts to entice them when we need to give them shots. When they come out for them, a quick grab by our groundskeepers, a quick shot, and no more bovine TB," Tony said.

"That's fascinating. I hadn't read anything about vaccinating them. Why don't more people do it?"

"Expensive. Trouble. There are other ways to avoid killing them, including the way the cattle are handled, but most farmers don't like having their ways challenged, so lots of badgers die every day."

"Oh, that's so sad," Coleman said.

He looked at her. "Are you really interested in this? Farming stuff?

"Yes, of course," she said.

"You're very different from the way I pictured you when Heyward told me you were coming to London."

She smiled. "What did you think I'd be like?" she asked.

"Oh, New York-y. No interest in country things—citified," he said.

She laughed. "I grew up in the country. Maybe I'll tell you about it someday. But not tonight. I'm too tired," she said.

"Oh, sorry. Let's go."

A few minutes later, they were in the car, speeding toward London. Coleman nodded off, and didn't wake until they pulled into the drive at Heyward's house.

•••

When Tony kissed her goodnight, she no longer had the slightest doubt about his sexual interest in her. He held her body tightly against his, and kissed her with unmistakable passion. His desire for her was overwhelming, and the strength of her response was almost frightening. When he put her down—she was so much shorter than he that his embrace had lifted her off the floor—she could barely stand. He must have said goodnight, and she hoped she'd replied, but she wasn't sure of anything. Was this what being drunk felt like? She had never had a sip of alcohol in her life, and tonight was no exception. Was she drunk on love?

She was unsteady and staggering slightly when she passed the door to Heyward's office. She tried to be quiet. She was in no shape for a late-night chat.

But he heard her and called out, "Did you have a good time?"

"Oh, yes. Hedgehogs, badgers, a cottage pie at a pub," she said, and to herself, "And the best kiss I've ever had."

"Good. Sleep well. I'll see you tomorrow. Here's Dolly," Heyward said. The little dog ran out to meet her. Coleman picked her up, and tucked her under her right arm. She needed her left arm to hold on to the banister when she walked up the stairs.

In her bedroom she threw off her clothes, pulled on a gown, and fell into bed, exhausted, and weak, overwhelmed with passion— hers and his. She was asleep in minutes.

CHAPTER TWENTY-EIGHT

Rachel

Monday morning, May, London

She got up, dressed, and went downstairs. She'd work on the book this morning, and try to put poor Stephanie out of her mind. She was determined to help other unfortunate girls, but it would not be the same.

An hour later, she was annoyed when Eileen tapped on the door of her office. She had left standing orders that no one should disturb her during the precious morning hours when she wrote.

"What is it?" she asked, trying not to sound irritated.

"I'm sorry to disturb you, madam, but when I went upstairs to change the sheets in the guest room, I found this paper under the mattress. The lady who was up there crying must have left it."

"Let me see it." It was a piece of the stationery kept in the desk drawer for guests to use. Stephanie must have found it, and the pen with it. Rachel stared at the few words, blurred by tears.

J and I will kill me—they boss the drugs. Killed my men. Will do me now. Princess Stephanie.

"Oh my God, we sent that lamb to her slaughterers. I'll have to get in touch with the authorities. You'll have to testify and say where you found this note," Rachel said.

She called Heyward, who—thank God—was available. "I have something terrible to tell you," Rachel said. "Stephanie left a note here. I'm going to read it to you." She read the horrifying note to Heyward, who said he'd be right over with one of the detectives. Rachel sat down to wait. Eileen was still hovering.

"What is it?" Rachel asked.

"Madam, when I took the woman upstairs to get Miss Princess, she searched that room—looked under pillows, wanted to know if Miss Princess had a purse or a bag with her. Miss Princess had put the paper I found way down under all the covers and sheets, and under the mattress. Then she remade the bed, or the woman would have found the note."

"Stephanie was a lot smarter than we gave her credit for. Her note will make sure her killers are punished. Nothing can bring her back, but she's helped put away two murderers."

"Yes, madam. The doorbell is ringing. Shall I answer it?"

"Yes, go ahead." It would be Heyward and the detective.

Rachel, who never cried, wiped her eyes with the handkerchief she always carried. *I helped kill that girl,* she thought. *I won't let her down. There are other Stephanies out there I can help.*

CHAPTER TWENTY-NINE

Dinah

Monday morning, May, London

Dinah was nervous about her return to the Art Museum of Great Britain. She had felt snubbed by her new associates on her first visit, and she expected the same cool treatment today. But then she had been vulnerable to their slights, and despondent about her living situation. Today she was a different person. If the work at the museum proved to be a bore—well, she'd been bored before. She'd do what she had to do, finish up, and go on to something else, like her new food project. If the people were unfriendly, she'd manage. She intended to make friends in the food world, and the art and antique world, and if the print people didn't like her, so what?

She dressed carefully, wanting to look businesslike, but not like an American showoff. She had a feeling that was how they thought of her.

The day was beautiful, but still chilly. She put on a gray-blue wool suit, with a blue silk blouse, gray suede boots, and a gray and blue scarf. She thought she had achieved the perfect look, but she was afraid it wouldn't help. The people she had to work with didn't want her there. They probably didn't pay attention to clothes, either.

She went out to the waiting car, and got in, thinking she should probably forget commuting to the museum with a driver, and take a bus or something to seem less like a one percenter, but Jonathan would have a fit, and she didn't want to. She was used to the car, and her few experiences on the Tube or on crowded buses had been awful. She arrived at the museum and braced herself for a cold welcome, if not outright hostility.

"I'll call when I know what time I'll want to leave," she said.

"Yes, madam," James said. "I'll be here."

To her astonishment, Lucy, the Keeper of American Prints—not curator but keeper, another word for Coleman's collection—greeted her warmly. Lucy had been stiff, formal, and off-putting at their previous meeting. She still looked like an uptight librarian in her Harry Potter glasses and plain black dress, but her manner was totally different. She showed Dinah the small office that would be hers, and handed her a stack of paper.

"Here's a list of the gift prints, and a list of our few duplicates, and another list of all our American prints—not many, as you'll see. I suspect there are catalogues raisonnés and other sources for most of the prints, but you'll find we have very few American books. Expensive, as you know."

Dinah nodded. She did indeed know.

"When you've had a look, maybe you could tell me what we should do about the sources—buy, borrow, or . . . ?" Lucy asked.

"Of course," Dinah said, thinking she'd help with this problem.

"The room where we make coffee and tea is two doors down on your left; the ladies' room is in the opposite direction. I've arranged lunch in the restaurant upstairs for a few of us. Will one o'clock suit you?"

Dinah had the same feeling she'd had when James had whisked her off to the florist—as if she'd been caught in a strong but warm and friendly wind.

"Lunch at one is fine," Dinah said.

"If you have any questions between now and lunch, call me—you'll find a phone directory on your desk, or drop by. I'm across the hall," Lucy said, and departed.

Dinah took off her coat, and hung it on the hook behind the door. The weather in the museum had changed. The ice had melted. Why, she didn't know, but she was grateful for it. She sat down at the desk, and got to work.

Her most interesting challenge was the black-backed color prints, all woodcuts. The donated collection included four of these mysterious works by Gustave Baumann, Anna Taylor, Margaret Patterson, and William Seltzer Rice. She had always been interested in those works, and had planned to study them, but had never got around to it. She'd have to put together some information about them for this project. The big question: what had inspired the handful of prints of colorful flowers against a black background? Patterson had made some as early as 1915, almost surely in Provincetown, when that seaside village was becoming an arts colony. It was populated largely by women artists who'd gone to Paris early in the century, but had fled back to America, mainly to Provincetown, with the start of the world war. Anna Taylor had worked in Provincetown, too, but later. Her black-backed prints were made in the 1930s.

Were they inspired by the exquisite paper mosaics or collages Mrs. Delany had made in England in the eighteenth century? Maybe, but doubtful. The Delany collages were in the British Museum. They were beautiful and might inspire any artist to place colorful flowers against black—it made the colors brighter. But there was no record of the Provincetown artists being in London, and why would there be? Paris was the center, and London a backwater, of modernist art in the early twentieth century, or so it was believed at the time. Could the American artists have seen Delany's work elsewhere? No, her collages stayed in England— the first exhibition in the United States had been at the Morgan Library in 1986. And there was no book published about them until just a few decades ago, long after these prints were made.

Compounding this mystery was the work by Rice and Baumann. They lived in the West, California and Santa Fe. Baumann passed through Provincetown early in his career, but the black-backed floral Dinah held was dated 1952. Rice was never in Provincetown or Paris or London. Where had his inspiration come from? And what about Baumann?

It would be great to be able to tie all this American work to Mrs. Delany, but there was no probable link. Could there have been another source—or sources—that inspired them? She didn't think she would be able to solve this problem quickly.

It was a great relief to be absorbed in interesting work, and to put Stephanie's death out of her mind. She had met the young woman three times, and disliked her every time. Dinah couldn't feel much about her death, except sadness that the girl had such a terrible life. Still, her knowledge of Stephanie's life and death hovered like a black cloud at the back of her mind. Only concentrating on something else would chase the cloud away.

CHAPTER THIRTY

Coleman

Monday, May, London

Coleman settled down for some serious thinking. She was glad she had some time to herself. She was looking forward to seeing and hearing a nightingale, but would seeing Tony again be uncomfortable? After that passionate goodnight embrace, they couldn't go back to their easy companionship, could they? Would she want to? What did she want? Although it was hard to do, she put the subject of Tony aside and took out her calendar.

She had arrived on Friday. She'd only been here three days, but it seemed like weeks. She'd had fun at the welcome party (except for watching Jeb and Stephanie) and she had enjoyed her two evenings with Tony. But the rest of her time in London had been grim. She was happy that she'd rid Dinah of her demons, but dealing with the situation at 23 Culross and the Rosses had been an unpleasant experience. Dolly's disappearance had been ghastly. Even her fairly distant involvement with the murders was awful. She'd had far too much contact with, and knowledge about, criminals since arriving in London.

Now that Rachel was cleared of suspicion, surely Coleman could return to the list of things she wanted to do, which included learning all about *Cottage & Castle*, and discussing the art book project with Rachel.

Just as important (or maybe more important, if she was honest with herself) was her original to-do list:

1. The nightingale
2. Bluebells
3. Shopping for hats and fabrics
4. Museums, especially the Victoria and Albert
5. Theater?
6. Have fun!

She decided to declare her independence from crime and criminals, and to an extent, her family, if they continued to stay involved with the dark side. She was taking charge of her life starting today, and she planned to make her visit to London rewarding, and, above all, fun.

She took the material on *Cottage & Castle* Heyward had given her out of her briefcase, and found the name and the phone number of Kathleen Mann, the editor and owner of the magazine.

A few minutes later she was speaking to Ms. Mann, and had made a date to meet with her at the office of *Cottage & Castle* Wednesday morning at ten.

She'd made a start, and a good one. She'd rescue this day, which had begun with crime news. She changed into a light green dress and matching jacket, and asked Mrs. Carter if she would keep Dolly for a few hours—maybe longer. Mrs. Carter had fallen in love with Dolly, and was happy to take care of her.

She planned to head out to Chapeau, the store on New Bond Street, where the great hats were. After hats, she'd go to Hatchards and buy books—mysteries set in England. Maybe she'd go back to Fortnum's and eat at the bar. Have fun! She wouldn't have Heyward's car, but that was just fine. She'd longed to ride in a London taxi. Dinah had ridden in one during her first visit to London and had enjoyed it.

Half an hour later, having left Dolly with Mrs. Carter, who was tossing a ball for the little dog to chase, Coleman was on her way.

•••

The cab ride was uneventful, and a little like films she'd seen. She was glad London still had some of the old-fashioned, boxy, black square cabs. She was also pleased that some of the red telephone boxes had survived. Maybe no one used them, but they were a London symbol; they should always be preserved.

The cab dropped her outside the door of Chapeau. The inside of the store looked just as she'd thought it would: big, airy, high ceilings, and lots of gorgeous hats. She'd seen similar hats in *Majesty*. Tall with feathers or other decorations. Huge and round. Odd shapes, all kinds of colors. She wandered around looking at all of them, and spotted two she wanted to try on. That was when she checked their prices. She gulped. Each cost more than five hundred dollars. She wouldn't dream of paying that much for a hat. To make sure she wasn't missing anything she liked that might be available for a lower price, she checked a few more price tags. Good heavens, there wasn't a hat in the store that cost less than five hundred dollars. So much for Chapeau. She left the store, and thought about walking to Hatchards. She changed her mind after looking at her street map. Too far to walk.

She hailed a cab and asked the driver to take her to the corner of Piccadilly and Duke Streets, where James had dropped her and Dinah her first day in London. She knew how to get to Hatchards and Fortnum's from that spot, and she was excited at being out and about in London alone.

•••

It was nearly six when Coleman arrived back at Heyward's house, in a taxi packed with books and goodies from Fortnum's. She was more than ready to sit down. She wasn't surprised to see Tony's car in Heyward's driveway, or to hear from the butler that

Tony and Heyward were having drinks in the library. The butler relieved her of her bags of books, and said that he'd have them taken to her room.

Coleman took the elevator upstairs, and went straight to her immaculate bathroom. She washed her face and hands, put on lipstick, brushed her hair, and collected Dolly from Mrs. Carter, before she joined the men in the library. They rose to greet her when she walked in the room. "Welcome home! Have a seat," Heyward said. Tony smiled, and blew her a kiss.

She was glad to see that the men looked cheerful. She wasn't in the mood to discuss dark subjects. She hoped they wouldn't talk about Stephanie or the murderers. She'd had enough of those topics.

"Would you like a drink?" Heyward asked. "Mrs. Carter had the kitchen make lemonade for you. I tasted it—it's delicious."

"I'd love it," she said.

"Have you been shopping?" Tony asked.

"Yes. Books—lots of books," she said.

"I thought you were off to buy hats," Heyward said. "I was hoping you'd model some."

"No, too expensive," she said.

"Let me buy you a hat, or hats," Tony said.

"I was about to say the same thing," Heyward said.

"No, thanks. I bought a how-to book, and I'm going to make my own hats if I can't find anything I like at a decent price," Coleman said.

Tony looked at her. "You never cease to amaze me," he said. "Here are two men trying to give you expensive hats, and you're rejecting our gifts, going to become a hat maker? Why?"

She laughed. "Growing up poor. Having to be thrifty. Unwilling to waste money," she said.

"Have you opened the package I left for you this morning?" Tony asked. "I warn you, it's time-sensitive."

"No, I'll open it now," Coleman said. "It's in the dining room."

She was back in a few minutes, unwrapping as she walked. "Oh, great! It's CDs of nightingales singing. Can we play it in here?" she asked Heyward.

"Of course." He put the top CD in the sound system, and a powerful and melodious song flooded the room. When it was over, Coleman felt dazed, but she couldn't wait to hear the second CD. When she heard it—the magnificent song with RAF bombers in the background taking off to bomb Germany—tears came to her eyes. She couldn't help thinking of how many of the boys in those planes didn't return. Was the CD contrasting the beautiful song of the bird with the horror of war? Whatever its intent, the recording was very moving.

"Wow," she said.

"I wanted you to hear those CDs before we hear the living bird tomorrow. You should know what to listen for. Speaking of tomorrow, I must leave you two, and go do a few chores since I'll be out of my office all day tomorrow. Have a nice evening. I'll see you tomorrow at eight," he said, and was gone.

Like it or not, she had to ask Heyward about his day. "How did everything go? Did Julia and Isobel talk?" she asked.

"Those two women couldn't wait to pour the blame on each other. Some of it was interesting, but most of it was tiresome or horrible. Do you want to hear?"

"Now that the story has ended, I'd like the answers to some questions: Why did they kill Stephanie's boyfriends?" she asked.

"Both men were buying drugs from Stephanie, and they had both figured out who the bosses were. They wanted in: They wanted a share of the money. Julia got them full of booze, and gave them lethal shots. Isobel cut their throats and arranged the literary scenes, to lead the police to think of Julia and Rachel, rather than herself and Stephanie. Julia would have alibis and they'd fix it all on Rachel. I think Julia would have eventually killed Isobel, unless

Isobel killed her first. Julia gave the death shot to Stephanie. Had enough?"

"Horrible stuff. Were they tied into the Ross crowd or Dinah's witches?"

"I don't think anyone knows, and maybe we'll never know," he said.

She shook her head. "That poor girl," she said.

"Here's some good news about Jane Ross: The lawyers have managed to tie up the little money she has so tight her greedy relatives can't get it away from her. And James, Dinah's driver, is one of our spies, and has been working undercover, trying to find out if she was guilty of anything. Since she's been cleared, he has put aside his role, and explained all to Jane. I hear he and Jane may be an item. That's good news, too: He'll help keep her safe from her relatives."

"How nice to hear some people are innocent, and may live happily ever after," Coleman said.

"I agree. Are you interested in dinner?" Heyward asked.

"Yes, I'm hungry again. If I stay in London much longer, I'll be very fat."

"Never mind. Tonight we'll eat lightly—I ordered shrimp and lobster salads. We'll turn in early. You look tired."

"I am. I'll be glad for an early night," she said.

CHAPTER THIRTY-ONE

Coleman

Tuesday, Nightingale Day, London

Tony, who acted just as he had the night before and on their previous outings, picked her up at eight on Tuesday morning. They whizzed off with scarcely a word exchanged, while he concentrated on the London rush-hour traffic. When they were out of London, and she thought it was safe to talk to him, she asked, "Where are we going?"

"We're taking a two-hour drive to the Minsmere nature reserve. It's a lovely place, half a mile from the North Sea, very wooded, and partly surrounded by marsh. We'll meet Jack, our guide, there."

"Why do we need a guide? And why do we have to go so far? Aren't there nightingales in London? And if we want to hear it sing, why are we going during the day? Don't they sing at night?"

Tony looked amused. "Did you think nightingales sing in Berkeley Square? Nightingales like thickets and woods. If a nightingale was ever in London, it was years and years ago. It's too crowded and the parks are too well kept and tidy these days to tempt nightingales. The nightingales don't stay very long in England. They migrate to warmer countries. Jack had to call all over England to see if he could locate one for us to see. He learned there were still three nesting in different locations in Minsmere. He's sure at least one of them is still there—at least it was there yesterday. We may have to do a lot of walking to find the bird, but it will be a beautiful walk. We'll probably see bluebells."

"Tell me more about nightingales," she said.

"They only sing when they are mating or nesting. They can sing either at night or during the day. They're small brown birds, hard to see, and they hide their nests. We'd probably never see the nest or the bird if Jack wasn't with us to point it out. I have binoculars, but he'll have to show us where to look."

•••

Tony parked the car outside the entry to Minsmere. Jack, a tall, thin man with longish hair and a beard was waiting by a battered and ancient Land Rover. He led the way into the reserve, walking slowly, and pausing frequently to listen. Almost as soon as they began their walk, they entered a small glade, deep in the shade of a dense grove of trees. The floor of the glade was covered with bluebells, a deeper blue than the Spanish bluebells Coleman had seen in American gardens. Coleman thought they were exquisite, but Tony was unimpressed.

"Wait till you see acres of bluebells. You don't see them at their best in small patches like this," Tony said.

In the first site Jack took them to, where he'd been told a nightingale had a nest, the nest was there, but it was empty. Jack said that meant the babies could fly, and they'd all left England. At the second place, the nightingale was at home, but it wasn't singing. The tiny brown bird, about the size of a wren, was perched on a twig in a dense thicket near the road. As Tony had said, Coleman probably wouldn't have seen it without Jack pointing out the bird, and, farther back, a tiny nest.

Shortly after they arrived, a school bus full of little boys shouting and yelling and making an enormous amount of noise passed them. "That's it for the nightingale," Coleman thought, when suddenly the bird exploded into gorgeous song. Long after the bus had disappeared, the bird was still singing. Its song was so loud, it was hard to believe a tiny bird was producing it, but they were watching the little creature, and every note was his.

"It's responding to the noise those kids in the bus made," Jack explained. "We think the bird sings to frighten off potential threats to its nest by anything noisy. A nightingale will sing when it hears a lot of noise. The bird believes the song we all love and think is so beautiful is threatening. You heard the CD with the planes? Some people think the bird was trying to scare the noisy planes away."

The song was magnificent, but indescribable, even more wonderful than the CDs. They stood for nearly an hour listening, while Jack taped the bird's song for Coleman to take home, and Tony took pictures of Coleman listening, and staring at the bird. Coleman was enraptured, hypnotized. When Tony asked if she was ready to go, she realized only her feet and legs were tired of standing. If she'd had a chair, she could have listened to the bird sing all day. Reluctantly, she followed the men back to the cars.

"This was unforgettable," she told Jack. "Thank you."

In the car, she felt dazzled, almost dizzy, but she came to her senses long enough to ask Tony where they were headed.

"Another pub—plainer than the one we went to Sunday night. But they do a typical English lunch you should try. They serve it all day. We'll be there in twenty minutes. There's water and lemonade in the cooler in the back seat, if you want something to drink."

"I am thirsty, thanks. I'll have some water."

•••

The second pub, named the Unicorn, with a carving of that magical animal over the door, was smaller and less decorated than the first pub, but it was snug and cozy, with a lovely garden and window boxes full of multicolored flowers. They were seated in the garden, and Tony ordered what the menu called "the ploughman's lunch," for both of them.

They sat at a round picnic table, which seemed far too big for the two of them, until the food was served. A large basket of freshly baked bread, still hot from the oven, and a pot of butter, came first. Next, a mammoth tray of cheese wedges, enough for a hungry family of ten, appeared. She looked at Tony for enlightenment.

"The typical cheese for a ploughman's lunch is cheddar, but this pub specializes in the ploughman's dish, and serves assorted English cheeses. Try the cheddar first, but the Stilton's a must-have."

Next, the waitress delivered a large bowl of salad—fresh mixed greens, tomatoes, cucumbers, tossed with a little oil and vinegar, and a tray of small dishes.

"What's in the little bowls?" Coleman asked.

"English mustard—be careful, it's very spicy. Some people find it too hot. Also pickled onions, various preserves, and other kinds of pickles. Beer is the usual beverage, but I got you some cider. Is that okay?"

"Absolutely," she said.

She promised herself that she'd eat sparingly—that cheese was not low-fat or reduced-calorie—but it was so good, she ate until she was far too full.

•••

In the car, on the way to London, she said, "What a charming place, what a delicious lunch, what a wonderful experience. Thank you, Tony." Less than half an hour later, she was sound asleep.

•••

When the car stopped, Coleman sat up, wide awake. "Where are we?" she asked.

"We're at my flat. I left a small supper in the fridge for us here before we left this morning," Tony said.

"Flat? I thought you lived with your father?" Coleman said.

"I do, but I have this place for privacy. I never have a moment to myself when I'm at home, or in my office. This is my secret getaway." He unlocked a glass and metal door, and led her through a red-carpeted entry with large vases of lilies on tables on either side. They stepped into a small elevator and rode up two flights to a corridor where he unlocked another door. A short hall took them to a very long room on their left, with a fireplace at one end, and a wall-to-wall bookcase at the other end. A table, seating eight, stood in front of the bookcase; two sofas and a coffee table stood in front of the fireplace. The wall opposite the door was all windows, through which a view of a park could be seen.

Looking at another wall, Coleman said, "I've seen these posters before in Dinah's gallery. Why have you decorated your flat with nineteenth-century American posters?"

"It's my tribute to your country," Tony laughed. "Seriously, I'm very fond of these images. Art Nouveau was just showing up in both Britain and America, and posters demonstrate this best."

"Do you have a favorite?" Coleman asked.

"Probably this one, by Will Bradley, *When Hearts Are Trumps.* It's the most romantic, with that title, and the image of a beautiful woman and a satyr surrounded by swirls of foliage."

"Yes, it's beautiful," Coleman agreed, intrigued by Tony's emphasis on romance.

Tony continued, "Will Bradley is my favorite poster artist. His *Blue Lady* is another good example. The elegant woman is standing in a woods, all very simple designs. This is Florence Lundborg's *The Lark*, set in California. That's the Marin Peninsula behind the soaring bird. Maxfield Parrish did these two, both of nude women, one reading. This is *Miss Träumerei* by Ethel Reed, and there's a story here: Ethel Reed came to Britain when she was twenty-three, after a successful early career as a poster artist in Boston. She made one poster here—that's it over there, *The*

Quest of the Golden Girl—then she disappeared. She might have had an affair, maybe she had a child, with the author of the book advertised by the poster."

"You know a lot about these," Coleman said. "You *are* a romantic."

"Guilty. I became interested, and there was little published information, so I did some research. But, yes, Art Nouveau is romantic."

"They are all so colorful," Coleman said. "But who would expect to find a collection like this in a London flat?"

"Do you want to see more, take a tour?" he asked.

"Absolutely," she said.

"The kitchen is on the right," he said, "with a table where I can have breakfast or a snack. Down the hall on the left is a bedroom, which I use as my office-library. Sometimes I watch TV or a DVD there. My bedroom is on the right. There are two baths, and a powder room."

"All for you? Do you entertain here?" she asked

"No, and before you ask, you're the first woman I ever brought here."

"I'm honored," she said.

"Don't say another word," he said. He put his arms around her, and picked her up. She had the same feeling she'd had when he'd kissed her Sunday night. She thought she might faint. He kissed her again and again, and she was afraid she'd fall when he put her down. But he didn't put her down. He laid her on the bed.

He undressed her, and himself with ease and absence of clumsiness. In a few minutes he was on her, and surrounding her. He made love to her, passionately and exquisitely. It was unlike anything she had ever experienced, and when it was over, she longed to start all over again.

He cradled her in his arms, and kissed her again. "I've jumped the gun. I didn't mean to rush you. I should have made my speech first, but I couldn't wait: Coleman, will you marry me? Before you answer, just know that, just as I said I've never brought a woman here, I've never said those words before."

Coleman was still in a daze, but she heard him, and she tried to sit up.

"Be still," he said. "I'm holding you until I get an answer."

"Tony, you can't be serious. I met you Friday night. We hardly know each other. Anyway, I'm not the marrying kind."

"It doesn't matter how long we've known each other. I knew on the Eye that I wanted to marry you. Do you doubt that we are meant to be together, after our lovemaking?"

"There's a lot more to marrying than lovemaking. Can we change the subject? I can't think straight."

"What would you like to do? Or talk about?"

"I want to know all about your family."

"My family is my father. My mother died when I was born. Theirs was a genuine love match, and he could never bring himself to marry again. But he's been after me to get married and have a family since I was in my teens. I was thirty on my last birthday, and he had hoped I'd be married and have a couple of children by now.

"I've told him I'll never settle for anything less than he had—I want a true-love marriage, like his.

"But he and all of his friends keep presenting me with potential brides. He's desperate to get me married and with children while I'm still young. He says old fathers are bad breeders. He makes me feel like a stud horse or a bull."

"How would he feel about you marrying an American?" Coleman asked.

"He'd welcome you with open arms. That's why I haven't introduced you to him—he'd tell you what a wonderful husband I'll be, and what a great life you'd have married to me and being a duchess. We'd both be uncomfortable and embarrassed."

"Does he know about me?" Coleman asked.

"Of course he does. He knows everything I do, every breath I take. He doesn't like me doing the art-antiques recovery work. He thinks it's dangerous. But he loved the story about you and your discovery at 23 Culross, and the triumph of the great Dolly."

"Sounds like you might be asking me to marry you just to get a wife, and get him off your back. Honestly, I'm all wrong for you," Coleman said.

"Oh, no, you're perfect," he said. "Please say you'll marry me."

"Tony, we've just met. I hardly know you, but I've enjoyed your company. Let's make a deal: Don't ask me again until the day before I go back to New York. I promise to think about it, but don't get your hopes up."

"I'll do anything you want," he promised.

"Okay. Let's have fun," she said.

He reached for her, and kissed her again.

CHAPTER THIRTY-TWO

Coleman

Wednesday morning, May, London

When Coleman woke a little after six, Tony was wide awake, lying on his side, and staring down at her.

"Why are you looking at me like that? I must look awful," she said.

"I'm staring at you because I'm afraid I'll miss something. And because you are beautiful."

She sat up, holding the covers around her. "Go away," she said. "I have to put on yesterday's clothes and go home. Call me a cab, will you? I'll be ready to go in five minutes."

"I'll drive you home," he said.

"No, no, I want a cab. Everyone in the neighborhood and all of the people working for Heyward will see your red car," she said.

"Heyward won't be surprised," he said.

"Go away. I have an important business appointment this morning," Coleman said.

"Will I see you tonight?" he asked.

"I don't think so. I think Heyward made plans. Here's the deal: I'll see you every night I can until I leave, but most of the time it will be with family—Jonathan and Dinah, Heyward. We'll all go to the theater, opera, ballet, and when it's a family party, I'll stay at Heyward's. When I don't have to be with family, and you and I go out alone, I'll stay here. Don't argue. Now go away. I have to get out of here."

•••

He stood with her on the street until the cab came, and helped her in. He leaned over to kiss her, but she dodged him. "Go away, I'm in a hurry," she said.

"You are a hard woman," he said.

"I'll call you later," she said.

•••

Coleman used her key to open Heyward's front door. She didn't see a soul. But she sensed that there were people all around, staying out of her way, to spare her the embarrassment of having come in at six thirty in the morning after staying out all night.

She'd left Dolly with Heyward, and he or Dolly must have heard her come in, because when she reached her bedroom door, Dolly was sitting outside it, waiting for her. She picked up the little dog and cuddled her. She stripped off yesterday's clothes, and took a long shower.

She put on the white robe she'd found in the bathroom when she arrived, and pushed the intercom button to the kitchen.

"What can I do for you, madam?" a voice said.

"Would you please bring me some breakfast? Orange juice, coffee, American bacon, toast with no butter, and a blueberry muffin. And will you also please bring Dolly's breakfast?"

"Right away, madam," the voice said.

Coleman was hungry. She and Tony had forgotten to eat supper last night. She was used to eating three light—non-fattening—meals a day. The meals she was eating here were far from non-fattening. She dreaded getting on a scale. There was one in her bathroom, but she was ignoring it. She'd pushed her weight out of her mind. When she thought about Tony, she shoved those thoughts away, too. She had things to do, and places to go.

What would she wear today? It was a business appointment, but with another woman. A suit, but not too uptight. The tangerine suit she'd worn her first day in London would be perfect.

Someone tapped on the door, and a maid came in with a trolley loaded with her meal, and Dolly's. Coleman put Dolly's dish out on the balcony, with a full bowl of fresh water, and sat down at the trolley to enjoy her breakfast. She ate slowly, savoring every bite.

When she had finished her breakfast, and was dressed and ready to go, she was still early for her ten o'clock appointment. She'd go downstairs and face Heyward. Would he mention her overnight absence? She didn't think he would. He was the soul of tact.

Heyward was sitting at the dining room table drinking coffee, and reading the *Wall Street Journal*. He'd already finished the *Financial Times*—it was folded neatly, lying on a chair. He read both every morning. He was always working. She smiled to herself; she was like him that way. She liked working night and day. This time in London had been a rare holiday. She joined him and accepted another cup of coffee. She told him she was on her way to visit *Cottage & Castle*.

"Great," he said. "I'll be interested to hear what you think. Will you be back here for lunch?" he asked.

"I think so. I'll call you when I know for sure," she said. "If she suggests we lunch together, I probably should do it."

"Absolutely," he said. "I think you have this on your calendar, but in case you've forgotten, we're going to the ballet tonight—Sadler's Wells. You and me, and Dinah and Jonathan. Is that all right with you? We can invite Tony, if you like. I'm sure I can get another ticket."

"No, just the four of us sounds great. After lunch today, I have to see Rachel, then I'm going to spend the rest of the day in my room. I'd like to sleep all afternoon, so I can be wide awake for the ballet."

"That's a good idea. Your stay here has been far from restful. I hope you like *Cottage & Castle*."

"Me, too," she said. "Am I going by car?"

"Yes, of course. William is waiting for you. Give me a call later about lunch."

•••

Coleman liked Kathleen Mann as soon as they met. She asked Coleman to call her Kathy, and they settled down to talk about *Cottage & Castle*.

"Why do you want to sell?" Coleman asked.

"I don't want to sell; I have to. I can't compete with *Country Life*. They're a weekly, with a huge staff. I'm a monthly with a small staff. I'm always behind—can't ever beat them to a story. We have a much smaller subscriber list, and can't come close to their advertising. I'm short of capital—can't afford to expand the staff. It's hopeless."

"I thought it must be like that. I have an idea: We buy fifty percent of your company's equity. With that, we can provide long-term debt financing to help you expand. We'll produce an American half of your magazine—*Country Life* has almost no American coverage—and you will produce an English section, which we'll put in *First Home*. I think we can come up with two winners. I've already begun to introduce some English ideas and products in my food department. I've been looking at fashion—like your wonderful hats, but they're way too expensive. Do you have any ideas?"

"Oh, yes. So many. Give me a little time, and I'll put together a plan. That sounds fabulous. What else would you be interested in—food, fashion, and . . . ?"

"Gardens, theater, films, book reviews," Coleman said. "I just bought dozens of books at Hatchards that have never made it to New York. Put your plan together, and I'll show it to Heyward. Do you have a money man we can talk to—or are you it?"

"My husband is our accountant. He's the one to discuss money."

Kathy had ordered salads for them to eat in the magazine's conference room so they could keep on talking. Coleman called Heyward to tell him she wouldn't be back for lunch. "Well, I think we've moved along a lot today. I'm here a week and a half more. We'll keep communicating, keep planning. Stay in touch," Coleman said. She didn't get home until two thirty and went straight to bed, sleeping until it was time to dress for the ballet.

•••

Her meeting with Rachel had also been successful, but not much fun. She hardly knew Rachel, but she could not miss the dark circles under her eyes and her sad expression. Rachel made it clear she wasn't interested in small talk, and went straight to the business at hand.

"I've concluded we can't do this without a partner. I think a museum would be ideal. What would you think of approaching Dinah's museum, the Art Museum of Great Britain? I'm sure they'd be happy to be a part of the program." Coleman thought that was a great idea, and urged Rachel to proceed.

Rachel had contacted several people knowledgeable about art to help identify and select out-of-print books to be republished, and Coleman thought her choices were ideal. She suggested Rachel stay in touch with Dinah and get to know Bethany, who would be her U.S. contacts for the project. They would have suggestions, too.

Rachel agreed, and tactfully brought their meeting to a close.

When Coleman told Heyward about her experience with Rachel, he wasn't surprised. "She's been through a bad time, but she'll get it all done," he said.

"That's what matters," Coleman said.

CHAPTER THIRTY-THREE

Dinah

Wednesday, May, London

Dinah came home Wednesday evening happy as a lark. She'd had a great day at the museum. She was humming to herself when she went upstairs to shower and change, knowing her new cook would come up with a delicious dinner, tonight featuring a crab soufflé.

She felt a sudden stab of guilt. She'd eaten crab soufflés with Rachel the day she met Stephanie. She should have called Rachel as soon as she'd heard about Stephanie's death, and called again when she heard Rachel's friend Julia was a murderer. There would never be a better time than now.

Rachel was glad to hear from her. The poor woman sounded very unhappy about Stephanie's death, and about her friend Julia's crimes. Neither of them knew the details of the girl's death, nor plans for a memorial service. Dinah had little to say other than how sorry she was, and she was about to hang up when Rachel raised a new topic: "Have you ever heard noises in the night at 23 Culross?"

"No, just shouts in the daytime from the horrible women," Dinah said. "Why do you ask?"

"Julia told me there's a rumor the house is haunted. She also told me a story about Lady Jane's nanny having hidden treasures in the house, treasures which have never been found," Rachel said.

"How exciting. I don't believe in ghosts, but there may be a door here somewhere that we don't know about, used by the thieves. I'll ask James, Hamilton, and Franklin to see what they can find. I'll keep you posted. So good to talk to you, Rachel. See you soon, I hope," Dinah said.

As soon as she hung up, she rushed downstairs to tell Hamilton what Rachel had said. He was as excited as she was.

"If there's an extra door here, it's in the basement," he said. "The basement is full of small rooms and cubbies. If we find a door, we'll make sure it's locked."

"Absolutely. I hate the thought of people being able to come in here at night," Dinah said.

"As for treasure, if it's small it can be anywhere, but we'll start with the attic. No one ever goes there. The last time I looked, it was full of junk, papers, broken furniture. Lady Jane might want us to clean it out. It would give us a good excuse to search. James should ask her if she'd like us to clean the attic and the basement," he said.

"Great. Let me know what she wants," Dinah said.

•••

After dinner, Hamilton approached her with the news.

"There is indeed an exit leading outdoors from the basement. It's now well-locked on both sides. And James spoke to Lady Jane. She'd be very pleased if we'd clean the attic and the cellar, but she was worried about paying us. James told her you wanted it done—you've heard mice—so you were paying. Of course, we'll do it for nothing, but if I told her that, she'd be upset."

CHAPTER THIRTY-FOUR

Dinah

Thursday, May, London

On Thursday evening when Dinah came home after work, Hamilton met her at the door, nearly jumping with excitement.

"We found what we think is a treasure: old postage stamps."

"I don't know anything about stamps, but I think Jonathan does," Dinah said.

While Jonathan was sipping his pre-dinner glass of wine, Dinah approached him. "Haven't I heard you mention stamp collecting?"

"Yes, a bit," he said. "Why?"

Dinah handed him the musty-smelling, worn, leather-bound book that Hamilton had found in the attic. "This was in a locked trunk. Hamilton brought the trunk downstairs and broke the lock. It was full of papers, invoices, receipts, financial records, all dating back to the 1890s and the early twentieth century. And this book, which seems to have old stamps in it. Please take a look," she said.

Jonathan opened the book. "It's a stamp collection, but an odd one. Not the usual stamp album, with little illustrations and numbers indicating where to place stamps. This is customized, and old—the stamps are secured by strips of paper. Probably before collectors started using paper hinges, let alone cellophane or plastic sleeves."

Dinah smiled. Her husband was revealing a side of himself she'd never seen. "You do know 'a bit' about stamps, don't you? How did you come by this esoteric knowledge?"

Jonathan blushed. "I collected stamps when I was young. But it was considered nerdish, and I kept my interest quiet. I should have been playing football, I suppose, but I enjoyed learning about places, people, events," he said. "A stamp collection is a great history teacher."

"But you were an athlete in college—you swam for Harvard," Dinah said. "We've got pictures to prove it. You didn't just collect stamps."

"I quit collecting by the time I was in prep school. But I've remained interested in news about stamps, when it shows up in the papers, or an auction catalogue."

"Tell me what you make of these stamps."

Jonathan squinted at the small squares of paper. "They are old, and they're all British Colonials. This is a very specialized collection. There's probably value here. The denominations are large, which adds to rarity, like one pound or five dollars, in the case of Newfoundland—yes, Newfoundland was once a separate colony. Large-denomination stamps were issued in small quantities, because they were little used. But if the mother country had a one-pound stamp, each colony wanted one, too. The African countries all have their colonial names, like Tanganyika, not Tanzania. This collection may be close to one hundred years old."

He was still looking through the book when his eyes widened and his voice rose. "This can't be true! This looks like a British Guiana One-Cent Magenta. Is it possible? I've never seen one, but I've seen photos. It's the rarest stamp in the world. I can't believe it—this is beyond belief. It's thought that there was only one in existence. We have to take this to an expert."

Dinah could understand Jonathan's excitement. She knew the thrill of finding a long-sought-after print. "What else can you tell me about it?"

"It has a storied past, and coincidentally, I'm up to date. Sotheby's just announced that it was about to auction the only known British Guiana One-Cent Magenta. I read an article about it last week. Sotheby's was quoted as estimating it would sell for over ten million dollars. The seller is the estate of its last owner, a DuPont heir who died in prison."

"Prison?" Dinah asked.

"He murdered his boyfriend," said Jonathan. "But the legend goes that there were two of these stamps in existence. The owner of both, a rich textile magnate, burned one with his cigar lighter to ensure there would be only a single surviving copy, thereby enhancing its value. If the legend is true, this must be a third. It certainly adds to the allure."

Jonathan's enthusiasm was contagious. Could they have found a real treasure? "What do we do now?" she asked.

"The largest stamp dealer in the world is right here in London. Stanley Gibbons, on the Strand. I've walked by and glanced in the window. We'll take the stamp to them. If this thing is for real, they'll faint. They'll want to do all kinds of tests on it—paper type, ink, exact size. If it proves true, Sotheby's will have a heart attack. Ten million dollars will become one or two million. The existence of two of the stamps rather than one will drastically lower the value."

"Should we tell Lady Jane? I guess she's the rightful owner—or do all of her horrible relatives have a share in the collection?" Dinah grimaced at the thought.

"No, let's find out if this rarity is for real. Anyhow, there's value to all of these stamps. We'll get Stanley Gibbons to appraise the collection, then tell her."

•••

Jonathan didn't go into the office the next morning, an unheard-of event. He—with the stamp album carefully stowed in his briefcase—and Dinah were at Stanley Gibbons when the door opened at ten in the morning.

Dinah had never been in a stamp dealer's gallery. It was a far cry from a New York art gallery. In contrast to the serenity and calm of a typical art gallery, Stanley Gibbons was blatantly commercial, with posters all over the walls advertising stamps for sale. Magazines promoting stamp collecting filled racks. A man seated behind a raised desk, right at the entry, greeted them with a cheery "Good morning" and "Please come in." Quite a change from the usual haughty receptionist in a New York gallery.

Jonathan spoke up. "We'd like you to look at this collection, and if you think it's worthy, appraise it for us."

The dealer took one look at the first page, and summoned a colleague. "This is a special group of stamps. These old Colonials are worth something. There seem to be multiple stamps from every colony in the Empire," the dealer explained to his cohort.

Jonathan turned to the last page in the book, where the single British Guiana was displayed. Stunned silence.

Then both dealers started talking at once.

"Could it be?"

"It can't be."

"It looks right."

"It's a forgery, for sure."

"Too perfect."

"I've seen the real one—this is identical."

"We've got to really analyze this. Can we keep it?"

Turning to Dinah and Jonathan, Dealer #1 said, "By coincidence, Sotheby's is about to auction . . ."

Jonathan interrupted. "Yes, I know. I've read about the upcoming sale."

Dealer #2 said, "What you might not know is that the stamp is in London today, at Sotheby's. It's on a world tour so collectors can see the real thing before the actual sale, without having to travel to New York. Hong Kong is next. Or maybe you did know. There's too much coincidence about this."

Dinah, recognizing the dealer's implication, spoke up. "Our butler and I discovered this stamp book yesterday afternoon in our attic. Neither of us knows anything about stamps. I showed it to my husband last night, and he knew enough to recognize possible value in the entire collection. We came here immediately."

Jonathan, annoyed, said with his Boston aristocrat manner, "We'll take this somewhere else if you don't treat us with courtesy. We are not thieves or forgers."

The dealer capitulated. "We can take your Guiana to Sotheby's, and put it side by side with the one that was thought to be the only one in existence and compare."

Dinah asked, "Will Sotheby's allow that? Won't they deny the existence of ours, or at least argue that it's a forgery?"

"If our paper consultant verifies the paper, Sotheby's will have no choice. Our consultant works in the city—he'll be here in thirty minutes, once we call him. We can check dimensions and ink with a direct comparison to Sotheby's copy. Can we keep it?"

Jonathan's suspicions were aroused. "No, we're not leaving it," he said, and turning to Dinah, "I'm calling Heyward. We need advice and backup."

•••

The paper expert, carrying a large case of special equipment, arrived at Stanley Gibbons's door with Heyward Bain, flanked by two of his lawyers.

One of the dealers, under Jonathan's watchful eye, gingerly handed the stamp to the paper expert, who put it on a tray beneath a microscope. Bain began instructing his lawyers to draw up a contract with Stanley Gibbons, and turned to Dinah. "You and your butler found this item, but I suppose Lady Jane Ross is the owner?"

"Yes, it was in her house, 23 Culross—in the attic, mixed with papers relating to financial matters, with Ross family names on them. There may be a problem for her with those awful Rosses, even if they're in prison or headed there."

"All the more reason to specify her name in this contract, and get this collection, with the British Guiana, into her physical possession as quickly as possible. 'Possession is nine-tenths of the law,' as they say," Heyward said.

The paper expert spoke up. "The paper type looks right. I've never seen the One-Cent Magenta, but I've seen other South American British Colonials of this period, and they are printed on the same paper. If this was forged, it was done long ago, when there was identical paper stock available. The stamp is 1856, and anyone interested in stamps knows that it was discovered by a young collector some twenty years later. Nobody dreamed it was unique, and therefore valuable, for some time after that. It wouldn't have been easy to create another copy. Where would the paper have come from? By the turn of the century, British Colonial stamps were completely different, with different paper, dimensions, and perforations. It's not impossible that it's a forgery, but improbable."

•••

Contracts written and signed, Heyward and his legal crew departed. Too excited to return to work, Jonathan called his assistant and instructed her to cancel his appointments for the day. Dinah let her coworkers at the museum know she'd be late, and called her cousin, who was busy at work in her office in Heyward's house.

"Coleman, hold your breath. We may have found a treasure at 23 Culross. It's an old postage stamp collection, certainly worth something, and it may contain what some call the most valuable stamp in the world—but it may not be if this one turns out to be the second extant copy. Just the same, it would be worth a lot. We're going to Sotheby's now."

Coleman broke in. She'd rarely heard Dinah so excited. "Slow down. Sotheby's? Where are you?"

"Some place you've never heard of called Stanley Gibbons. It's complicated. Meet us at Sotheby's and I'll fill you in. You'll want to call Zeke at *ArtSmart*—it's a story he'll love."

•••

Dinah, Jonathan, Coleman, the paper expert, and the two Gibbons dealers huddled around the grim-faced Sotheby's stamp expert, all staring at two small scraps of oddly shaped paper.

Jonathan was the first to speak up. "Identical. What else is to be said?"

The paper expert, also an avid stamp collector, agreed. "Everything's right: color, size—and I know the paper is genuine. This powerful magnification confirms the lettering—it's the same on both copies, down to the slight imperfection in the 'G.' The cancellation is in the identical style, and we can get a handwriting expert to bless that, but it's obviously the same hand. The ink can be tested, but it looks the same to me under this infrared light."

Other Sotheby's curators arrived looking worried, muttering, "What do we do now?"

The Gibbons dealers spoke in near unison: "We're prepared to authenticate this as an 1856 British Guiana One-Cent Magenta."

Coleman started taking notes, and questioning the Sotheby's curators, who were offering confused and contradictory answers. She announced to the room at large, "*ArtSmart* has never done a story on stamps or stamp collecting, but we're going to tell the story of this great discovery. We'll have a special announcement online, and the complete story, fully illustrated, in this month's print edition."

The Sotheby curators retreated, summoning their PR minions.

Dinah asked, "How are they going to handle this? Their seller will be devastated. They might get sued. What can they do?"

Jonathan answered, "That's their problem. Let's go see Lady Jane."

•••

Dinah, Coleman, Jonathan, a Stanley Gibbons representative, and Heyward converged on Lady Jane's modest cottage. As expected, she was in her garden. Heyward gave her the news.

Jane was overcome. She sat down and began fanning herself. The Gibbons man told her he was confident the entire collection was worth at least £2 million, possibly close to £3 million. They were prepared to handle the sale for her. Coleman was busy taking pictures with her iPhone—action shots of Stanley Gibbons breaking the news to the owner of the rare stamp that she would publish in *ArtSmart*.

Heyward explained about the contract, handed her a copy, and said, "Lady Jane, we will get this album back in your hands today. Better yet, will you let me put it into a bank safe, the location of which only you and I will know? There must be no opportunity for any of the Ross clan to claim ownership. The lawyers have worked hard to protect you from them, but this is an unusual situation."

"Oh, there's no chance of that. The stamp collection belonged to my nanny. It was her greatest treasure. She left everything she owned, including the collection, to me. I have the will in my safe. I'll give it to you, and you can put it with the collection in a bank you choose. But the collection disappeared after she died. I thought it had been stolen. I can't thank you enough for finding it for me," Jane said.

Dinah looked back at Jane as they were leaving. Her face was glowing. She looked happier than Dinah had ever seen her. When she'd first seen this place and its owner, she'd thought it looked like a fairyland. She'd just seen a fairy tale come true.

CHAPTER THIRTY-FIVE

Coleman

Saturday, May, London

Coleman stuck to her plans and the list of things she wanted to do. She managed to slip away from Tony long enough to do her shopping. She didn't tell him where she was going, or what she planned to buy. He'd want to accompany her, and he'd try to buy things for her.

She went to Liberty, and was entranced by the fabrics. She bought samples of upholstery fabrics to take back to the decorating department at *First Home*. She bought yards and yards of delicate silks in green, blue, lavender, and pale yellow to turn into party dresses in New York. She bought another copy of her how-to book on hats—*The Modern Girl's Guide to Hatmaking*—to take home to Bethany, who, like Coleman, made most of her clothes, and would leap at the opportunity to design hats.

The hats at Liberty were less expensive than those she'd seen, but they were disappointing—pedestrian and lacking in glamour. Coleman had asked Kathy Mann if there was any place that had great hats for reasonable prices.

Kathy knew and had responded. "If you mean those grand hats worn by the Royals, no. But you can get some fashionable caps and berets and other plain hats at a place called Beret in Pimlico. After you buy them, you can dress them up. I'll give you a list of places where you can buy trimmings—feathers, flowers, beading. You'll love those shops."

Coleman made the rounds, and bought lavishly. She could hardly wait to begin designing hats.

•••

She spent a bluebell day with Tony, a delicious day of beauty and love. Was she in love with Tony? She asked herself that every day. She supposed she was, but it didn't matter: She couldn't marry him.

Another day, he took her to Oxford to see his college, Christ Church, and the Dreaming Spires. She was as impressed as he'd hoped. She pictured the young Tony walking in that beautiful town, and wished she'd known him then.

"Did you like it here?" she asked.

"Oh, yes," he said. "I liked Eton, too. I'll take you there so you can see the area and what the boys look like."

He took her to all of his favorite restaurants. Her favorites were those in beautiful locations. The Waterside Inn at Bray was not only on the water, its large glass windows revealed swans drifting by. Tony pointed out Windsor Castle, and young Etonians in their top hats and black coats. She could see Tony the schoolboy in that attire, and thought he would have been adorable.

He took her to the French Horn, Sonning-on-Thames, where the specialty was roast duck, and the windows framed a wide spot in the river surrounded by willow trees. Another lovely day, a lovely view, and delicious food.

He flew her and Dolly to Paris for a day, and took them to a restaurant set in a grassy garden, where petals from the blossoming trees drifted into her hair and Dolly's fur and all over the table. They ate asparagus, a cheese soufflé, and strawberries. She was exhausted at the end of the day. It was a night she and Dolly spent at Tony's apartment. She rarely slept on nights in this apartment, and usually spent the next afternoon asleep in her room at

Heyward's house, only getting up to go out to the theater or a concert with her family, or dinner with Tony.

Would she change anything? No, but she had the sense of the candle burning at both ends. Her dreams were a blur of unicorns and hedgehogs and badgers, of bluebells and nightingales, and soaring through a star-studded sky. She knew these were the dreams she'd take home with her, and that when she woke from them, the pillow would be wet with tears.

CHAPTER THIRTY-SIX

Dinah

Monday, May, London

Dinah endeared herself to her new associates by ordering and donating all the catalogues needed for their new American collection. She called Bethany, at the Greene Gallery, and asked her to round up the rare books, and Bethany was pleased to help, and create a library to match the collection.

•••

As absorbed as she was in her work at the museum, Dinah found the time to begin her study of English food. She started with collecting cookbooks. Hatchards had a good selection, and she found older, out-of-print books at a small bookstore, Heywood Hill, located near Rachel's house. The first cookbook she looked at provided a piece of information that made her angry as a hornet: To make a house smell the way 23 Culross had when cooking kidneys *had to be deliberate.* People cooked kidneys properly all the time without causing an odor. She hoped those wretched women would be in jail forever.

•••

Her first writing for *First Home* was "Upper Crust: The Very Best Savory Pies." She included recipes she'd found in English cookbooks, but she usually modernized them by cutting down the work required. She'd use frozen pie crust from the market, or refrigerated pie dough, instead of making the crust from scratch. She tested the pies on James, William, Hamilton—anyone available—and they gave her rave reviews.

Some of the most popular pies were crustless: crustless crab quiche, crustless shrimp quiche, crustless tuna quiche, crustless chicken asparagus quiche. Less work *and* fewer calories. She sometimes used mashed potatoes as a topping instead of crust, pointing out that the English cottage pie (made with beef) and shepherd's pie (made with lamb) both had mashed-potato tops, and no bottom crusts, and they were absolutely delicious. Ellen, the cook, was always willing to experiment and came up with great ideas.

Dinah decided her next project would be "Favorite London Soups." She'd put together a long list of future projects, all of which excited her. She was busier than she had ever been, but found time to go shopping with Coleman, and to great restaurants and great theater with Jonathan, Heyward, Coleman, and sometimes Tony. Every day was an adventure, and she had two jobs that fit perfectly with her two main interests. Bliss.

•••

When Coleman came to 23 Culross to say goodbye, the day she was leaving London to go back to New York, Dinah said goodbye with only a few tears. She would never be as strong and certain as Coleman, but she knew for the first time in her life that she could deal with whatever came up. She would remember that angels were fearless, and try to be like an angel. She would always love Coleman, but she was sure she would never again need Coleman to fight her battles.

CHAPTER THIRTY-SEVEN

Coleman

Tuesday, May, London

Coleman, with Dolly in her carrier, boarded Heyward's plane—the same plane that had picked her up in Paris. She'd asked Heyward if she could avoid the Omnium landing strip, and Paris. Both had associations with Tony, and she didn't want to be reminded of her times with him.

The plane took her to the airport at Nice, where she and Dolly boarded a flight to Kennedy. She'd asked for and got a window seat. She wanted to be able to stare out into the dark and avoid speaking to anyone. She was relieved when an elderly man sat in the aisle seat. He didn't say hello, or look friendly. Good. She turned her back on him, stared out the window, and thought about farewells.

Saying goodbye to Heyward hadn't been sad; he'd be in New York in a few weeks. Dinah was cheerful, and Coleman was happy for her: Their goodbyes were lighthearted. But then there was Tony. She'd told him almost daily since he'd proposed that she couldn't marry him, couldn't stay in London, but he couldn't—wouldn't—believe her. He loved her, and he was sure she loved him. She did love him. She was sure she'd never love anyone as much as she loved Tony. But she couldn't marry him. His kind of life wasn't hers, and never would be. She hoped he'd find someone else—someone who was young and adoring, someone who'd enjoy being a duchess and the mother of the heir or heirs. Coleman rarely cried, but at the thought of never seeing Tony again, or seeing him married to someone else, tears welled up in her eyes.

She felt movement in the aisle seat. The grumpy old man was leaving. Maybe she wouldn't have a seatmate. Oh, drat, someone else was taking his seat. She turned to look. Good Lord, Jeb Middleton was sitting beside her, beaming at her as if they were close friends. Was he stalking her? What a nuisance. She'd lost interest in him when she saw him drooling over Stephanie. She sighed. This would be a long trip. She'd like to snub him, but he worked for her half-brother. She had to be polite.

•••

When Coleman was in New York and looked back on her two weeks in London, she saw herself constantly busy, with her family, with work, and, of course, with Tony. Some days stood out, for good or bad. Others were a blur. She'd tried to keep a diary, but some of her entries were short.

She'd had several more meetings with Kathy Mann. Heyward and Bob Brinkley, Kathy's husband, joined them once. Coleman didn't like Kathy's husband—he was arrogant and patronizing—but Kathy looked at him worshipfully. She seemed to think every word he said was precious. Heyward didn't like him either, and turned him and the money issues over to Hicks, his number-one "go-to" assistant, who settled all the financial issues about *Cottage & Castle*. He undoubtedly put Brinkley in his place.

Her meetings with Kathy alone were productive and fun. Coleman was confident their venture would succeed, and Kathy and she were becoming friends.

There had been tears on the pillow over Tony, and memories of their delicious days of adventure, beauty, and love. Was she in love with Tony? She asked herself every day. She was, but it didn't matter: She couldn't marry him. She would always remember him. She couldn't imagine she would ever meet a man as attractive as Tony. But she had to forget Tony, and get on with her life.

CHAPTER THIRTY-EIGHT

Heyward

Tuesday morning, May, London

Heyward was in the library thinking about Coleman. He'd have enjoyed seeing his sister a duchess, and he'd never met a man he liked better than Tony, but they were not a match. Coleman could never live the life required of the woman who married Tony, and Tony could only live the life laid out for him in England. He feared that Tony had been seriously hurt. He wasn't worried about Coleman. In time, she would recover.

The phone rang. He glanced at the number, and answered it. He paled, and hung up a few minutes later. What terrible news. He couldn't reach Coleman—she was on the plane to New York. He had to alert Rachel, but first he touched the intercom to summon Mrs. Carter, who appeared immediately.

"I must leave for New York as soon as possible," he said. "Please pack for me—you'll know what I'll need. Get me on a BA flight tonight, leaving around six or seven, and alert the New York staff."

"Is anything wrong?" she asked.

"Yes, some bad news. But it needn't worry you. Thank you for asking," Heyward said.

ACKNOWLEDGMENTS

Bloody Royal Prints, covering many topics, was a difficult book to write. A number of people contributed to it. Without their help, it never would have been completed. My thanks to Clair Lamb; Erin Mitchell; our friends at the British Museum who helped arrange our visit to the Windsor Castle Print Room; Elisabeth Norton and Judy Rudoe, who helped with food and restaurant information; and all our English friends, who discussed with me a variety of topics, from where to buy a hat to protecting a dog from dog-nappers. Most of all, thanks to Dave, both for saving my sanity when the refrigerator went crazy and for being Coleman's and my companion at all the places we visited. And Dave, many thanks for arranging the nightingale!